RELUCTANT CASSANDRA

RELUCTANT CASSANDRA

Ellen Smith

Copyright © 2015 by Ellen Smith.

All rights reserved. No part of this publication may be reproduced, distributed or transmitted in any form or by any means, including photocopying, recording, or other electronic or mechanical methods, without the prior written permission of the publisher, except in the case of brief quotations embodied in critical reviews and certain other noncommercial uses permitted by copyright law. For permission requests, write to info@ellensmithwrites.com.

Publisher's Note: This is a work of fiction. Names, characters, places, and incidents are a product of the author's imagination. Locales and public names are sometimes used for atmospheric purposes. Any resemblance to actual people, living or dead, or to businesses, companies, events, institutions, or locales is completely coincidental.

Cover Design by The Thatchery at http://www.thethatchery.com
Edited by Kris Kendall of Final-Edits at
http://final-edits.blogspot.com
Book Layout ©2013 BookDesignTemplates.com

Reluctant Cassandra/ Ellen Smith. -- 1st ed.
ISBN 978-0-9961999-0-2

Dedicated to my husband, A.B.S.
and our children
G.B.S. and R.N.S.
with all my love

1

I feel change rolling through Eagle Valley like mist
before a storm. It's a vague, unsettling feeling, enough
to make me stop work around my store and take a
look out the front window. Main Street looks the same,
from the herringbone brick sidewalks to the American
flags on the lampposts. I look again, studying each
detail slowly. To my right, the street curves uphill and
ends at the stone face of Eagle Valley Presbyterian. To
my left, the street rolls downhill. Brick storefronts
eventually give way to gravel roads and low-hanging
trees. Just outside town, I can see the outer fields of

my parents' farm, and beyond that, the September indigo of the Blue Ridge Mountains.

Nothing looks out of place. In fact, I'd bet all the money in the till that our Main Street looks about like every other historic district in Virginia. Still, the whole town has an odd sheen. Frozen and perfect in a way it never will be again.

I trace my gloved finger along the gold stick-on letters in my front window. They spell out "McCrae's Antiques," though it looks backwards from inside the store. The edges of the "Q" and "T" are starting to peel up again. All that window washing I do is taking its toll.

I shake my head and turn away from the window. I need to get back to work. It's been a slow month, and these antiques aren't going to sell themselves. It's probably nothing, anyway. Since breaking up with Jeremy, seems I've gone from ignoring premonitions to imagining them.

I can't shake the feeling of dread that's sinking deeper into my gut. I dial my parents' number and leave a message, asking Mama to call me back. After a second thought, I send a little how-are-you text to my sisters, Eliza and Lila Beth. Better safe than sorry.

I look over the front displays, the glass counter full of antique jewelry, and the display shelves of odds and ends. Everything's already been scoured clean and dusted twice today. I haven't had a customer in here since three o'clock. Since then, I've been taking pictures and uploading product descriptions to the store website. I don't love selling things on the Internet, but at least I'm getting customers there. Being the only person in this big store is starting to make me antsy. Makes me feel surrounded, like everything in here's just bursting to tell its history.

"Go for a walk, Thor?" I call. My Boxer puppy comes bounding and skidding out of the back room, dragging his leash behind him. After six months of pet ownership and devoted doggie training, I still haven't managed to teach him how to play fetch, shake hands, or roll over. But going for a walk, well, that he's got down. I strip off my rubber cleaning gloves and switch them out for a clean pair of knit mittens. Thor's practically dancing with excitement. I flip my sign from "Open" to "Come Back Soon" on our way out.

For once, Thor isn't pulling on his leash or trying to run ahead of me. He seems happy to stop and inspect the small blades of grass peeking through the brick sidewalk. It takes forever to steer him around the side of the building to the back alley. Every few steps, Thor stops and sniffs the breeze intently. For a second, I think he must be able to sense a change, too.

Probably not. He probably just smells a cat. Or a squirrel.

"Arden!" The voice comes from just around the corner. "Arden! Yoo-hoo!"

Only one person in Eagle Valley would actually yell "Yoo-hoo." I plaster a smile on my face and turn.

Miss Paula Abernathy is tripping down the sidewalk in her not-quite-practical pumps. "I saw your sign and thought I'd missed you!"

"I just stepped out for a minute," I call back. "What can I do for you?"

"I need a little help with the webpage for the Festival," she says. "I was wondering if you could stop by and get it all up on Google for me."

I've been building web pages for Miss Paula since the Internet was invented. Actually, I've been designing her brochures, fixing her printer, and putting attachments on her e-mails, too. Since Miss Paula is the head of the Eagle Valley Historical Society, she has a lot to do. Since she's my mother's best friend, I have to help her.

"Sure," I tell her. "How about after the meeting on Monday?"

"You're a lifesaver, Arden," she says. "We're going to be busy, busy, busy from now until Festival comes! How are we coming along? Are we prepared?"

Translation: Have I touched up the paint on my store's window frames? Do I have enough inventory to last all four weekends of the Eagle Valley Living History Festival? Am I ready for weeks of emergency meetings and last-minute detail planning? Answers: yes, getting there, and no.

"It's all coming along," I tell her. "You have a good evening. I'll see you at the meeting."

"You too, honey. Only one week until Festival!" she trills.

I watch as she changes direction and walks back towards the museum. Thor chooses this moment to squat. I wonder if I should read anything into that.

The sun's setting now. I take another hard look at Main Street, studying the way the low orange light sets off the brick sidewalk, the street, and the windows of the stores across the way. The streetlamps are glowing softly, too. It's undeniable now, this feeling. The mist-like sense of change I felt rolling through earlier has turned into a thick blanket setting over Eagle Valley. What this future is, I don't know, but it's closing in.

I hope this premonition doesn't take too long to break. In my experience, the longer the build-up, the bigger the change that's coming. When my coffee maker broke last month, I got about five seconds of warning before I saw a vision of it going up in smoke. When Jeremy and I broke up six months ago, I knew something was wrong for days before I got the vision of Jeremy driving away.

There's nothing I can do to make a premonition break before it's good and ready. Nothing I can do to change the future once I see it, either. I know that from experience, too. So I do what I've learned to do best. I settle in and wait.

Nobody else comes in before closing, which gives me plenty of time to balance the books. Doesn't take too long these days. Not a lot of folks are buying, so nothing much is moving in or out of the shop. I haven't been to an auction in weeks.

I hold the pen and my ledger with my bare hands. There's a good long history of worry buried deep in both of them. It practically jumps off the pages and crawls all over the fingerprints I left on the pen. Earlier this year, I had enough extra to make some real progress on fixing up my little house. New floors, new paint, new almost everything. Now I wish I'd held off. The last few months, I've been juggling bills like a circus clown.

I'm holding out hope for October. Most folks would say a month-long Festival of Living History Days is crazy. It is crazy, but these days, it's crazy-important. Festival does more than put our little old town on the map. It brings tourists, and tourists bring money.

Owning an antique store in Eagle Valley, Virginia should be a business owner's dream come true. The setting is perfect, right in the middle of a small-town historic district. Everybody who comes to Main Street is primed and ready to buy a little piece of history to take home.

I bought the place from Bryson and Sadie five years ago. I was twenty-six and they were just retiring. Well, not retiring exactly. They owned this store plus two others, plus a few booths in an antique mall in Roanoke, and Bryson had some side work managing estate sales. Their version of retirement was scaling back to the antique mall and estate sales.

Most people don't leave Eagle Valley when they retire. We're born here, we're raised here, and we die here. It ended up working out well for them, though. A couple years later, Sadie started having some health problems, and now she has an oxygen tank and breathing treatments to deal with. I think it's best that they're closer to the hospital, all things considered.

Back when they decided to sell, I probably seemed like the natural choice to take over the store. I'd been working here since I was eighteen. College wasn't really in the cards for me, and I've always had a knack for selling antiques. Even Bryson thought so.

"I've never met an antique dealer that wouldn't bargain," he used to say, shaking his head every time a customer left. "Don't you know people like a little back-and-forth?"

I do know that, and I also know that nobody should be bargaining with me. Fact is, I'm too good. If I wanted, I could read people to find out how bad they want a piece and then drive the price up as high as they'll pay. Or if they're looking for something special, I could convince them that something not-so-great is exactly what they want. That's just taking advantage, though. Nobody knows about me and the way I can sense things. But I know. So my rule is, the price on the sticker is the price I'll take, no exceptions. Fair's fair.

My other rule is just as simple: always sell it with a story. That's what people really go antiquing for. They want something different, something with a history they can tell their guests and show off to their family. Lucky for me, I always know the story behind a piece. Unlike visions of the future, which hover and hesitate and shift at random, visions of the past are clear. If I brush my fingers over a piece, I'll get a hint of the stories it holds, the same way I could get a whiff of old varnish or a glimpse of a worn patina. If I wrap my hands around a piece, really take the time to feel and listen, the stories come out just as clear as if they were spoken aloud.

All I need to do after that is listen to the people that come in to buy. This morning, I sold a little wooden rocking chair to a retired couple from Lynchburg. When you get right down to it, they could have gone and bought a brand-new rocking chair for half the price, if they just wanted a chair to rock their grandchildren in. Probably would have been more comfortable, too.

But that's not what they wanted. The husband was in the army for thirty years. There's not a day that goes by that he doesn't look around and feel proud to be here in America. Plenty grateful, too. The wife moved all over and raised their children at Fort This and Fort That, selling all their things and buying used whenever they moved somewhere new. What these folks wanted was an heirloom, a genuine piece of American history they could pass on to their children. So I told them how that rocking chair once belonged to a young German immigrant. She bought it with the first paycheck she made in America so she could rock her babies to sleep at night.

Granted, the whole time that poor woman was rocking her babies, she was praying they wouldn't turn out to be no-account dead beats like their daddy. I left that part out, though. There is always a part of a story people are happier not knowing. I don't think that's lying. I think that's just kindness.

Whether or not Bryson agrees with my business policies, he can't argue with success. He gave me a good deal when I bought the store from him. All things considered, I haven't done too badly for myself. Up until now, the ink in my account books has been more black than red, and that's something. I've made a few changes to the store, here and there. Right after I bought it, I changed the name to McCrae's Antiques. When your father's the former town mayor and your mother co-founded the Eagle Valley Historical Society, using the family name doesn't hurt.

The best change I've made so far was building the store's online presence. I did that two years ago, when the recession first started to hit Eagle Valley. Truth is, if I hadn't, the store would have gone under back then. Now I'm almost back in the same boat, and no more tricks up my sleeves. If I am having a premonition, I hope it's not about my business.

I tap my pen against the last page of the ledger, sending electric shocks of anxiety through my fingers. *Come on, October,* I think.

When I go to lock up the store, the air is heavy with foreboding. Outside my window, though, everything is still Norman Rockwell perfect. I try to tell myself that maybe it's all in my head. Maybe I'm just sensing the rollover from summer to autumn, or maybe I'm just wishing Jeremy will come back. Sometimes you can want something so much you almost imagine it into existence.

Come to think of it, wishful thinking is probably how Jeremy and I stayed together as long as we did.

Enough. I shake my head, as if I could rattle that thought loose for good. If there's a point after a breakup when you can actually stop thinking about your ex-boyfriend, I'd sure like to get there. I hate that I'm stuck remembering someone that's already forgotten me.

It's Thursday, so I've got other things to think about anyway. On Tuesdays and Thursdays, I drop by Mama and Daddy's, just to check in and make sure they're all right. My sister Eliza drives up from Roanoke on the weekends to visit, too. It's been a rough year. Maybe this premonition is a good one. Maybe we're going to get things rolling for Mama and Daddy to go into assisted living. Maybe some nursing care or round-the-clock help. Maybe Mama will stop being so stressed. Maybe Daddy will get better.

There's that wishful thinking again. Daddy's not getting any better.

I call Thor, and big oaf that he is, he stumbles awake from where he's been snoring happily in the stockroom. Dog doesn't know how good he has it.

Thor's pretty calm while I turn the lock on the front door. As soon as he sees the truck parked in the back alley, though, he winds himself back up, nails clacking on the sidewalk like a tap dancer.

"Sit!" I say firmly, and God love him, he tries. Thor sits and wiggles his butt so much he's standing again, then sits, wiggles, sits. I take pity on him and open the truck door then help him hop inside.

Once I start the truck, Thor settles down and rests his front paws on the armrest. His nose is busy, snorting and sniffing the breeze out the truck window. I imagine he smells things in the wind the way I hear things by touch. If I didn't have to keep my hands on the wheel, I might try petting him just to see what he's picking up. *Who's grilling outside one last time before autumn really hits? Who's ready for the weekend or a vacation or to leave this town, once and for all?* We get a lot of those, around the time school starts up. Angsty high school seniors ready to make their plans and move on to see the world. In five years, about half of them will be back. A place like Eagle Valley, people never really leave behind.

2

The smell of pine trees hits Thor and me a good half-mile before we turn into my parents' driveway. The McCrae Christmas Tree Farm is relatively new by Eagle Valley standards, operating for only twenty-five years. For three generations before that, it was a dairy farm. I was so little when we had the cows that I barely remember them. My sisters Eliza and Lila Beth remember better. They were old enough to help with things like watering and feeding. As far as I'm concerned, farm chores always meant fertilizing the trees, making wreaths to sell, and running the apple cider table during tree-selling season. Whenever I smell pine, I feel like I'm late to work.

I pull up and park behind my mother's car. I let Thor out into the backyard, and he's only too happy to get out and run. "Stay here," I tell Thor, even though there's nowhere else for him to really go. The road's a good way back and the nearest neighbors are more than a mile away. He'll spend the whole visit inspecting every blade of grass. On cool days like this, he's happier outside anyway. In my parents' house, he wouldn't be allowed to sit on, lay down near, or sniff anything too historic. Which is to say, most of the house.

I crunch up the gravel driveway, pausing to blow a kiss towards the dogwood tree by the porch. I can see lights in almost every window downstairs.

"Hello!" I call through the back door, clambering past the swinging storm door. The kitchen looks clean. Everything's been wiped down and the floors have been swept. Things must be going well today.

"Hello, Arden," says Mama, poking her head out of the laundry room. The older she gets, the more she reminds me of a little bird. She can't be more than a hundred pounds soaking wet, and she moves like a sparrow hopping from one branch to another. "It's so nice to see you. Get yourself something to drink."

I'm not thirsty, but I open up the refrigerator anyway and scan the shelves. Eggs, yogurt, a ham, hot dogs. Plenty of water bottles and Sprite, which is the most exciting drink Mama allows herself. The top shelf is full of condiments and dishes of leftover peas and pot roast. I make a mental note for when I call Eliza. No need for her to stop by with groceries this weekend.

"How are things at the store?" Mama asks. She comes fully into the kitchen, carrying a basket of folded shirts and jeans. The basket is so big it looks like it might snap her in half. She puts it on the kitchen table.

"Made a good sale today," I say lightly. "Sold a cute little rocking chair."

Mama nods, but her eyes are focusing past my shoulder, out the back window. I turn to see if Thor's getting into something he shouldn't in the backyard. He's actually behaving himself, lying down in the grass with his nose resting on his paws. With the pine trees and the mountains as a backdrop, he makes a pretty picture.

I figure I'll let her have a minute to herself. With Daddy the way he is, she doesn't get many of those. "Mind if I use the bathroom?" I ask. Mama barely acknowledges the question. She just nods.

I walk extra slow and brush my hands against the walls, trying to catch stories as I go. Trying to pick a specific story out of a family home is worse than that proverbial needle in a haystack. Mostly my fingers catch faint hums of activity, some from today and some from way before I was born. Daddy paced this hallway dozens of times last night. My sister Eliza played Barbies here when she was six years old. There's another note here I can't place, but I keep moving. I don't have all day.

I pass the front room, which I notice is covered in a fine coat of dust. I'm itching to clean it, but keep going. It's not like they're going to use that room anytime soon. The front room in my parents' house is a homage to 1889, the year my great-grandfather built this house. It's used exactly once a year, when my parents host the Eagle Valley Legends Gala after Festival's over. By "Eagle Valley Legends," they mean the mostly-untrue stories of the town's history. By "Gala," they mean punch and polite conversation on the politically incorrect horsehair couch.

The back rooms of the house are a little cozier. Daddy is in the family room, stretched out on the couch. His mouth hangs wide open while he snores, and his glasses sit lopsided on his forehead.

Despite all that, when he's sleeping, Daddy looks almost peaceful. That's why I walk toward him, lean down and inhale the dark, spicy scent of his cologne. I pretend to adjust the quilt Mama spread over him, so it covers his shoulders. Then I get brave and lean in for a hug.

Hugging is not my thing—touching objects is complicated enough. Generally, I touch people the way I would a live grenade: quick and light as I can, and only if I have to. The last few years with Daddy, hugs are more of a barometer for where he is each day. His story feels a bit like a sliding scale. Instead of being all in the present with a clear past, scenes from his whole life seem to bubble up and take turns rising to the top. I hold nothing back when I wrap my arms around his shoulders. He's having a good day. I'm glad.

When I lean back up, I catch a glimpse of Mama standing in the doorway. She's looking away, mouth stretched taut.

"He looks so peaceful," I say. "Has he had a good day?"

"Better than most," Mama says. The truth hangs between us as heavily as the premonition that's been threatening to come all afternoon. We don't come out and say "Alzheimer's" in our family. That's not how McCraes handle things. We say he's "absent-minded" or "feeling his age" or "having a hard time."

I walk back to where Mama is standing. She holds herself stiff and straight as a board, arms crossed. She doesn't understand why I can't hug her as easily as Daddy. I want to reach out to her next, maybe catch her hand or something, but I can't. Even on a peaceful day, hugging just about drains me to the core. I feel like a dishrag, all wrung out.

"I'll just go up to use the bathroom," I say instead. Mama nods.

Upstairs, I run the water for a few seconds while I snap on a new pair of rubber gloves and quickly scrub the tub, toilet, and sink. I run one of the old wash-cloths around the floor with my toe. Then I whip the used towels into the hamper and replace them with fresh ones from the linen closet. My record is five minutes total. Today, I finish in just under seven.

A quick look in the bedroom shows Mama was able to change the sheets and make the bed this morning. I pull one crisp twenty-dollar bill out of my pocket and place it half-hidden behind their penny jar. I crumple up the other twenty I brought and put it in Mama's robe pocket. Forty dollars is the highest amount that Mama won't question. Once I left a fifty, and the next time I visited, Mama tucked it right back into the pie plate she returned.

I don't take the rubber gloves off when I dust. I try to focus on the picture frames, the tops of the tables, and the railing. When I finish, I throw the rag in the hamper and snap off the gloves. That should hold them for a bit. Next week, I'll ask to use the down-stairs bathroom and do my once-over there.

I take my time walking back down the stairs. The stairwell is decorated with tasteful wood frames and sepia-toned family pictures, all labeled at the bottom in my mother's neat curlicue writing. The pictures range from my great-grandfather (Charles McCrae II, 1889.) to my parents' wedding picture (Vaughn McCrae II and Dorothy Davison McCrae, June 1, 1969.) to Tripp's baby picture (Vaughn McCrae III, 1970. Six weeks old.)

Tripp was my parents' first child. He died when he was two months old, at a time when people were just starting to use the term SIDS. As if there was actually a way to put a label on heartbreak. It took three years before Lila Beth arrived. There aren't any vacation photos or picture albums from those three years. No memorabilia meant to remind them of every aching day. I feel like those stories are engraved into this house, though. Engraved into my parents, too.

Sprinkled throughout the wall are happier times in the family history. Also featured on the wall is Eliza's wedding portrait, Lila Beth's college graduation, and Daddy by the town sign the day he was elected mayor. And we can't forget, Mama and Miss Paula cutting a giant ribbon on the newly restored Main Street.

Other than a picture of me standing by Bryson and Sadie on the day I bought the store, my most recent appearance on the wall is my high school senior picture. I look about the same, thanks to my baby face and a lifelong devotion to sunscreen. I have McCrae curly hair—you can't see the reddish-brown tint from the pictures, but Daddy and both my sisters have the exact same shade. I have a sharp chin and sharper knees and elbows, courtesy of the Davison side. Brown eyes, like Mama and Lila Beth, and a pert nose last seen on my Grandfather McCrae. Looking at our picture wall is like seeing my reflection in a shattered mirror.

When I get to the bottom of the stairs, Mama is waiting for me. She looks more like a bird than ever, as if any second she might just twitch into flight.

"There's something you should be aware of," she begins, and I freeze for a minute. *Here it comes.* I feel like the premonition is hovering just overhead now, ready to break.

"We got the call," says Mama. "A room opened up for us at the assisted living facility. We've got thirty days to move in."

"Good!" I tell her. I wait for the heaviness to leave the air, holding on to the railing in case it's a strong premonition. Nothing.

Mama nods absently. "We still have the farm to sell," she says. "And...we won't be needing much when we move. Could you get Bryson to do an estate sale for us?"

"Sure, I can ask him." I'm still waiting for that premonition to break, but the air is just as dense and heavy as when I walked downstairs. "When do you need it done?"

"By the end of October would be nice," Mama says. "So I guess that gives us a month. If Bryson can manage it."

It's a tight timeline, but I'm not telling Mama that. "I'll call him," I promise. "Didn't the Historical Society put in an offer on the farm? Wouldn't they want some of the furniture?"

"They did make an offer," Mama says. "But nothing's final yet."

"I'm sure they'll do right by you," I tell her.

The faraway look in Mama's eyes is almost too much for me. This moment shouldn't be any great surprise. Eliza and I were there to tour the assisted living place with Mama and Daddy. We were there when they made a deposit and heard the timeline for the waiting list. We were there when they put the farm on the market. Doesn't make it any easier though.

I have to be slow about it when I reach out to her. Unlike Daddy, Mama carries her hurt just under the surface. It knocks my breath away if I hug her too quickly. It's all there when I manage to get both arms around her. Me, Eliza, Lila Beth, Tripp, the farm, the town, and Daddy... especially Daddy.

"I'm sorry," I say. I wish holding her could actually do something. I wish I could pull off all her hurt and carry some of it for her. When I start thinking that, I get kind of panicky. Everything she's feeling starts buzzing against my skin like a live wire. I pull away before I can stop myself.

Mama smoothes back an imaginary stray hair and acts like she doesn't notice.

"I'm sorry," I say again.

"We have to do what we have to do," she says simply.

I nod. I couldn't feel worse if I'd slapped her. "I'll be by again soon. Just to say hi. And you'll call if you need anything," I remind her.

"We are fine," Mama says, smiling with a firmness that reminds me she is still the mother, and I am still the child.

I barely hear the storm door creak closed behind me. Thor comes loping towards the truck, excited to go for another ride. It's only out of habit that I remember to blow a kiss towards Tripp's dogwood tree before I buckle my seatbelt and turn the key in the ignition. Thor sniffs out the window, investigating the pine-scented breeze as if it had all the secrets the world could hold.

The change I felt rolling over Eagle Valley feels heavier, thicker, like it's coating my skin and infecting the air. I breathe it in all the way home.

3

By the time I wake up on Friday morning, my cell phone already has three missed calls. They're all from Miss Paula. I roll over and wedge the phone between my mattress and the wall. Some days are just easier to deal with if you've lost your phone. I lose mine at least once a month. Works wonders.

Thor is already prancing and dancing on the floor, so I make myself get dressed and take him outside. I sit gingerly on the porch swing. I'm almost afraid to move or breathe, in case that's what will shatter this moment and unleash whatever's coming next. Thor, oblivious to my stress, finishes his business and tries to catch moths in his mouth. If there's such a thing as reincarnation, I want to come back as my dog.

I sit still long enough that the air starts to feel like it's shrink-wrapping around me. I need to move. If this one's going to last for days, I can't let myself get crushed by the wait. I push off with one foot to make the swing rock, which sends Thor running back to me. He still hasn't figured out what to make of the swing. He always looks caught between wanting to leap on and wanting to run away from it.

There are thousands of things I could be doing right now. Since I don't open until noon on Fridays, these mornings are usually reserved for errands and projects. I have a whole stack of things for the store in my basement that need repairing, refinishing or polishing. The kitchen and bathroom could be scrubbed. The store needs a window display for Festival. And then there's my house.

After a year and a half and thousands of dollars spent at the hardware store, my fixer-upper is mostly fixed up. It's structurally sound, anyway, and the inside's looking pretty good. Last year, when Jeremy and I were still together, I impressed him with my ability to find beams that needed replacing and floorboards that were starting to rot. "With almost no experience," he marveled. I took the compliment, although it's not terribly hard to track down termites and water damage when you can hear the stories left behind. Not that Jeremy would know that.

Now that most of the big things are done, it's starting to feel more like a home and less like a never-ending project. On the inside, that is. The outside is about as awful as the day I bought it. Maybe even worse. I'd meant to paint the house this summer, but I only got as far as the left side before I decided light gray paint didn't look the way I'd hoped it would. Then sage green didn't look right, and neither did blue. Now it's fall, and I have ten empty cans of sample paint and a house that looks like Frankenstein.

I walk around to the side of the house to survey my samples. Thor, good dog that he is, comes trotting over to investigate. He takes an unnecessarily high leap over a patch of dandelions. I haven't even thought about the front yard yet. The only thing I can do with plants is cut them or kill them. So far, I've got a survival-of-the-fittest deal with the flora around my house. If it can make it on its own, it gets to stay. A Darwin garden. This is how the oaks in the backyard got big enough to overshadow the house and why the pansies Eliza gave me died the day after I planted them.

Thor is happy to take an investigative sniff at the siding, but then he's off trying to pounce on a grasshopper. I stand back and consider the house. The problem is, none of the colors I've splashed up there—pearl gray, smoky blue, sage green—looks right. Nothing fits.

I've touched the clapboard siding before, of course, so I already know that originally it was white. Then it was a shocking yellow, then gray, and now it's white again. What I don't know is what color it needs to be next. What color will give it a new life and make it look like a home again? I lean in and try to really listen past the superficial whispers of the trial paints and the rain and wind that's pelted the siding. I listen all the way down to when the house was new and this was a jewel on wooded acreage instead of a fixer-upper in a jungle.

I love the sound of this house. I love the deep, buried murmurs of families that lived here before. A history that's almost a hundred years old. I love that the newer notes of Thor dancing across the floors and me hammering in new beams float on top, like a descant. A present that's new and hopeful, and a future that's ready and waiting to be filled.

Lilac. I see it suddenly, and it's exactly right. A dusty, weathered color, but with a hint of lavender to warm it up and set it apart. I'll paint the trim cream to contrast with the slate gray of the roof. I could kick myself for not just listening from the beginning. I would have saved myself a lot of paint samples.

"Go for a ride, Thor?" I ask, and he takes off for the pickup. I guess I'm not fast enough for him, because he comes back and bounds in circles around my feet before leaping ahead again.

I'm hoping Eagle Valley Hardware has the color I have in mind. They'll mix whatever color you want, but I can just see the look on Russ Wainwright's face when I go in and tell him how many gallons I want of lilac paint. I hold on to a vain hope that I can just grab my cans and get out.

Sure enough, it's a special mix, and Russ gives me a side-eye the entire time he programs the mixer. "You sure about this, Miss Arden?" he asks. Twice. "What about that blue you had last time? That'd look real nice on your place."

"Positive," I tell him, keeping an eye on Thor by the entrance. Russ isn't much for dogs, but by now, he's got Thor trained to sit just inside the door and wait while I shop. Thor never strays from his spot, but from here, I can see his nose twitching like crazy, picking up all the scents.

"Have you ever seen such a patient dog?" I gloat to Russ. "Smart, too. I've never heard of a dog that trained so fast."

"I've never heard of anyone painting a house purple," grumbles Russ, but he rings me up anyway. "You have a sixty-day return guarantee on that paint," he says, circling the bar code in blue pen and pushing it across the counter towards me. "Start with the sample. If it doesn't look the way you want, bring those cans back and get your refund."

"I didn't pick up a sample, Russ."

"It's on me. You paint a house purple, Miss Arden, you better be sure."

I have just enough time to pop into Golda's Diner before I open the store. Unlike Russ, Golda doesn't mind if I bring the dog into her place, so long as I keep him out when the health inspector shows up. Golda fears very few things in life, but the health inspector is one of them.

Golda's Diner has established Eagle Valley credibility for three reasons. One, there isn't anywhere else to eat for at least thirty miles. Two, Golda's great-great granddaddy was a baker in the army during the Civil War. And three, her diner has outlived almost every other business on Main Street. If Golda ever stands still long enough, Miss Paula might just nail a brass historical plaque on her.

I like stopping by here at least a couple times a week. I don't come for dinner much anymore, on account of wanting to get Thor back home, but sometimes I'll slip in for a quick coffee before work or a sandwich for lunch. There's almost always someone here that I know. Russ stops by a lot, and even Mr. Carson likes to come in and shoot the breeze for a while. Cliff is usually there when he's not out on a job. He and Golda got married six years ago after a whirlwind romance that surprised absolutely nobody but them.

Thor strains on the leash when we get closer. I stop and wait for him to mind his manners and come back to my side before we go in. I have to keep Thor close while we're at Golda's. The smell of frying bacon sends him into a panting, drooling frenzy.

Today, I've got just enough time for a coffee before opening. Golda's food is more what you'd call serviceable than good, but she makes a strong cup of coffee and remembers to make my stuff vegetarian. I don't suppose there are many ways to get through a premonition, but a cup of Golda's coffee is good as any.

"Mornin', Golda," I call out when I open the door. Sometimes she gets sidetracked in the back room and forgets to listen for the bells she's tied to the door.

"Mornin', sugar," she hollers from the grill. The customers at the counter turn and give a little half-wave as I come in. It's Cliff and Mr. Carson, the librarian. My heart sinks a little when I realize Gordon Johns is here too. Jeremy's dad. I try to give him a sincere smile. For some reason, I feel like I'm just baring my teeth.

"Just a coffee, please," I say to Golda.

"And a doughnut," she tells me, lobbing a glazed homemade pastry on a plate. "On the house."

I don't even pretend to argue. "Thanks, Golda," I say and tear off a bite while she gets the coffee. I chew. And chew. The dough is tough and the glaze so sweet it makes my eyes water. Too late, I notice the others have doughnuts partially hidden underneath their napkins.

"How's your dad?" Golda asks the way people do when they know the answer isn't good. She tosses Thor a small piece of bacon. He settles on his haunches, smacking his lips over the treat. Dogs that live with vegetarians don't get a lot of bacon.

"Daddy's hanging in there," I say, gratefully accepting the coffee she passes me. "Mama is too."

The men bob their heads without making eye contact. There's a short silence, and I have a quick pang of fear that somebody's going to break it with more sympathy.

"I was just at Russ's buying some paint for the house," I say quickly. "I'm going to get a start on it this weekend."

"What are you painting?" Golda asks. "Not that living room again."

I've painted the living room three different shades of blue in search of the perfect color. When I started looking at paint chips for a fourth try, Golda practically held an intervention.

"No, for the outside," I say. "Finally decided to get the siding fixed up."

"Should I ask what color?" Golda asks.

"Lilac."

Mr. Carson and Gordon both get the exact same frozen smile. Cliff's face gets a squinchy look, like he's trying to figure out what color lilac is.

Golda nods approvingly. "I could see it," she says. "With white trim? That could look real nice. A little unexpected."

"I'd like to see what Paula thinks of that," Mr. Carson says, smiling faintly. "Are you going to tell her first or let her find out when it's done?"

"She doesn't answer to Paula Abernathy," Gordon says, shooting Mr. Carson a look. I hate that it's Jeremy's dad sticking up for me.

"Of course she doesn't," Mr. Carson says quickly. Normally, he makes himself talk in a deep voice everyone knows is fake. When he's caught a little off guard—like now—he slips for a minute, and his voice is high and reedy. "I was just thinking of how Paula's going to react, is all."

If Miss Paula ever gave up the museum, Mr. Carson would leave the library in a heartbeat and take her place as the town historian. Except Miss Paula will probably never give up the museum, so Mr. Carson has had to satisfy himself by writing reports on the history of the Eagle Valley Library for over twenty years. My guess is he's thought about going up against Miss Paula a time or two.

"I think you should go for it," says Golda. "The town could use a little shaking up."

The town's about to get a little shaken up, I think. If my premonitions mean anything–and they always do–the town's about to get shaken to the core. I take a last swig of coffee and push my mug and plate back across the counter.

"Got to go to work," I say. "Have a good one."

"You too," they say, almost in unison. Golda tosses Thor another tidbit of bacon, which he smacks and gulps all the way out the door.

Outside, the sky is so shockingly blue it knocks the breath straight out of me. Across the street, I can see Thor and I won't be the only ones opening my store today. Miss Paula Abernathy is waiting for me at the door.

"Arden!" Miss Paula says brightly as I approach. "I was worried about you when I didn't get a little call-back this morning. Glad to see you and Thor are okay."

"Did you call? I can't seem to find my phone. Lost it again," I say. It's only a little lie, but my cheeks still burn with shame.

Miss Paula doesn't move away from the door, so I have to shimmy sideways to fit the key in the lock. She walks in first. Thor tears past her and runs into the stock room to lie down on his bed. Smart dog.

I turn on the lights, open the cash register, and go about opening the store. Miss Paula stands uncomfortably close, observing. She makes my skin crawl without even touching her. If that premonition breaks today, I hope it happens without Miss Paula watching.

"I was calling about your parents, Arden," she says. For a second, I actually wonder if something happened to them and Miss Paula found out before me. "Of course we're all so sad they're moving, but naturally everyone wants what's best for your father. Your parents really made this town what it is today."

I am about three seconds away from swatting at Miss Paula and running away, like Thor. I can't keep breathing this thick air, turning away from the sharp light, listening to Miss Paula talk louder and closer.

It takes everything I have to walk back to the counter, unsnap a fresh pair of dishwashing gloves, and slide them on. My hands are instantly quieter. All I feel is the clean rubber against my skin instead of the dozens of stories coming at me. It's already easier to breathe. I take a cloth and glass cleaner out, wipe down the counter like it's all just part of my morning routine.

"Of course, you know your mother came to the Society first. And, Arden, I just want you to know that we made them a very reasonable offer. I told her, "Dottie, don't you worry about a thing. You've done so much for Eagle Valley, now Eagle Valley's going to take care of you."

I'm scrubbing at the edges of the counter now, where all those fingerprints collect and it's hard to get everything good and clean. I push so hard I wonder if the glass will break and snow shards all over the display of jewelry and watches underneath.

"That's good of you," I say to Miss Paula. "I'm sure Mama and Daddy appreciate it." I find it in me to look up again, and she's right there. Her and her clear blue eyes boring into me.

"I just hope they'll take us up on our offer," she says. Her words come at me slowly. I look down again and concentrate on scrubbing that corner. "It would mean so much to all of us to keep their house as part of our historic district."

That part surprises me. "Are they in the historic district?" I ask. "I thought they were barely in the town limits." What I don't say is that I remember when Daddy wanted to run for mayor, and he couldn't because our house was just outside town. Miss Paula led the petition to extend the town limit past our mailbox, so he could run.

"If they sell the house to the Historical Society, I guarantee you I'll get it added to our register," Miss Paula says. "Tell your mother not to worry for a second about that."

Tell my mother... Why would I tell Mama anything? If Miss Paula is telling me, Mama must already know. I look up at Miss Paula, but she's still just looking at me, waiting for some sort of answer.

I suppose I could just reach out and touch her arm or brush her shoulder to find out what the real story is. She's standing close enough, for sure. Thing is, Miss Paula's so intense that trying to listen to her is like tuning an air horn.

"Mama and Daddy are smart," I say finally. "They'll do what needs to be done."

Miss Paula leans back a bit, looking satisfied. "Yes," she says thoughtfully. "They always do." She flashes a brilliant smile. "Good talking with you, Arden," she says. "You have a good day, now."

Have a good day. Like it's that simple.

4

Talking to Miss Paula reminds me to call Bryson and arrange for an estate sale. There's a call I'm not looking forward to. But the store's quiet, so I reach for the phone on the counter. I keep my gloves on to pick up the receiver and dial. It's easier to talk when I'm not picking up reminders of every other conversation I've had on this phone.

Sadie answers. "Arden!" she says before I get a chance to say anything. "I saw your number pop up on the machine and I just about had a fit. Didn't I, Bryson?" In the background, I hear Bryson's deep voice mumbling assent. "Just last night I was saying to

Bryson, 'How long has it been since we heard from Arden?'"

Two weeks, I'm about to answer, but Sadie keeps right on talking.

"Must be two weeks at least! How're things going with you? How's the store? No, don't start with that. How're your folks? I just bet your mother's up to her ears in work, with Festival around the corner."

"Actually..." I say, half-expecting Sadie to cut me off. She doesn't, so I keep talking. "Actually, that's what I called about. Mama and Daddy got a spot at the assisted living place, so they're moving out this month. I was wondering if Bryson could help us with the estate sale?"

"Oh," Sadie says. "Oh. Oh. I'm sorry, honey. Let me get Bryson for you. Here he is." There's a brief scuffle while she passes him the phone and gives him a heads-up.

"An estate sale for her folks," she's saying in a not-quite-whisper. "Going to the assisted living place. Her daddy must be going downhill fast."

Then it's Bryson on the other end of the phone. "Hey, kid," he says. "What can I do for you?"

"Mama and Daddy just got word that their room at the assisted living place is ready." Saying it for the second time hits me harder. I can just imagine how a spot became available. "Mama wanted to have an estate sale for everything they're not taking with them. Can you help?"

"Course I can," Bryson says. "Let me get my calendar out here. When were you thinking?"

"Mama said by the end of October. If you can."

Bryson is grimacing. I know he is. "It'll have to be the very end of October," he says slowly. "Think a two-day sale will be long enough? I can do the last Friday and Saturday. The 30th and 31st."

"Two days should be fine," I say. "One for the early birds, one for the bargain hunters."

Bryson gives a little chuckle for that. "My boys can help me the day of the sale," he says. Bryson and Sadie have two grown sons that help them out on estate sale days. "Only thing that's going to be tough is getting everything tagged. When will your folks be moved out?"

"I'm not sure," I admit. "I think Mama wants to get them out and settled pretty quickly. Thirty days from now is, what, the 24th? Maybe a week before? I'm sure they'll be moved out before then."

"We'll make it the week before the sale, just to be safe." Bryson clicks his tongue. Sadie hates it when he does that.

"I can help with the tagging," I volunteer. "I think Eliza can too."

"I don't know about that, Arden," Bryson says. "You know I don't like it when the family's involved. Too personal."

"And I know this timeline is way too tight," I say. "Would you and the boys really be able to get it all done in a week?"

"I can find help." Bryson is starting to sound stubborn. I'd better ease up.

"What if you write us up a price sheet?" I say. "You know the basic stuff all tends to be the same. Eliza and I can tag the kitchen utensils and things like that. Leave you guys to handle the rest."

Bryson doesn't say anything.

"We'll just be an extra set of hands You set the prices, we'll write the tags," I say. "You know I'm good at sticking to a price."

"All right, Arden," Bryson says. "All right. You talk it over with Eliza, and if y'all are up for it, that's what we'll do."

I look out the store window after we say our goodbyes and hang up. I guess the premonition that's been threatening to break isn't about my parents' estate. Outside, everything looks sharp and crystalline. A perfect snapshot before everything changes.

By the end of the day, when Janie comes in, I'm polishing the dust off the furniture in the back. It's been another slow day for customers. Just one couple from Salem, and then a mother and daughter passing through on their way to North Carolina. I've spent most of the day arranging, rearranging, scrubbing, and dusting. Thor has only ventured out from the stockroom twice to be taken outside.

"TGIF, Miss Arden!" Janie calls out, slamming her backpack down behind the counter. She stops. "Whoa. You've been busy."

At the tender age of seventeen, Janie is already something that most adults never become: a good assistant. She has her opinions, but she does what I ask her to do around the store without contradicting, and that's worth what I pay her.

"Just a little busy," I say, dropping my dust cloth and coming over to her.

"Is everything...okay?" she asks, eyeing the front displays.

"I've done some rearranging," I say. "Just getting things ready for First Friday."

"And Festival," she adds. This is another reason I like Janie. The first weekend of Festival is a week away. She's smart enough to know the store doesn't need a floor-to-ceiling scrub right now, but she goes along with me anyway.

I get her started in the stock room, writing price tags for the second-string merchandise I've set aside. It'll be good to have those pieces on hand. I'm hoping that when Festival comes, we'll be restocking the shelves faster than we can write price tags.

The air fairly hums with tension. I've had premonitions all my life, and I know by now that nobody else can hear the stories of the past that I pick up or sense the future I see coming. It'd be enough to make me feel crazy, if my visions weren't always right. Can't tell anyone about them, either. Half the time, I feel like I'm lying to people, spouting out guesses and "I don't knows" so I'll seem normal. People will forgive too much honesty about the present, and they'll even admire honesty about the past. But spot-on honesty about the future, that's just creepy.

Take Janie. She's a smart cookie. Straight A student, first-chair violinist, and already taking college math classes even though she's still in high school. She's got her eye on an Ivy League education, and a little premonition told me she'll get it. Someone like Janie would never understand about visions or how I have to clean things to help keep stories from the past at bay. She'd use words like "coincidence" or "déjà vu" or "overactive imagination." That's why she gets jobs like marking price tags and cataloging inventory. She's all about accuracy. If it were up to her, the whole store would be arranged by time period, with merchandise lined up by height on matching shelves.

Me, I like a vignette. I keep the jewelry in the glass display case at the front of the store, but other than that, I arrange my displays like little scenes. Right now, my front window display is a gorgeous oak dining set. I have table linens and hand-crocheted doilies spread over the buffet and spilling out of the drawers, like the hostess was just deciding which one to use. China sets and silverware are arranged on the table and in the china cabinet. It's enough that people can walk in and picture these things in their homes, but it's not so perfectly arranged that nobody wants to take something and destroy the scene. People are funny like that.

"I'm going to close the store this weekend," I tell Janie conversationally. "I owe myself a couple vacation days, and we'll need to rest up before October."

Janie nods. "With your parents moving and all, I guess there's a lot to do."

I stop. "You knew my parents were moving?"

Janie flushes, like a little kid caught stealing a cookie. "I just heard, on my way here. Miss Paula told me your parents were selling their house to the Society and moving to Roanoke." She skips a beat before adding, "I'm sorry about your dad."

"Oh," I say. "Thanks."

So they already settled things, I guess, and told Miss Paula. It makes sense. The Historical Society is probably the only one willing to buy a Christmas tree farm in the middle of nowhere. Have to preserve all that almost-significant town history.

"I didn't mean to upset you," Janie says. She's practically squirming in the little office chair.

"You didn't," I tell her. "I'm sure everyone knows." It even sounds fake to me, so I drop it, and we work in silence. It's not surprising when Janie suddenly remembers a paper she needs to research and asks to leave early. I decide to follow suit. I wave off the pang of guilt I get over closing for the weekend. I always have Mondays off, so I'll actually get a three-day break.

"Closed for the weekend. Back next week!" I scrawl on a piece of paper and tape it to the inside of the front door. All this stuff will be waiting for me when I get back. It's the weekend, and I've got a house to paint.

I wake up three times before dawn on Saturday. I know Thor is starting to worry. He's not allowed up on the bed, but he inches closer until he's sleeping right beside me, down on the floor. I let my arm hang down, and he snuffles it reassuringly.

The air is so heavy I'd swear a thunderstorm was rolling through, but the skies are clear and cloudless. I hate nights like this. When I was little, I used to give up on sleep and go make myself Ovaltine. I'd take deep swigs and try to breathe while I watched out the window for the first glimmers of dawn.

That's where Daddy would find me when he'd clomp through the kitchen in his work boots. "Well, hello there. What are you doing up so early?" he'd ask.

"Just thinking," I'd say.

Daddy would measure me with his eyes at the same time he measured coffee grounds into the coffee maker. "Something troubling you?"

I never quite managed to say *no*. Days like this, it's hard enough just to catch my breath.

He'd sit down next to me while the coffee brewed. "Spill it, kid."

Eventually, I'd manage to come up with some version of the truth. If the vision had already come, I'd give it a half-baked spin. "I'm worried I won't get invited to Bethany's birthday," I'd say, when actually I had a vision of all the other girls in class laughing and talking about me. Or, if I was waiting for a premonition, like now, I'd say, "I just feel like something bad's about to happen."

"Don't you go worrying about problems before they get here," he'd say. "If something happens, we'll handle it. If not, you'll wish you'd had more sleep and less Ovaltine."

Early on, I'd try to explain myself. "But if she doesn't invite me to her birthday, then I'll be left out. And if I'm left out, I won't have any friends next year in fourth grade or the next year, either."

Daddy would shake his head. "That's my little Cassandra," he'd say. "Always seeing problems two steps ahead."

"I'm not Cassandra. I'm Arden," I'd say.

That's when he'd tweak my nose and take my empty Ovaltine mug. "Cassandra was a prophetess in Greek mythology. Do you know what a prophetess is?"

"Is it like a princess?"

"It's someone who can see the future," Daddy said. "Cassandra saw visions of bad things happening to Greece, and she'd go around warning people and telling them what was coming."

The first time he said it, I felt like I'd been turned inside out. So he did know. Maybe everybody knew. Then he kept going.

"Good thing is, Cassandra is just a story. People can't really see the future, and you don't really know that this problem of yours is going to happen. Go on back upstairs, now. You need your sleep."

Then I'd go back to bed, and he'd go outside to start the chores. He didn't understand, not really. No one did. But at least he tried.

Thinking about Daddy the way he used to be sends a sharp pang deep in my gut. There's no way I'll get to sleep now. Might as well get up.

I've moved beyond Ovaltine when it comes to dealing with my premonitions. Some good hard work usually helps. If I'm straining every muscle, it takes my mind off myself. Kind of like stepping on your toe to distract yourself from a broken finger. It's not a perfect solution, but it works.

Painting the outside of a house is a lot like painting the walls or refinishing one of my pieces for sale. Go too fast, I have to go back and re-do it. Go too slow, and the paint starts drying while I work, making it streak. I start at the back of the house, which is convenient because the sun is on the other side in the morning. It also gives me a less-obvious place for mistakes. I finish a wide swath under the kitchen window and stand back before I get the ladder.

The lilac paint stands out against the September-green grass, like a thistle in a patch of clover. Even freshly painted, the paint looks dusty and slightly weathered. It is exactly what I pictured. Mostly gray, but with a hint of lavender thrown in. A little something special that makes you look again. I'm in love. I get the ladder and keep going.

By mid-afternoon, Thor gets tired of running around the backyard and lays down, face planted on his front paws, to supervise. I know he wants me to take a break to play with him, but I know myself too well. It's easier to press on through my throbbing muscles than it will be to pick the brush back up once I put it down. The only breaks I allow myself are spent perched on the ladder like an eagle, looking out over the yard. It's not really that high. My house isn't even two full stories. The master suite on the upstairs is so gabled and pitched that I can't stand up fully in most of it. Still, from up here, my house feels bigger than it really is, and my erstwhile yard looks lush and large.

By the time the sun is setting, I've actually put one coat on a good portion of the house. Even I didn't think I'd get that far in one day. My arms are shaking with exhaustion when I fold up the ladder and lean it against the porch. Then I hammer the lid back on the open can and put them on the porch too. It's not supposed to be windy tonight, so I fold the tarp and tuck it under the ladder. It'll have to do.

Before I go to bed, I indulge in a full, soaking bath. First, I pour in half the vanilla–scented bath salts Eliza gave me last Christmas. The water is turned up so hot that sweet, heady steam fogs up the bathroom mirror.

The bathroom was the first room I renovated floor to ceiling. I figure I did the house a favor. That much mint-green subway tile wasn't meant to exist in one place. Now it's an oasis. It has black and white tile that I set on the diagonal to make the room look bigger. There's white wainscoting and pretty robin's egg blue paint on the upper half of the walls, a pedestal sink and a claw-foot tub like I always wanted.

I peel off my sweaty clothes next, and it's like a rush of white noise, feeling cool, clean air against my skin instead. While I'm at it, I get a fresh washcloth and scrub off the faucet, the shampoo bottle pump, and the soap bottle. It's not until I turn off the water and step into the tub that I let myself really breathe. This is as close to quiet as my life ever gets.

That's the great thing about baths. The whole world is quiet and clean and I don't have to think or feel anything at all. I wash my hair twice and scour my skin until it's red and blisteringly clean.

When the water cools off, I turn the faucet with my toes to inject another rush of warmth in the tub. From where I sit, I can see Thor's shadow under the door. He's been lying there ever since I came in. Every time I run the water, I hear him get up, sniff under the door, whine for a few seconds, and lay back down. As much as that dog hates baths himself, he sure gets jealous when I take one.

Thor is the best thing that came out of my break-up with Jeremy. In those first days, I'd thrown myself into all kinds of projects just to keep myself from hearing the same sad story everywhere I went. I tore all the doors off my kitchen cupboards and replaced them with glass. After that, my plates and boxes of cereal stood as stark and exposed as I felt. Then came the haircut. I lopped off twelve inches of wavy reddish hair, leaving me with a mess of curls that bounced around my chin and tickled my neck. Finally, the dog. He's the one change I'm still glad I made.

Thor was the runt of the litter, so tiny all the other pups just toppled right over him. I'd picked the strongest name I could think of for him: Thor, after the Norse god of thunder. People thought I was being ironic, calling to this tiny Boxer puppy like he was a force to be reckoned with. He was big-hearted, though, strong in the way most people only hope to be. I knew it as soon as he came and nestled right up to my knee, like he was choosing me instead of the other way around.

That's about the opposite of how things had started out with Jeremy, so I'd taken it as a good omen. I spent most of our relationship trying to convince myself that he wanted to be with me just as badly as I

wanted to be with him. If I'm being honest with myself, I guess I knew from the beginning that it wasn't
going to work out with Jeremy. That's the thing. You
can hear the future that's coming all day long, hear it
every time you brush hands and stand with his arms
around you and especially when you kiss, that this is
ending before it even began. That this is never really
going to happen. But if you really want something—if
you really want some*one*—you just don't listen until
it's gone.

Suddenly, the bathwater feels like soup, full of feelings I wish I could send spinning down the drain. I
can't wait to get out, dry off with a fresh towel, and
get into clean pajamas.

Another day down, I think, letting the water out.
That's what it comes down to. I got through another
day.

5

I finish painting the next day. I figure I have until dark, but I get the job done in half the time. It's ruthless, pushing my sore muscles to move. By noon, my knees and elbows are shaking under the strain. A few times, I start to buckle, and I have to lean over the next rung of the ladder. I want to stop, but I push on anyway. It's my only hope to tune out the way the sky is more brilliantly blue than I've ever seen it. The air is so clear and still I feel like the whole town is holding its breath.

Either I'm upsetting Thor or he's sensing the same thing I am, that we're in our last few moments before everything changes. He spends the day pacing by the ladder, occasionally curling up by the paint cans and fixing me with watchful eyes.

When the job is done, I can't even get excited. I can barely manage to fold up the ladder and half-carry, half-drag it back to the shed. I even throw away the paintbrushes rather than try to clean and save them. *Money down the drain,* I think, but I don't have the energy to summon up guilt.

The future is still closing in. I can feel it hovering. My heart beats faster and my chest aches from the strain of waiting, waiting, waiting for this premonition to break. I shower just to hear the rush of white noise as I scrub the sweat and paint from my skin. *It will break any second,* I think, steeling myself for the moment the pressure will release and visions of the future will flood in instead.

It has to be soon. I turn the water off and wait. When minutes pass without a break, I wrap myself in a towel and sit on the edge of the tub, ready to wait it out. I don't like being hit by a premonition unexpectedly. Once it happened when I was in middle school, and I almost passed out. A couple years ago, I was driving, and I'm just glad I was able to pull the car over.

When I was younger, these times were sympathetically referred to as anxiety attacks. After my first disastrous attempts at honesty, I've always been happy to hide behind that excuse. Anxiety attacks make sense. Seeing glimpses of the future does not.

Minutes tick by, and the only change is the water running off my body and turning cold. I can't take another second of this pressure. I can't make the future come any sooner than it's going to.

I get dressed and run a handful of gel through my hair. In the mirror, my face looks pinched and my eyes are wide from tension. The sight of my hair drying in odd directions doesn't help the overall effect. Anxiety is the nice way of putting it. I look crazy.

I know I'm not crazy, because my premonitions, when they come, are always right.

I lay down across my bed, just for a few minutes. Just to sink in to my pillows and close my eyes to the day that keeps pressing in. Thor leaps up next to me, and for once, I'm too exhausted to remind him he doesn't go on the furniture. *I'm going to start bad habits,* I think, but then Thor rests his chin on my knee and I decide I don't care. I lean against his warm fur.

Thor loves me. He doesn't think it, not in so many words, but it shines through him just as pure and natural as anything. He nuzzles in closer, like he wants to make sure I know he's not going anywhere, not until I'm better.

I could fall asleep this way. I could take a nap and wake up to find the future already here. It could be over. I close my eyes and fall fitfully to sleep.

I wake up off and on, to take Thor out, to turn my pillow over to the cool side, and to check the clock to see how much time has passed without any change. Fifteen minutes, then an hour, then two minutes. I let Sunday night pass and watch Monday dawn.

I stretch and dig my cell phone out from the space between the mattress and the wall. Hard to believe it was only Friday morning I left it there.

I have six voicemails. The first two are from Miss Paula on Friday, asking me to call her back. Then a voicemail from Eliza, also from Friday. She was just checking in to say hello. Call her back soon. She loves me.

The next two voicemails are from Mama. One on Saturday and the next on Sunday. The two messages are nearly identical. "Hello, Arden. I was just calling to check in on you. (pause) I also wanted to give you some news about the house. Have you talked to Bryson about doing an estate sale yet? Please call me back. I love you."

I start to break into a small sweat when I click on the last voicemail. Another from Eliza, this one from

Sunday. "Hi, Arden. Just wanted to check in with you and see if you'd talked to Mama and Daddy yet. Call me soon."

This is it. This must be it. There's news, which means change, which means soon the premonition will break. I hit the button to redial my parents' number. It rings eleven times before switching to the answering machine message. It's narrated by Daddy, before he was sick. I ask Mama to give me a call back and hang up.

They must still be asleep. Mama turns the ringer off at night, so the phone won't wake Daddy if someone calls too early. Someone like me, their daughter, who can't be bothered to remember her phone or call her parents or even let them know their estate sale was set up. What if there had been an emergency? What if Daddy fell again and I had just been off painting my house, oblivious?

Next I try Eliza. It rings straight to voicemail. Of course her phone is off. I picture her orchestrating her little family's morning routine. She's kissing John goodbye as he heads off to work. Then she'll get the twins ready for the day in coordinating but non-matching outfits. She'll call me back when she gets a break, which, knowing how active my nephews can be, will be halfway through their afternoon nap.

I should have checked for my phone. I should have thought of my family and called before now. Instead, I've been painting and cleaning and thinking about me. Selfish, selfish, selfish.

I groan out loud as I get out of bed. Every muscle is stiff and sore from painting the house. I need to keep moving.

Thor whines when I leave him behind, but I'm so tired I know I won't be able to control him on a leash if he sees a squirrel or something. If the premonition hits, forget it. I bypass my pickup truck and walk, step by aching step, down the gravel road towards Main Street.

In the middle of the traffic circle, Eagle Valley Presbyterian stands serene. It's Monday morning, which means the pastor has the day off and the church will be deserted until the cleaning crew comes in the afternoon. Pastor Drew always leaves the doors unlocked, but I don't like turning the lights on for just me. I let myself into the sanctuary and watch the early morning sunlight filter through the stained glass windows.

The church is impressive in its stillness, quiet in a way few other buildings can be. I walk slowly down the aisle, keeping my eyes trained on the altar, taking deep, greedy breaths of silence.

I started coming here last year, when Jeremy was still my boyfriend. Back then, I would sit in the back pew and picture the aisles lined with tulle and bouquets of white roses. The church doesn't hold that future, anymore.

It does hold some of my history. I was baptized here, like my sisters and Tripp. We didn't go to church much. After Tripp died, Mama and Daddy went from being every-Sunday Christians to only attending for baptisms, weddings, and Christmas.

I search the words I memorized years ago for the right ones. "Our Father who art in Heaven," I think when I slide into a pew. "Blessed are the meek, for they shall inherit the Earth." When I first put my palms on the pew in front of me, I feel the buzz of stories waiting deep inside the weathered wood. "Though I walk through the valley of the shadow of death, I shall fear no evil." I hear a car driving slowly down Main Street.

Relief. Sometimes I think I'll die seeking it—soaking in bathtubs to wash away stories, working myself sick, running all over town trying to hide from this oppressive future that won't reveal itself. I wipe the sweat beading on the back of my neck and rest my forehead on the pew in front of me. If the future decides to break while I'm here, at least I'll be alone.

Until it breaks, there is no relief. I can escape for a little while, but this premonition will always be here with me, hanging over me, waiting. History–with its unchangeable facts, its cool certainty–is the perfect escape.

If Miss Paula or Mr. Carson were giving the history of the building, they'd focus on all the wrong things. There's a printed page in the church vestibule of the highlights. It started out as a log cabin, built over two hundred years ago by Scots-Irish settlers. It was replaced by a brick church building in 1816, until it burned to the ground in the 1930s. After the Great Depression, no one could afford to rebuild, so they worshipped in the town hall and in people's houses and even outside until the 1950s. Story goes that Reverend Bob Childress stumbled on one of those outside services and, impressed by the faith of the Eagle Valley congregation, helped them build a church in the style of his famous six Stone Churches.

I don't know if Reverend Childress really helped design this church or not. Thing about trying to draw out a specific story in an old building like this is that it's nearly impossible. It's hard enough just trying to fit my hands in the exact handprints someone else left, put my feet in their footprints. It used to drive Mama crazy when I was a kid.

"Arden, please stop whatever it is you're doing," she'd whisper whenever I'd line my feet up on invisible footprints or move my hands around just so. I used to try and pick up stories that way all the time when I was little. I finally stopped when I hit middle school. Some stuff you don't want to hear so clearly.

Now, trying to get one consistent story is the perfect distraction. As much as it hangs over me when I sense the future, it's a nice relief, sometimes, if I can lose myself in someone else's past for a bit. Shifting ever so slightly this way or moving all the way over, I try to adjust myself until I'm fully in the place of someone who came before me. The way I am now, I'm picking up thousands of snippets of experiences and histories and songs and stories. I edge my feet over a little to the right and run my hands along the pew and the hymnal rack, looking for matching handprints.

Eventually, I give it up and stretch out along the pew. My shoulder and hip are digging into the wooden back, and yet I feel cradled, immersed in the presence of all the people who've come and gone.

I hope the future breaks now. A glance at my watch reveals I've been here too long already. My poor dog is probably driven to distraction wondering where I am.

Please come, I think, almost sleepy in the comfort of the pew. But willing a premonition to break is about as pointless as willing a storm to come or the sun to shine or a boyfriend to love you back. It doesn't matter what I want. The future will be ushered in when it's good and ready, and there won't be anything I can do to stop it once it comes.

My little Cassandra, Daddy used to say. He didn't know how right he was.

My muscles, if possible, are even more sore and shaky. The church is almost lit up from the sunlight now, and I feel slightly creepy walking back down the silent aisle, closing the door carefully behind me when I leave.

I pull out my cell phone and check again, even though it hasn't rung once since I got up. No missed calls. Mama and Daddy should wake up soon. Or maybe Eliza will get a spare minute over her cup of coffee.

Coffee. There's an idea I can get behind. Instead of walking towards home, I turn toward Golda's. I'll just get a little cup, clear my head, then go home and get my day started.

The air is so thick I feel like I'm swimming through it. Is this a premonition, or is there a heat wave? I try to focus on the other people walking down the side-walk. They're wearing coats, scarves even. Not a heat wave. Just a premonition.

I have to stop to wipe more sweat off the back of my neck. My hair is slick and plastered behind my ears. *I can get through this,* I think, even as the sun suddenly moves closer and hotter and brighter. I can hear my footsteps and the crickets and passing cars all at once, all loud, like they're trying to rush in.

Three more steps to Golda's.

"Arden?" I hear a voice behind me, tinny almost, then louder. "Arden, are you okay?"

I stop and try to sort out how to respond. Am I okay? I don't think so. I want to sit down. I should sit down.

The door to Golda's swings open right in front of my nose. I blink. It's Miss Paula, huffing out the door in a red-pantsuited rampage. She looks as surprised to see me as I am to see her.

"Arden, I am just not ready to talk to you," she says. *Did I say something?* I wonder, dazed. I don't think I did. My lips feel stuck together and my tongue feels heavy. Miss Paula keeps talking anyway. "I don't know what to say to anyone in your family. After this many years of serving this town together, after all I've done for your parents, and after being *friends*, I'm just shocked. I really am. That your mother would sell to a housing developer and you would try to pull the wool over my eyes. 'I'm sure they'll do what needs to be done,' you said. That's *exactly* what you said."

Her eyes are bluer than I've ever seen them. I wonder if they could swallow me whole. I think they could.

"This is not over," Miss Paula says, low. "If you or your parents think Eagle Valley is just going to roll over and lose our town to your selfishness, you're wrong. We are not losing our standing as a historic site. We are not losing out to a developer. We will get that farm."

She turns her back and clicks down the sidewalk, her pumps making a deafening staccato sound. I'm suddenly freezing. I wrap my arms around my middle to keep from shivering. It's happening.

"Arden? Are you all right?" The voice behind me is louder, but not as loud as the rumbling in my ears. It gets louder until I turn my head and look.

Main Street splits in two, making a fault line that rolls from the top of the hill all the way down, past the pavement, over the gravel road, down to my parents' farm. It crashes into the house and bursts into flames. I watch my parents' house smoke and smolder until it leaves nothing but the burned-up frame and ashes.

It happened, I think, before it goes dark. The future is here.

6

I feel cold. Cold feet, cold chair, cold all the way down to my core. I crack open one eye. I'm sitting in Golda's diner, resting my forehead on the slightly sticky Formica table. There are some stories there, demanding to be heard, but they ping off my forehead like dull pins. Somebody put an ice pack on the back of my neck. It's dripping now.

"She fell before I could get to her," says a man's voice. It sounds like Mr. Carson. "Right after Paula walked off, down she went."

"We'll keep her here," a woman says. Her voice rattles with irritation and a smoker's cough. Golda. "I'm not calling her parents at a time like this."

"No, of course not," Mr. Carson agrees quickly.

They're kidding themselves if they believe there's such a thing as a secret in Eagle Valley. I dredge up a middle-school memory of returning to French class after having a premonition and fainting right in front of everyone. By the end of the day, the entire school knew.

That premonition hadn't been so bad. I'd seen my best friend Emily looking straight through me, like I was made of glass, seeing me but not seeing me. It was a creepy vision, but ultimately pretty close to the truth. For the rest of middle and high school, Emily hadn't seemed to notice I existed at all. At the time, I'd tried to tell myself it was because I'd made a spectacle, passing out right in the middle of class. Now I know better. I know that the visions I see are going to happen, sure as death and taxes.

I cross my arms to ward off another shiver. It's enough to make Mr. Carson and Golda realize I'm awake, because next thing I know, Golda is putting a big glass of water in front of me and Mr. Carson is taking off the dribbling ice pack.

"My sister used to have spells too," Mr. Carson tells me, kindly. "Just take some deep breaths and it'll pass."

For a minute, I think he means his sister had premonitions until I remember that when normal people say "spells," they mean anxiety attacks.

"Drink the water," Golda says. "It'll help."

It does help. With every sip, I think ahead a little more. I need to look like I'm recovering slowly, but not too slowly.

"Thanks," I say, a little too weakly. I swallow and say it again. "Thanks."

They buy it. Golda smiles and goes back behind the counter to start prepping for breakfast orders. Mr. Carson stays with me, but he shifts his weight slightly from one foot to the other.

"I'm going to go on back home now," I say. "Start my day. Thanks again for everything."

"No problem," Mr. Carson says, walking me to the door. "And don't mind Miss Paula. Everybody loves your parents. They'll understand about the farm."

I think back to my premonition— the fault line through the town, and the house smoldering in flames. I force a smile. "Thanks, Mr. Carson," I say. "I'm sure you're right."

When I get home, I go down to the workshop I set up in the basement. Thor follows so closely I almost trip on him a few times. I guess I won't be going back out for a while, at least not until the Historical Society meeting tonight. My stomach sinks at the thought.

Right after a premonition is when it's hardest not to tell somebody. I wish I could call Eliza or Mama and get it all off my chest. "The town's going to be divided over all this," I would say. "Eagle Valley's never going to be the same again. Our farm is gone for good."

I know better. As bad as it is to hold it in, it's worse to hear the responses I'd get. Responses like "You don't know that." Or "Think positive." Or "Don't borrow trouble."

I need a distraction, I decide. Too bad I already finished painting the house. I should have paced myself. Since I didn't, I suppose now's as good a time as any to look through some of my extra merchandise. I scored a box of hats, evening bags, jewelry, and gloves at an estate sale months ago. Some of it's junk, but it should sell at First Friday, when everybody's looking for period clothing for Festival. Well, almost everybody. Our family usually attended in normal clothes, scurrying around behind the scenes. Even now, I don't dress up. It feels strange to wear someone else's clothes. Like I'm hijacking their life.

I spread the jewelry out over my workbench and start sorting. Usually, I wear gloves for this. No need to get bogged down in each piece's life story when I need to be sorting watches from bracelets and checking for broken clasps. Today, I'm enjoying the light, airy feeling that comes after a premonition. Now that the future-to-come isn't weighing down on me, it's kind of fun to listen to the stories each piece holds.

The rose gold pinky ring I liked hasn't had much of a life. It was worn twice and put away in a jewelry box. There's a fake-diamond choker that's been to a hundred parties, easily, and worn by at least three different women. Two of them didn't like each other. Sisters, I think, but there is so much history here it's hard to puzzle out one story from another. Whoever owned all this jewelry must have been a bit of a collector. I can't find one consistent story, not one common thread. I think it's sad to have a house full of things that have never been used and loved. Guess I'm not in any danger of that, myself. I'm an antiques dealer living in a restored hundred-year-old house. Just about everything I own is pre-used and pre-loved.

In an hour, I've finished sorting. I have piles of costume jewelry, a set of nice things I'll put under the glass counter, and a few rings that need to be appraised. I'm left with a tangled mess of odd chains with broken links, a bracelet that's missing a stone, and three unmatched earrings. Usually, stuff like this gets sold for the gold or thrown out. Today, I coax the chains out of a knot, carefully separating each piece once it's free.

My cell phone rings. Thor jumps up and props his droopy chin on my knee, like he's waiting to see who it is, too. It's Eliza, so I answer.

"I'm guessing you've found out about Mama and Daddy by now," she says without preamble. I think I hear Wyatt and Ian, my nephews, giggling in the background.

"Some of it," I tell her. "Miss Paula got to me first."

Eliza mutters half a cuss word. She's been trying to watch her language since the twins were born. At this point, she's two and a half years in and not much progress. "I was hoping you'd be able to avoid her. Mama said Miss Paula took it badly."

"That's an understatement," I tell her. "This morning she went off on me about how we lied to her and pulled the wool over her eyes, and how she was going to get the farm."

"She's welcome to it if she'll pay what it's worth," Eliza says. "The Society only offered half of what the developer did."

"Half?"

"You haven't talked to Mama about this yet?"

"Not yet," I say. "I was just about to try calling again."

"She'll tell you more about it when you get a hold of her," Eliza says. "But that's about the size of it. What Miss Paula offered— sorry, what the *Historical Society* offered—it wouldn't even touch the value of the land. Don't they know about Daddy? They can't just take a hit for Eagle Valley and move into a cheap little apartment."

I think about this summer, when Eliza and I went with Mama and Daddy to check out the assisted living communities. I had to keep my hands wedged in my pockets the whole time because I couldn't bear the stories. We chose the community around the corner from Eliza. That way Mama and Daddy could still live together, but nursing care would come around to help.

Thor barks, just once, a gruff little sound that makes me startle. He nudges his head against my stomach.

"Is that Thor?" asks Eliza. "You're not getting stressed out about this, are you?"

"No," I tell her.

"Promise me you're not cleaning," she orders.

I look down at the necklace chains that I've now arranged in straight lines, shortest to longest. "Nope," I tell her. "Just putting stuff together in the workshop."

"What stuff?" she asks.

"Some jewelry I thought I'd sell at Festival," I tell her. "I'm fine, Eliza."

"I don't want you getting all...upset about this stuff," she says.

"I'm not upset!" I tell her. Of my two older sisters, I'm closest to Eliza, but she thinks she understands me better than she does. Sometimes I wish I did have anxiety. There are ways to treat that. Visions of the future, not so much.

Eliza changes tracks. "Well, Mama's pretty unhappy with Miss Paula. I think she expected her to be more understanding. I mean, the historical stuff is nice and all, but you have to take care of your family."

"Did you think she'd understand?"

"Miss Paula?" Eliza asks. "I'm not sure. I guess I didn't expect her to lowball Mama and Daddy. You'd think they'd be willing to put up what the house was worth, at least. Kind of weird to leave people who've been so involved in the town high and dry."

I try to think back to my conversation with Miss Paula here in the store, before the premonition. It feels like decades ago. "I don't think she imagined that Mama would consider selling to anyone but the town. I don't think she really believed there was another way it could go."

"Do you think she took advantage?"

I want to answer no. Nobody would pull the rug out from under a friend like that. But wasn't that exactly what Miss Paula thought Mama did to her?

"I don't think it was on purpose," I say.

Over the phone, I hear a crash. "Ian and Wyatt!" Eliza hollers before she remembers to pull the phone away from her face. She says it again, like their names are one word. "Ian-and-Wyatt!"

"I'll let you go," I say. Eliza barely mumbles, "Thanks," before she hangs up.

Thor is practically head-butting me now. I reach down to scratch his ears, and he turns his head to lick my hand. I should call Mama. I should hear her tell what happened and tell her it's okay, she did the best thing and Miss Paula will get over it. I should tell them about the estate sale.

I stare at the cell phone on the workshop table, but I can't bring myself to dial it. Calling Mama feels like admitting it's all over. I remember my vision of the farmhouse going up in flames. There's a sign if ever there was one. No going back now. Daddy is sick, and they really can't make it on their own anymore.

I twirl the chains into a spiral. Idly, I pull the remaining stones out of the bracelet and arrange them in a starburst. I choose the longest chain with no missing links and arrange it at the top of the starburst, like it's all one necklace. If I reset the stones, I could make it into a pendant. Something new.

Making new things isn't what I do, I think. But then, maybe it should be.

Mama calls me back around lunch. "Do you have a minute?" she asks. Her voice is tight with stress.

"Sure, Mama," I say. "Need me to come over?"

"Daddy had a bit of a rough night," she says. "He just got settled in for a nap."

Which doesn't answer my question, except it kind of does. I motion to Thor to come with me and let him outside.

"I guess you've heard we decided to sell to the developer," she says flatly. "I'm sorry Paula got to you first."

"My fault for not getting to my phone this weekend," I say. "How are you holding up?"

Mama lets that question pass by, too. "I heard you had a spell this morning? Is that right?"

"I did. Must have been more worn out than I thought. I painted the outside of the house this weekend."

"The whole house?"

"Sure did. Got on a roll."

"So long as that's all it is," Mama says. "This business with the house is between me and Paula. You don't need to let all this worry you."

"I just pushed myself to hard. Wanted to get the house looking nice on the outside, that's all."

"Well, all right," Mama says. I can tell she doesn't believe me, which is fine, since I don't believe she's all right with the farm sale either.

"Tell me more about how Daddy's doing," I say. "Why don't I come by?"

"I know it's your day off," Mama says. "If you're that tired, you should be resting."

"I did, Mama," I say. "All morning. I could stand to get out of the house." I gesture to Thor again then let him back in and fill up his food and water bowls.

"Well, if you'd like," Mama says. "You're always welcome."

As soon as I open the screen door to Mama's kitchen, I can tell it was more than "a bit of a rough night." There are two barely-touched breakfast plates on the kitchen counter, and Mama didn't get a chance to clean the skillet, either. I check to make sure the burner on the stove is off. It is. That's a relief, at least. I put the skillet in the sink to soak and scrape the plates into the garbage.

"That you, Arden?" Mama calls. "Come on in."

I follow her voice down the hall and into the front parlor. The lingering scent of bleach tells me that Mama had to clean up at least one accident. I shake my head a little when I realize that. Poor Daddy. Poor Mama.

In the parlor, there are handprints and streak marks all over the dust on the good antiques. Daddy is pacing around the room. He sits down on a chair and then stands back up. Then he walks over to the sofa and sits. Then he stands again. It makes me dizzy to watch. I recognize something in his hands. It's a drawer pull, the fancy kind that belongs on the washstand. Mama is standing with her feet planted squarely in the middle of the room, following him with her eyes.

"Vaughn," says Mama, firmly. She holds out a crossword puzzle book. "Do you want the book?"

Daddy looks at her and then back to the drawer pull. He sits down and scowls. He stands back up and holds the drawer pull up to the end table. Tries to twist it like he's screwing it in.

It doesn't go there, Daddy, I think to myself, but I know better than to say it out loud. Instead, I walk quietly into the room, slow and steady. "Hi, Daddy," I say. "Good to see you."

He tosses a look my way and goes back to twisting the drawer pull.

I walk over to the washstand and find the empty hole. "Let's try it here," I suggest. "Daddy. Help me with the drawer pull."

Daddy stops. He looks at me like I'm speaking a foreign language.

"Daddy. Can you put it here, please? It goes here."

Slowly, shuffling, Daddy walks over and tries to put the drawer pull into the hole. He only gives it one twist, and it falls. Without thinking, I reach out and catch it.

The noise he makes is unreal. Half-scream, half-growl. With one quick swipe, he slaps the drawer pull out of my hand and stalks out of the room.

"I'm sorry," Mama whispers to me before she turns to go after him.

In thirty years, Daddy has never raised a hand to me. That fact doesn't hurt so much as the stinging cacophony he left behind. He's frustrated, yes, and he has a headache and doesn't want to be talked to like a child and he doesn't know how to fix this stupid thing. But more than that, the lingering story in his slap is despair. It's the same story that's been buried deep inside him since I can remember. That helpless feeling he's had since Tripp died. That feeling isn't buried anymore. He doesn't wear it just under the surface, like Mama. Now he wears it over top of everything else, like a coat.

"Vaughn," I hear Mama saying from the next room. "Vaughn."

I'm not helping. I'm confusing Daddy and complicating things for Mama. I stand in the doorway of the family room and gesture to Mama—*I'm leaving.* She nods.

I give the skillet and plates a good scrubbing and put them away. Back in the family room, I can hear the rise and fall of their voices, Daddy stomping and Mama's deep sighs. I let myself out.

I'd give anything to get out of the Monday night Historical Society meeting. I don't need a premonition to tell me it's going to be bad, but I get one anyway. Halfway through my lunch of macaroni and cheese, I get a vision of Miss Paula talking a mile a minute, only instead of words coming out, it's clouds of black smoke, making it so hard to breathe I actually choke up a little.

The way I see it, though, it's better to show up than stay home. The weekly meetings are mandatory for Main Street storeowners. The Society's actually levied fines for frivolous non-attendance. Only way to get out of it is illness or an actual emergency. I don't think a fainting spell counts. When Russ cut his thumb open last year, he showed up, compressing the wound and holding it over his head to stop the bleeding. That's the kind of dedication you expect in the Eagle Valley Historical Society.

"Sorry, Thor," I tell him just before I head out. I feel bad leaving him behind again. Usually, he's glued to my side all day. "Trust me, I'd rather stay here with you. Be good, okay?" He wags his tail and licks my hand. He has no intention of being good. Guess I'll have that to deal with after the meeting.

I take the truck into town. Usually, I try and get there five or ten minutes early, but today, I'm aiming for five o'clock on the dot. I might have to make an appearance, but no sense dragging it out.

Nobody looks directly at me when I come into the Town Hall. That's pretty bad. Most Mondays, the pre-meeting chatter goes on so long Miss Paula has to bang her gavel three times to make everyone wrap up their conversations and listen. Today, it's dead silent.

Miss Paula is at the podium, shuffling and reshuffling her papers. She has an especially thick stack this evening. My stomach sinks even lower.

"The meeting will come to order," she says crisply. "We'll postpone discussing the usual business and begin with a matter of critical importance to the Society."

Nobody moves. Gossip travels like wildfire in Eagle Valley, so everyone knows what Miss Paula's going to say next.

"As you know, Vaughn McCrae has been having health problems for some time. The McCrae family has decided it would be best for Vaughn and Dottie to move to an assisted living facility. As you also know, when their house went on the market, the Historical Society offered to purchase the property and extend the town limits to include the house and farmland, so that it could be preserved as a Historic Landmark. It behooves the community to know that Dottie McCrae chose instead to sell the farm to a housing developer who will demolish the farmhouse, tear up the trees, and build a neighborhood of new homes on the property."

Miss Paula looks up, making eye contact with every person in the room. Except for me. "With the obstruction of the mountain view, we will lose a large part of the historic atmosphere we have all worked so hard to preserve. You should also be aware that new homes will naturally mean more residents, which will mean more traffic. We should expect that the roads will need to be widened. An influx of newcomers will be inconvenienced by driving to the next town for groceries and schools and clothes shopping, so we can expect that those will be built here in the near future. And most importantly..." Miss Paula makes a dramatic pause. "This development threatens the standing of Eagle Valley as a Historic Preservation site."

She stops to let that sink in. One by one, people raise their hands and start to ask questions.

"What type of development? Are we talking about a neighborhood of cookie-cutter houses, or some spaced-out homes with a farmhouse feel?"

"Do we know that the development will threaten the town's historic status?"

"How will this affect the Main Street businesses?"

"Is there anything we can do?"

Miss Paula takes each question without comment, writing them neatly on the dry-erase board. Finally, she turns back. "I've spent most of the day on the phone attempting to find a solution for this issue. So far, the developer is not willing to work with us. I've contacted some of our major sources of grant money to ask about emergency funds for purchasing back the land from the developer, and we're in talks to try and work out a solution. In the meantime, we need to stay positive and we need to stay focused. Festival is around the corner, and for many reasons, we need to make it our best yet."

Finally, the air shifts. Chairs squeak, and a few people even mumble assent. In the midst of everything, there is one small straw of hope. There's always Festival.

7

Eleven months out of the year, First Friday is a relaxed, family-friendly night out on the town. All the Main Street shops stay open until nine, the library hosts a reading night, and Golda marks all her dinner specials down to half-price.

In October, First Friday, like everything else, is completely overshadowed by Festival. The Main Street shop owners use it as a kind of dress rehearsal for the Living History Days, which will take up every weekend for the rest of October. Like all dress rehearsals, everybody feels pressured to get it right. And like all dress rehearsals, it's a disaster.

Even Janie looks frazzled today. She practically runs into the shop after school and drops her backpack on the floor by the counter. "Are we ready?" she pants. "Is everything set up? What do you need me to do?"

I point her towards the front display. "Do something with it," I order. Then I remember my manners. "Please. I just can't get everything to look right."

I decided on an "antique toys" theme for this month. I'd piled half the dolls and wagons and dollhouses into the front display, but I couldn't focus.

"No problem," Janie says. I go back to mopping the floors. During October, I'll clean the floors and shelves once a day, sometimes twice. Only so many hand and footprints I want to land on.

I catch Janie looking over at me. "Yes?" I ask.

She has the good grace not to pretend she wasn't looking. "Have you seen the museum?" she asks.

Everyone has seen the museum. They can probably see the museum from space. Miss Paula's been busy this week, arming herself for battle. She's draped a banner across the front of it that reads, "Save Eagle Valley's Historic District." A larger-than-life thermometer poster is propped in her window. To track donations, I suppose.

According to town gossip, that's all part of Miss Paula's new plan. The developer finally agreed to consider selling the farm to the town, but only at a huge mark-up to the price he paid and only if the Society has the money by the first week of November. Only one of Miss Paula's contacts was able to offer help, and that came in the form of a matching grant, giving rise to Miss Paula's new plan to accept donations throughout the Festival, all in the name of preserving the town's historically-appropriate view of the mountains. Not sure how that's going to work out for her. Mama didn't give me an actual number, but the developer definitely paid a good price for the land. Buying it back from the developer would probably cost more than Miss Paula can get from passing the hat and matching grants. With the deadline a month away, it seems downright impossible.

Well, even if it is impossible, Miss Paula's sure doing her darnedest to make it happen. I turn away from the window and go back to mopping.

"Wonder how long she's going to keep that up," I say. "What's done is done."

Janie's forehead furrows the way it does when she gets a B instead of her usual A. "What's the matter with you?" I ask.

From her pocket, she unfolds a long, glossy brochure and passes it to me.

It's the usual publicity picture of Main Street, looking downhill and ending at a rolling view of my parents' fields and the mountains behind. Printed in block letters below, it reads, "Save Eagle Valley's Historic District."

Inside, there's a brief history of the town. Ripped off of the write-up Mama did years ago, I happen to notice. At the end, Miss Paula has written in bold, "The Historic District overlooks a parcel of land belonging to the McCrae family farm. Unfortunately, the homeowners are selling the property and have rejected the Historical Society's offer to buy and preserve the farm's legacy. The property has been sold to a developer. Current plans call for the development of pre-fabricated homes, which will obstruct the view of the Blue Ridge Mountains and threaten the standing of Eagle Valley as a Historic Preservation site."

"The homeowners." Nice to see Miss Paula resisted the juicy intrigue of putting "The former mayor." "The former co-founder of the Historical Society." "My former friends."

"I just wondered if you knew," Janie says.

I shrug. "Nothing I can do about it." The biggest problem I can see with Miss Paula's pamphlet is the part where it says, "McCrae family farm." Even the out-of-towners are going to put that together with the "McCrae's Antiques" sign in my store window. That could start gossip or slow business. Or both.

Sure enough, when the people start trickling in at six o'clock, every surface is buzzing with their unasked questions. They sidle in and pick up this or that, feigning interest in a piece of furniture or acting like they're just browsing, but everyone is looking at me.

The first person to come out with it has the decency to make a purchase first. It's an out-of-towner, but one I've seen around here before. "So you're Arden McCrae," he says, pointing toward my business card on the front desk.

"Yes." I'm not giving him more than that. He left his questions all over the little crystal vase he's buying for his wife. He almost forgot their anniversary and remembered just in time to buy a present and save his butt.

"Any relation to the McCraes that are selling that farm?" he asks. Like it's just some story I might want to tell. Just some juicy piece of gossip.

"Yes," I say. I wrap the vase in newspaper and put it in the bag with his receipt. "Thank you for your business! Have a good evening."

He lingers a bit by the counter, but moves away when I motion toward the next customer. *That's right, buddy. It's not story time around here.* Janie shoots me a sympathetic look.

I'll say this for First Friday: awkwardness aside, I'm getting more business than I've seen in weeks. For the first time since the premonition, I'm starting to feel a little hopeful.

I had plans for how I would spend my evening recovering from First Friday. I'd thought I would relax on the couch with Thor, drink some hot tea and enjoy an hour or so of trashy reality TV.

Problem is, by the time I roll in the door, I'm too exhausted even for channel surfing. Thor curls up and falls asleep almost as soon as I get home. He managed to fall asleep with his chin on my ankle, pinning me to the couch. Even held captive, I'm not in the mood for television anymore.

Just sitting and moping won't do, either. Usually, I like to kill time on the computer, visiting the community forums on some of the antiques and furniture restoration websites. It's nice to read posts about how to use chalk paint or asking opinions on seat coverings. If I knew these people in real life, I'd be able to sense their pain and joy and untold stories at the first handshake. Since I just know them on the Internet, I can pretend we're all just calm, blissfully boring people who obsess over spray-painting techniques.

Careful not to disturb Thor, I reach for my laptop on the coffee table and grab a few tissues, too. I tend to keep a box of tissues by the computer and cover the keyboard with them before I sit down to type. I learned to touch type in school by covering the keyboard with a scarf, so that I could feel the keys without reading the letters. It also works nicely for keeping built-up stories at bay. Can't focus on what I'm trying to say now if my fingers are flooded with reminders of all the things I've typed before.

"I like the blue better," I type to a poster asking for opinions on paint colors. "Not worth the money. If you're just going to refinish it, you can find a table like that for a lot less. Check out your Goodwill," I type to another.

My foot starts to fall asleep under the weight of Thor's chin. Gently, I try to move it out from underneath him. Thor grumbles and twitches his paws before falling back into a deep, snoring sleep.

I wish I could relax like my dog does. He feels everything intensely, like me, but he can let it go almost instantly. Me, I'm left with remnants of old stories wherever I go.

I open another window on my browser and type in the address to another forum—one I haven't been writing on, only reading. It's an Alzheimer's support group site. I came here once to read the articles, but when I started reading posts in the community forum, I couldn't stop.

One person posted a discussion thread with the title "Respite care options?" It has 53 comments already. I guess a lot of people need a break. Another thread is titled "So angry. Just angry (vent)." I decide to skip that one. Don't know if I can take on anyone else's anger right now, even through the Internet.

I read through the threads that start with things like, "Never thought I'd be here (long)" or "Need help, what to do?" None of the posts sound exactly like our situation with Daddy, but they're not so different, either. Some people are still deciding whether to continue home care or move to assisted living or a nursing home. I'm suddenly grateful Mama decided already and we don't have to carry that decision for them.

One woman has posted five threads in two days. After her father died, she moved to New Mexico to take care of her mother with Alzheimer's. All five of her siblings live back in Ohio. The oldest sends money every month, the second oldest visited once and did one load of laundry, the youngest is in college and just calls to check on her mom, and the other two have dropped off the face of the earth.

"I can't make them understand how hard it is and how much she needs," she writes. "She has one good day where I can take her out to the grocery store with me, and they think, great, Mom's fine. When I talked about adult daycare or assisted living, my brother yelled and said he wasn't sending money for me to push her off on strangers. If he wants Mom to be with family, then where the hell is he? You'd be surprised how much you need your family through stuff like this. You really need all hands on deck."

I have to close my laptop for a minute after reading all that. Thor moves his head to look at me, and I scratch his ears.

There are so many things I wish I could control. Right now, I wish I could get a glimpse of the future on my terms. I want to know how many more good days Daddy has left. I want to know if Mama has it easier after the move to the assisted living home, and if Miss Paula calms down or if the damage she does is irreparable. I want to know whether the store fails or if I'll be brave enough to close it, and what I'll do next. Most of all, I want to know what our family will look like as Daddy slips away.

The phrase that the forum poster used comes to mind. *You really need all hands on deck.* Eliza and I have done the majority of the work checking up on Mama and Daddy, but this move feels bigger and more final than anything we've done so far. It's time. I open my laptop again and go to my e-mail.

My sister Lila Beth moved out when I was only nine years old. She went to college up in D.C. and never looked back. Eagle Valley was too small for Lila

Beth. She's a big fish, and I guess she felt like she needed a big pond. I made one disastrous attempt to visit her in D.C. when I was sixteen. It was so bad, neither Lila Beth nor I ever suggested doing it again. Other than that, I've only seen her on Christmas and Easter when she comes down to visit.

"I guess you've heard by now that Mama and Daddy sold the farm and they're moving to an assisted living facility," I type. "Miss Paula's all annoyed that they sold to a developer because she thinks it'll ruin the town's historic status, so things are pretty tense around here. Mama and Daddy are handling it well, but there's a lot going on this month. We're having an estate sale at the end of the month too, which doesn't give us much time. Will you come down? The estate sale will be right around Halloween, but anytime you could make it during the last week in October would be great. We need some help with all the tagging. Mama and Daddy could use some moral support, too. Things have changed a lot since Easter. You could come during the week and stay at my place. Let me know. Love you."

I read back over the e-mail. What if she doesn't want to stay with me? She'd probably rather stay with Eliza when she comes. Or in a hotel.

I delete it all and rewrite, "I guess you know that Mama and Daddy are selling the farm and moving to

Roanoke. Can you come? The estate sale is on a pretty tight timeline, so we need help with tagging everything. Mama and Daddy need you, too, even if they don't come out and say so. It's been tough. Let me know. Love you."

I debate a few seconds more then click "send." She'll come or she won't. Nothing I can do about it.

8

The next morning brings clear blue skies, a crisp breeze, and the faintest scent of wood smoke. The weather is so perfect for the first Saturday of Festival that I wonder if Miss Paula dreamed it into life. I'm glad one thing this weekend is going right.

The Festival kicks off with the Founding Days, paying homage to the Revolutionary War and the settlement of Eagle Valley. This first weekend always has the lowest turnout of any of the Living History Days. Guess we don't do enough for the real Revolutionary War buffs to bother.

By far, the best thing about this weekend is the Eagle Valley Ghost Tour. The town does one every weekend of Festival, but the acting and storytelling is definitely best on the first weekend. I've been plenty of times, and the stories—all untrue and hardly ever based on real people—are the same every year. By the last weekend of Festival, Mr. Carson practically yawns through his narration.

Even if it isn't the most popular weekend, I'm hoping there will be enough new faces to stir up some business. If I can sell a few of my bigger pieces this weekend, I might be able to pay all the bills without juggling too much. That's not too likely, though. Festival tends to bring in customers that want a little something to take home, not a major piece of furniture. More likely, I'll have to make a lot of lower-priced sales.

I do a little mental math while I walk to the store from my house. A good walk should help clear my head, and it's easier than fighting for a parking space during a Festival weekend. Plus, Thor won't be so jealous if he doesn't hear my truck start up. I'll just have to walk back a few times to check on him here at the house. I don't want to take him in with me on a day when we'll have so many customers. I hope.

My shoes make a crunching sound on the gravel. I reach out and touch a tree branch by the side of the road. A leaf crackles and breaks off in my hand. It leaves behind a dusty story that sticks to my palms even after I brush the leaf away.

As I turn past the church and start down Main Street, I keep my eyes trained on the brick sidewalk. I slow down so I can catch snippets of stories as I walk through. I brush my hand against a lamppost and get a quick snapshot of the banners and flags being hung early this morning.

When I touch the door handle to my store, I feel like I've been shocked. My hand landed smack dab where someone else's had been. Earlier this morning, given how fresh the story feels. Someone peering in the glass door, looking for me. Miss Paula.

She hadn't wanted to talk to me, exactly. I can tell that right off. I'm not even sure she wanted to see me. Feels more like she couldn't resist looking in, the same way people poke bruises to see if they hurt and look up their exes to see if they've moved on.

Betrayal. That's the real story Miss Paula left behind. It's plain as the chrome of the door handle and the glint of sunlight reflecting off the door. She never thought this could happen, her losing everything she'd worked for. How could the McCrae family up and do this? She never realized how fast things could change. How quickly everything could turn upside down.

Well. Neither did we.

By nine o'clock, the first customers are descending on Main Street. Within ten minutes, the store is so full of people it's actually hard to walk through without brushing up against someone and getting blasted with their story. Fortunately, I have plenty of reasons to dash back to the stock room for more merchandise. People are buying so fast that I don't have time to arrange things the way I usually do. Janie mans the cash register.

By lunch, the customers have slowed to a trickle, so I take a minute to unwrap my sandwich. Across the street, I can see a line snaking out the front door of Golda's Diner. I take a moment to send a silent plea to the forces of the universe. *Please don't let Golda forget and leave a wax paper square on someone's cheese. Please don't let her mix up the diet and regular soda orders. Please let her remember to put out her cigarette when she comes back from a break.* Golda needs the business this weekend almost as badly as I do.

By afternoon, the first rush is over and business is decidedly slower than the morning. I can hear the fife and drum corps playing all the way down the street, from the open field by the mill. Most people are probably down there, listening to the music. The town's hired the same Corps for the last ten years, and they're actually pretty good. The music gives a nice lilt to the breeze, and for a minute, I feel happy.

I leave the store in Janie's capable hands and go for a walk. I have a feeling I need to get out for a minute. It's a quick vision, so small I barely even notice. Just me, chatting with someone. Can't make out who I'm talking to or what it's about. I don't like visions like that. They come on and leave so fast I'm not quite sure if it really happened or if I just imagined the whole thing.

Soon as I turn the corner, my cell phone rings. It's Mama. So that's what my little vision was about. No wonder I felt like I had to leave the store. Eagle Valley is close to the mountains and short on cell towers, so reception is always a little spotty. I position myself by a lamppost on the curb.

"Glad you called," I tell her. "How's Daddy?"

"He's napping," Mama says. "He had a rough morning."

I wait a beat to see if she'll tell me more. She doesn't, so I go on. "So you're doing okay."

If we were having this conversation in person, I could lean up against a surface she just touched and find out for sure. Over the phone, it's harder to guess what to say.

"We're holding up," Mama says. "I'm sorry about what happened with Daddy. You know he doesn't mean it."

Thinking about it, I imagine I can still feel the sting of reproach where he slapped my hand.

"I know," I say. "I'm more worried about you."

"I'll manage," Mama says. Her voice gives me the message her words won't. *I'm the mother here. It's my job to worry about you. It's not your job to worry about me.*

I live spitting distance from my mother. I hear her thoughts and feelings with every touch and I know the story of her life as well as my own. Still, it's easy to forget who my mother really is.

Mama lives side-by-side with the future that might have been, the same way I live side-by-side with the future that's coming. There's always a part of her that's imagining who Tripp would be, what he would be doing, how different life would be if he was still here. It takes a lot out of a person to live like that.

"I love you," I say, shocking both of us. That's not the kind of thing McCraes tend to come out and say.

"I love you, too," Mama says. I can count on both hands how many times I've heard her say that, but I can't begin to count how many times I know she felt it. Feels good to hear, anyway.

After we hang up, I keep walking. I act like I'm just out for a breath of fresh air, enjoying the fife and drum music drifting all the way up from the mill. I look like I'm window shopping, strolling by each of the stores, laying a hand up on a front window or a lamppost as I look at the displays.

The first few times I do it, it hurts. There's too much here. I hear a lot of snippets, little bits about all the people passing through and what they bought and why they're here and who they're with and where they've been before and a thousand other things that steal my breath. A few times, I manage to find a surface that's more or less out of the way, something untouched enough that I can get some clear handprints and parse through some of the stories.

Most of it's boring, but there's plenty here about the McCrae family. The pure resentment feels red-hot. Thanks to Miss Paula's pamphlet campaign, Eagle Valley's historic status seems to be on everybody's mind. If the town loses its status, there goes Festival. There goes the historic district. There goes Main Street and our businesses.

I think back to my morning at the store. So many people were milling around me that I could barely keep anyone from brushing up against me. I hate that feeling. Just getting through high school was a nightmare—all that angst crammed into one space. That's enough to make your skin crawl right there.

Down by Felicia's bookstore, New Chapters, I brush up against a whole pile of worry. Felicia's pretty new around here. Two years ago, after she got divorced at twenty-seven, she moved to Eagle Valley to open a bookstore and find herself. I give her business two more years, tops, historic status notwithstanding. No animosity—I like Felicia—it's just that there isn't a huge market for a bookstore in a town with an active library and not much money.

Felicia doesn't see things that way, that much is clear. She spent the morning pacing the sidewalk and fussing over her window boxes. She can't afford to start over again. Once was bad enough. If Main Street goes the way of the dodo, her little bookstore is going with it. What's she supposed to do then? Get a fresh start to recover from her last fresh start?

I look in the window and see Felicia smiling and chatting up a customer. She doesn't look worried about a thing. If I didn't know better, I'd think she'd never had a bad day in her life.

Just as I turn to go, Felicia sees me. She smiles wider, waves, friendly as you please. If she's ever had a bad thought about my family, no one would know it.

No one but me, that is.

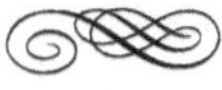

I skip the ghost tour that night. My feet are aching, and besides, I need to get home to Thor. Last year, when I still had Jeremy and didn't have a dog, I could stay out all night if I wanted to.

The roads are predictably quiet. I give a wide berth to the tour group by the church as I walk by. I don't know why. Nobody's looking for me, and they're all busy listening to Mr. Carson giving the introduction to the ghost tour. It looks eerie, watching them all light their candles. Every year, the Society debates whether it's safer to move towards battery-operated candles or flashlights for the ghost tour. Every year, someone makes a case for the ambience of real candles, and that's how we all end up with shoes spotted from the dripping wax.

This weekend's ghost tour will start with the story of the three brave rebels. As Mr. Carson would say, "Their names are lost to history but their courage lives on." Story goes that during the Revolution, Eagle Valley wasn't keen to rebel against England. The town was too close to the mountains to make money off of growing cash crops. Even if farmers had been able to grow them, the costs of transporting down to Newport for trade would have eaten all the profit. It was usually the gentry that supported the Revolution, since they were the ones rich enough to be worried about taxes and voting rights. Here in Eagle Valley, folks were mostly worried about keeping their nose above water and making enough money to see the next year. If the gentry supported the Revolution, it couldn't mean anything good for everyday farmers. Most folks tried to stay out of it or sided with England.

That is, except for the three brave rebels. All were eldest sons who should have stayed in place to help run the family farms. They disappeared in the night to join the Continental Army. They were feared dead until they all came slowly stumbling home, war-torn but victorious, bringing news of an independent America.

Russ, Cliff, and Gordon will be playing the brave rebels this year. They're out by the mill, waiting for their cue. When Mr. Carson finishes his narration, Golda will flash her lantern, and the three of them will come stumbling up Main Street, crying, "Independence!"

I doubt it really happened that way—haven't looked into it, one way or the other—but it's chilling to watch. Maybe there's a point to the candles after all. In the shadows and the flickering lights, it's easy to forget that the actors are the same people we see every day.

I wouldn't mind a candle myself, dripping or not. I forgot it would be dark by the time I got home. Even though each step takes me farther from the ghost tour, I feel deliciously spooky as the pavement ends and my boots crunch on the gravel road instead. When the light from the street lamps is too far behind me, I turn on the little flashlight on my key ring. It's a firefly-worth of light, not enough to brighten more than a foot in front of me. I stop and tense whenever I hear a rustle in the grasses beside the road.

Thor will be anxious to see me. I stopped by a few times to let him out, and he just about toppled me when I came through the door. Predictably, he greets me by shooting past me on his way to hoist his leg over my azaleas, glaring at me over his shoulder.

"Poor baby," I say. "Not used to being alone, are you?"

Relieved, Thor trots back over and walks past me into the house. I turn on the entryway light.

At first, I think someone must have broken in. Then I see and feel the truth. Doggy chomp marks all over the couch, pillows open with the filling scattered, overturned lamps, and my carefully-stacked piles of books knocked over.

"Bad dog!" I say with all the firmness I can muster, but it's too late. Whenever he did this, it's too long ago for him to remember having done it now. I snap on a fresh pair of rubber gloves and get to work cleaning it all up.

"He did what?" Eliza asks, incredulous. I push the speaker phone button on my cell and prop it up on a table. Might as well keep cleaning while we talk.

"Practically ate the living room," I say. Thor, smart enough to know when he's being talked about, slinks off to the kitchen.

"Crazy dog," Eliza says. "What are you going to do? You have Festival again tomorrow."

"Take him with me to the store, I guess."

"How'd the first day go? Lots of customers?"

"More than usual, so that's good."

"Was it weird not having Mama and Daddy there?" Eliza asks.

Last year, when we could still pretend Daddy was just forgetful or distracted or feeling his age, Mama helped set up and took him up and down Main Street to see the lights and the people. "It was hard," I say. "Miss Paula's got everyone in a frenzy about the town's historical status. Nobody's coming out and saying anything to me, exactly, but... it's tense."

"Arden," Eliza says, and I can tell she's winding up for a big-sister-level speech. "You can't let people have that kind of power over you. Maybe they're surprised how it all played out, but they'll get used to it and everything will settle down."

I snort. "Tell that to Miss Paula."

"Don't even bother telling Miss Paula anything. She's just talk. We both know that and so does everybody else."

I consider telling Eliza about the pamphlets, but decide not to. "Guess what we're doing the last week of October," I say instead.

"Going to the Bahamas."

"Helping tag before the estate sale," I correct her.

"I like mine better. Can we stick with mine?"

"Only if you're paying."

Eliza sighs. "I wondered how you were going to get Bryson to swing an estate sale this soon. Now I know."

"I e-mailed Lila Beth and asked her to come, too," I say.

"Why?"

"I thought I should ask. Families need each other for things like this."

"Families need each other all the time," Eliza says. "Don't get your hopes up."

9

Thor and I are up early on Sunday to set up for Festi-val. I don't love having to take him with me on a Festival day. I don't know how he'll do with the crowds or the noise. I'm guessing he'll like being cooped up with me at the store better than he'll like being cooped up at home. Hope I'm right.

We're early enough that I actually get a good parking spot behind the store. I take Thor out for a quick walk and let him stretch his legs.

If it was an ordinary year, I'd be heading over to Golda's right now for a cup of coffee. I don't know what to do with myself this year. If I keep coming around people like normal, I might find out what they're thinking, and maybe it'd be better not to know.

Then I remember what Eliza said during our phone call yesterday. *Don't let people have that kind of power over you.* I figure she's right. Thor and I go across the street to Golda's.

Half of the Main Street shop owners are there. Felicia is talking to Mr. Carson at a table. Cliff and Russ are sitting at the counter. My heart sinks a little when I see Gordon and Miranda Johns—Jeremy's parents. They restored one of the oldest houses and turned it into a bed and breakfast. I bet their place is hopping with out-of-towners. I'm a little surprised to see them both out getting coffee. I wonder who's watching the B&B.

Golda is in the middle of a dramatic reenactment of her role in the ghost tour last night. "I changed it up this year," she's saying. "Instead of coming out with a lantern, I changed it to just a single candle. So that it lights up only my face at first, and then when I come around the bend towards the group, all they see is this." She demonstrates by clasping her hands around an imaginary candle and making a long, mournful face.

"That's enough to scare anyone," remarks Cliff. Golda smacks his arm lightly with a wooden spoon. She's laughing, though. For all their kvetching about nearing retirement and aching joints, watching those two together is like being at junior prom.

Mr. Carson notices me first. "Well, hey, Arden," he says, and everyone turns.

"Hey," I say. I have to pull back on Thor's leash. He smells bacon, so he's straining towards the grill. "Can I get a coffee, Golda?"

"Sure thing, sweetie," she says.

There's a vibe so strong I wonder if I could reach out and feel the air thickening. Felicia smiles, just like she did yesterday, but she looks away when her eyes meet mine. Russ is suddenly very invested in finishing his omelet. Cliff waves hello, but Miranda and Gordon Johns don't.

"Here's your coffee," Golda says. "Extra sugar, no milk. And a little bacon for Thor."

"Thanks, Golda." I dig out a few crumpled dollars for her.

She waves it off. "Your money's no good today. We're celebrating a good first weekend."

"And only three more to go," adds Cliff. Russ chuckles a little for that.

I don't know where to sit. Thor decides for me. He settles on his haunches by the table between Felicia's and the Johns'. I sit and put his saucer of bacon on the floor.

"How's business?" asks Miranda. She's looking at me awfully hard. I'm not sure if I want to know what she's thinking.

"Fair enough," I tell her. "How's yours?"

"Just wonderful. Everybody's in town for Festival. Jeremy came down to help with the B&B this weekend. Wasn't that nice?" Miranda asks. Her husband shoots her a discreet warning look.

So Jeremy is in town. I feel a strange mix of exhilaration and horror. "How nice," I say. It sounds weak, even to me.

Russ stands and stretches. "I better get to the hardware store," he says. "Can't open late on a Festival day."

"You got a lot of customers driving in to buy hardware?" Cliff asks, smirking.

"No, those dang potted plants," Russ says. "Historical Society says I've got to have some local color in my store, so I figured I'd do flowers. Can't get more colorful than that."

"He's got a different kind of flower for each weekend," Felicia adds. "They're potted up real nice with ribbons. I made the little cards for them that say what flower and how it's local to Eagle Valley."

Russ grunts. I'm guessing most of that little togetherness project was Felicia's idea.

Everybody starts taking their last sips and getting their things together. Golda comes around the counter to start collecting the plates.

"Let me help you with that," I say. I pick up each cup, plate, and fork carefully and bring it to Golda.

"Don't take too long," Golda says. "You've got to head in too." I nod, bringing her the rest of the dishes and heading for the door.

"And Arden," she says. "Buck up. Things are going to work out just fine."

I smile at Golda and thank her again for the coffee and the bacon. Things are not going to be just fine. I heard it when I picked up Miranda Johns' coffee mug, and Russ's saucer, and Felicia's fork. They'd been talking. Cliff and Golda are okay with Mama and Daddy and me. That comes through loud and clear. Felicia's heard a lot around town. She doesn't know what to think about our family, but she sure doesn't want to lose historic Main Street. Russ never liked Miss Paula, but he has a healthy fear of her, so he's staying away from all of us. Miranda Johns thinks I'm only two steps above the devil, but then, I dated her son, so that's nothing new.

That's what I get for listening in. Should have kept to myself. No matter. The truth tends to come out sooner or later.

As a whole, Sunday is slower than Saturday was. I'm on my own in the store this morning because Janie goes to church with her family every week without fail. I tried to give her this afternoon off, too, but Janie insisted she could do it and I'm not about to turn down good help. Usually, she only comes by on one weekend day and a few afternoons a week, after school. During October, she comes on First Friday and every Festival day.

Since things aren't quite so busy, I spend a little time getting the merchandise arranged. Yesterday, I was in such a rush I just grabbed things from the stock room and threw them on the shelves. Now, I take a minute to get the place looking nice, set things up in vignettes the way I like. The customers that come in this morning are mostly older couples. They're planning to hit the stores and leave before the crowds come back in the afternoon. They're good if I just wave and welcome them when they come in.

Every time the bells on the door jingle, I wonder if it's Jeremy. I don't think he'd seek me out, but then, maybe he would. I don't know which I'd prefer. I wish Miranda hadn't told me he was in town. I didn't get a premonition, but maybe it was a quick one, or I wasn't paying attention. I hate how hopeful that thought makes me feel.

If he does come by, I'll have to act casual, like it doesn't matter to me whether he's here or not. Which it doesn't. We broke up. It's over. No skin off my nose where he spends his weekends.

Someone taps me on the shoulder, shocking me. It's a little older lady who comes just up to my nose. She looks at me so intently I feel about ten years old again. "I'm interested in this little school desk," she says.

"Right," I say. "That's a great piece. It belonged to one of the first Eagle Valley residents—"

She cuts me off short. "I don't need you to sell it to me, honey," she says. "I just want to know if this is the best price you can do."

That's what I get for trying to tell a story without listening first. I try to think back to the tap on my shoulder she used to get my attention, but I'm too muddled and it's no use trying. "My prices are firm," I say. "But if you're more than sixty years young, I give a ten percent discount on Festival days."

"That'll do," she says. "And you can say I'm more than sixty years old. I've replaced two knees, two hips, and two husbands. I know I'm old."

"Yes, ma'am," I say and ring her up.

While I'm counting out her change, another lady comes over. Same age, I'd guess, and they talk with the kind of familiarity that tells me they're old friends. "That'll look just perfect in your living room," she says. "Are you thinking it's for the grandkids?"

"Sure am," the first lady says. "I'm going to tell them that's what I used in school back when I was their age. I sat on my behind and put my mind to it." They laugh.

"Do you need any help carrying it outside?" I ask. "Where are you parked?"

"Oh, we've got it," says the second lady. "We do this all the time." And they do. They pick up the desk and carry it between them like it's easy, and having moved that thing myself a time or two, I know it's not.

They remind me of Mama and Miss Paula, I realize. Not in age–Mama's hair may be going silver, but she's a far cry from elderly. My two newest customers act the same way Mama and Miss Paula used to. They'd go out and spend the weekend on Society business or shopping or antiquing. Mama might be on the quiet side generally, but she'd get going and chatter away when she was out and about with Miss Paula.

A wave of sadness hits me so suddenly I have to stop and check that's what it is. I'm not Miss Paula's biggest fan, never have been, but I'm sad to see how quick things changed between them. Everybody needs a good friend like that.

10

During Festival, the Monday evening meetings are moved to the mornings. It's a double-edged sword. We're all so dog-tired as the month wears on that nobody wants an evening meeting. On the other hand, getting up early right after a Festival weekend is pretty tough to do, too. I guess I'm lucky since I take Mondays off anyway. After an early meeting, I can scoot right back home and into bed. For the poor schmucks who are working a full day, well, there's always coffee. About three years ago, Golda convinced Miss Paula to move the morning meetings to the diner.

"If you want people to get up early, you got to give them something to eat," she'd said.

Five minutes before the meeting is due to start, I head in with Thor on a leash and green tea in my thermos. I can tell I chose wisely when I walk in and see Golda's coffee pot has hardly been touched. I take a sniff. She's trying out that hazelnut coffee again. No wonder no one's drinking it.

The diner is already packed full. Cliff has set up the big standing fans to help circulate the air, so the smell of sweat and hazelnut coffee blows freely in every direction. I take a seat by the door with Thor at my feet. Unfortunately, that makes me the first person Miss Paula sees when she swoops in.

"Good morning, Arden," she says, the way people do when they've had to practice sounding casual.

"Morning," I say, the way people do when they're cornered into politeness. Nothing like some high-stakes awkwardness to start off my Monday. I take a sip of my green tea.

Miss Paula makes her way to the counter, where she lays down her notebooks and sits up on a barstool like she's surveying her kingdom. "Thanks for coming, everyone," Miss Paula says. "I think we're ready to call this meeting to order."

All the noises stop, except one poor soul that got caught slurping his coffee. I'll give Miss Paula this much, she can command a room.

"We had a fantastic turnout for our first Festival weekend," says Miss Paula brightly. "And let's have a big round of applause for everyone's hard work!" She claps louder and longer than anyone else. "The Historical Society collected just over $2,000 from admission. If we can get just as high a turnout the next three weekends, we may be able to check off some of the action items on the Society's budget. We got several comment cards back, so I'll go ahead and share a few of them while we're all here."

Miss Paula takes out a stack of cards from her notebook. She clears her throat and slides on her bifocals. "Love the atmosphere and the decorations. It's like a step back in time!" she reads aloud from one of them. "Loved the ghost tour last night—we were planning to leave Sunday morning but decided to come back to Main Street instead." Miss Paula smiles, as if that was a personal compliment. "Beautiful town. We come every year. See you next year!"

Miss Paula lays the comment cards down on the counter and takes her bifocals off. "And on that note..." she says. "Our special fundraiser to buy back the McCrae property from the developer is off to an excellent start. I know some of you helped by handing out pamphlets to your customers, but I really want to encourage everyone to help out more significantly. This affects all of us, so we all need to pitch in."

The only sound in the room comes from the fans. I refuse to look up. Not at Miss Paula, not at anyone. I imagine most everyone is looking down, trying not to get caught staring at me.

She drones on for another twenty minutes. I stare at my shoes the whole time. I wish I could think up an excuse to skip these meetings. Until the developer takes over the farm, at least.

"So that wraps it up, unless anyone else has business to discuss," Miss Paula says finally. Still no sound, not even a cough or a throat-clearing. "Fantastic! Let's make it another great week, everybody." When I hear chair legs scraping across the floor, I pick up my thermos and Thor's leash, ready for a quick escape.

Except Felicia is standing in front of me, holding the door open for Ben, the mayor, who's moving as quick as he can. Unfortunately, he has two trick knees and it takes some time. And then Felicia drops the door and Russ catches it and holds it for someone, and then just about half the town files past me and out the door before I can leave.

Thor bolts, and I have to pull back the leash and lean on the door to steady myself. That door handle might just be the most storied thing in all of Eagle Valley right now. They might not be saying it, but the whole town is thinking about Miss Paula and my parents. Judging.

After a meeting like that, I wouldn't mind getting out of town for a bit. I don't feel like that very often. With a pang, I remember the trip-that-wasn't to D.C. with Lila Beth, and the million-and-one fights with Jeremy back when we were together. Time was that I couldn't imagine leaving Eagle Valley, not even for a day trip. Well, times are changing. Guess I'm changing too.

Once I get home, I gather up some of the nicer pieces of jewelry I sorted through. I need to take a few of the rings to be appraised in Roanoke. Normally, that's a chore I put off until the last minute. I've been to the jeweler a few times, enough to know the stories I'll probably run into, but it's still unnerving. Roanoke has a lot more people than Eagle Valley. What if the jeweler doesn't wipe the door handle for a few days? What if I put my hand on the jewelry counter and land in the handprint of an arguing couple? That happened once. I walked out knowing the whole story behind a woman who shopped for engagement rings with her boyfriend while she mentally listed out all the reasons she didn't want to marry him. I about scoured my skin off later, trying to forget that story.

Well, whatever stories I hear in the city, they can't be worse than what I'm overhearing in town. "Go for a ride, Thor?" I call, and he jumps up like he won a prize. Well, maybe he has. He likes long car rides, which is funny, since I don't like driving out of town.

Thor adds another problem to my little adventure. I'm not leaving him home alone again, not after he tore everything to shreds last night. But I can't take him with me to the jeweler, either. Everybody in Eagle Valley knows Thor, but in Roanoke, I won't get away with taking him everywhere. Maybe I should have gotten a Chihuahua and carried it around in my purse like Paris Hilton.

As if he can tell what I'm thinking, Thor licks my hand and leaves a big trail of slobber behind. "I love you too, Thor," I tell him. "I wouldn't trade you for anything."

On our way out to the truck, I call Eliza. "You busy today?" I ask.

"Who, me? Nah, I'm just sitting here, tending my pedicure. The twins are playing chess and teaching themselves to read Latin." In the background, I hear a crash. "Ian and Wyatt!" Eliza bellows.

"Thor and I are headed into Roanoke," I say. "I need to stop by the jeweler. Mind if we stop by your place on our way?"

"You're driving to Roanoke?" Eliza asks. "Well, sure! We'd love to see you guys."

"Okay. We're leaving now," I say. "Any chance you'd mind dog-sitting for me while I'm at the jewelers?"

"And here I thought you just wanted to visit little old me. Sure, we'd love to. Thor will keep the boys entertained, anyway."

"I owe you one."

"You owe me much more than that, little sister. See you soon."

I've driven to Eliza's house exactly twice in the last year. Once for Thanksgiving, and once for the twins' second birthday. That was only three months ago. Hard to believe how much they grow in between visits. I half-expect them to be six feet tall and shaving by Christmas.

Ian and Wyatt have met Thor dozens of times, but always at my house or at Mama and Daddy's. They're the best of friends by now. Thor loves kids. Can't imagine how excited the twins will be to have him visit in their very own home.

Eliza and John bought their house right after they got married. It's a brick split level in a good neighborhood. Lots of good stories here. On my last visit, Ian and Wyatt convinced me to roll down the hill with them in the backyard. I felt like I was flying, catching little glimpses of their lives with each turn. Ian and Wyatt play catch out here. Well, more specifically, Ian throws and Wyatt runs off with the ball. John takes an unhealthy pride in cutting and trimming the lawn. Eliza raked twelve bags of leaves last fall before she gave up and pitched the rest of the leaves into the creek.

Thor and I are halfway up the walk when Eliza pops open the door. "Boys! I have a surprise for you!" she hollers. "It's Auntie Arden and Thor!"

Ian is out the door and down the steps in a flash. "Wait, wait! Gentle!" I cry as he practically throws himself on Thor. My good dog doesn't mind. He backs up a step before he softens and wags his tail.

"Pet him gently, Ian," Eliza says, showing him how to stroke Thor's ears.

"Good doggy," Ian coos as he pets. Thor rewards him with a wet lick on his cheek.

Wyatt shows up in the doorframe, holding half a banana. "Dog!" he offers. "Big dog!"

"Come on over," I say. "Remember? Nice touches. Gentle touch."

Wyatt bypasses Thor and snuggles up against me instead. We have a good connection, Wyatt and me. Where Ian tackles the world full-throttle, Wyatt likes to hang back and take it all in. The little stories I get from him are pure sweetness. He's totally absorbed in his train puzzle, and he's still picturing the pieces in his mind. He wants me to see his puzzle, too. He loves me. He wants me to have some of his banana. I look down at my shirt, where sticky smudges are already covering my front. Mission accomplished.

"Let Auntie Arden and Thor get in the house," Eliza says, finally, peeling Ian off the dog.

"Are you sure?" I ask, looking down at Thor's dirty paws. "I didn't think about your floors."

"If the floors are twin-proof, they're Thor-proof," Eliza says. "Come on in. Do you have to go do your errands right away, or can you sit for a minute?"

"I've got time," I say.

As much as Mama and Daddy's house pays homage to the past, Eliza and John's house embraces the present. Most of their furniture was bought online and assembled with not enough screws and too many cuss words. The hallway is lined with canvas prints of their family pictures, taken when the boys were just a year old. Eliza stenciled inspirational words all over the family room, like "Love" and "Family" and "Laughter."

In the kitchen, Eliza pulls plastic wrap off a pitcher of sweet tea and pours us each a glass. "So what's so special that you came out here to see the jewelers?" she asks. "Must be important to make you drive all the way out here."

I shrug. "Not much, actually," I say. "Just need to get a few things appraised. No big deal."

Eliza passes me the glass of sweet tea. I lace my fingers over the spot where her hand rested. She doesn't believe a word of it. She knows how much I hate leaving Eagle Valley.

"I thought I'd try getting out for a change," I tell her. "Started to feel a little hemmed in back home."

"Sweetie, Eagle Valley's made me feel hemmed in since I was eighteen," Eliza says. "If you're feeling that way, things must be bad. What's going on?"

I tell her, briefly, about the pamphlets, the fund-raiser, the meeting this morning. Even though I try to gloss it over, Eliza's eyes get big as dinner plates.

"Well, that's a nice way for Paula to carry on," she snaps. She's so mad she dropped the 'Miss.' "Has Mama said anything about it? I can't even imagine. As if she needs to deal with all of this on top of getting help for Daddy."

"You know Mama," I say. "She's not going to say anything to us about it."

Eliza nods. "Well, I think it's awful," she says. "When you think how close they used to be. Even if she doesn't say it, I know Mama never saw this coming."

"Neither did Miss Paula," I say without thinking. I'm caught up in remembering how Miss Paula's story sounded from that snippet I got off my door handle. But Eliza doesn't know that, and she just about topples out of her chair.

"Arden McCrae," she says. "You're not siding with Paula, are you?"

"Of course not. There's just always two sides to a story, you know?"

Eliza calms down instantly. "You're right," she says. "Though I don't know how you can be that nice to someone like her."

I shrug.

"You were always like that," Eliza says reflectively. "Even when you weren't any older than Ian and Wyatt. Always seemed like you were listening."

I feel the heat rising to my cheeks. She doesn't know how right she is.

"It's a good thing," Eliza says, misunderstanding my blush. "You were so sensitive, always trying to figure out what was going to happen and how everything was going to work out. What was it Daddy used to call you?"

"Cassandra," I say. "He called me a little Cassandra."

Talking about Daddy leaves a glimmer of pain hanging between us.

"Well," says Eliza. "Don't feel like you have to work out all this stuff with Eagle Valley. That's all I'm saying. Don't let it get you down."

I drive slower than I have to when I leave for the jeweler's. I know I should hurry to keep Thor from overstaying his welcome. Even buoyed by a successful trip to Eliza's, it's nerve-wracking to stare down a trip outside familiar territory.

Once I park, I talk myself through, step by step. Get out of the car and up to the front door. I get that far without touching anything. Safe. Okay. The door handles are the pull kind, so I can't get away with just leaning against it with my thick-sleeved elbow. No problem. I can deal with this. I pull out a pair of my heavy winter gloves, even though it's barely chilly outside. Well, if someone questions it, who cares?

Safely wrapped up in my gloves, I pull the door open and let it slam shut behind me. I've been in here before. It even smells about the same, like jewelry cleaner and lemon Pledge. That feels comforting.

The regular jeweler, Mr. Harris, isn't behind the counter. Instead, I see a girl about my age.

"How can I help you?" she asks, extra-polite. She must be new. She has that eager-to-please look about her.

"I'm just here to have some pieces appraised," I say. "Is Mr. Harris in?"

"He stepped out for a bit," she says. "I can help you, though. I'm his new assistant. I'm a certified Gemologist. Just graduated. Would you like to see my credentials?"

I wouldn't, not really, but I can tell she's anxious to show somebody, so I pinch her business card between my gloved fingers and pretend to read it. Sylvie Harris. Getting her start in the family store, I gather.

She's watching me, narrowing her eyes a little when she takes in my early-fall sweater and my late-winter gloves. "It's so hard to know how to dress for this weather," I say with a smile. "I have three rings to be appraised, if you've got the time."

Sylvie goes straight to business, taking the velvet boxes from my clumsy hands. "The first two aren't worth too much, I'm afraid," she says. "The settings are in good shape, but the stones are cloudy, and this one has a chip. This third one, though. This is something."

She knows her stuff. I can tell by the slightly show-offy way she's examining the ring, furrowing her brows. She's not going to be anybody's assistant for long, that's for sure.

"I'd put the value at this for the first two, and this for the third," Sylvie says, passing me a neatly-filled out card. "If you'd like to sell the third one, I'll offer the full value. It's striking."

"I didn't know you sold antique jewelry here," I say, surprised.

"We don't, but I do," Sylvie says with a mischievous smile. She flips over the business card. She has a website, an online store, I'm guessing.

"Really? I'm an antiques dealer," I say. "Let me give you my card." Only I still don't want to take off my gloves, so I peel off three instead of one and fumble some more down to the floor. "I have a storefront in historic Eagle Valley, and I have an online store too."

"I hope you'll keep my card on you, then," Sylvie says. "I don't know where you found this little treasure, but if you have more pieces like this to sell, I'm happy to work with you."

"I'll keep that in mind," I say. I agree to sell her the third ring, and tuck the other two in my purse, along with their neat little cards.

I did it, I think jubilantly as I leave the store. So what if I kept my gloves on the whole time? I got out there. Talked to someone new without breaking a sweat. If change is in the air, it might as well take me with it.

11

When Thor and I get back home that night, I'm too wound up with my own success to focus. I sort through the mail and leave it all in an untidy pile on the front table. Then I walk into the dining room and kitchen and back out without doing a thing. Thor follows me as I wander from room to room. Clearly, his owner has gone right over the deep end.

Used to be that I never thought I'd leave Eagle Valley. Partly because it's home but mostly, if I'm being honest, because I'm scared. I've gone to Roanoke now and again to do business with Bryson and Sadie. I've even met up with other antique dealers here and there. I've been known to drive to estate sales all around Central Virginia.

But that's different. Hunting down antiques and holding other people's stories in my hands—I knew how to deal with that. Meeting new people, going into banks or office buildings or new towns, that's a whole different ball of wax. There are handshakes. Doorknobs and handrails and buses. Cities covered with so many stories from so many people, all demanding to be heard. It's impossible to think in a city. Impossible to hear, to see. Impossible to breathe.

Not impossible, I remind myself. I did it yesterday. It's not impossible anymore.

It's not that I haven't tried before. There were all those class trips until my parents finally stopped signing the permission forms and let me stay home instead. Then the failed family vacation to Virginia Beach. The disastrous trip-that-wasn't to D.C. with Lila Beth when I was sixteen. The list goes on and on.

Well, I'm different now, or trying to be. A year ago, I would've waited until the last minute, maybe even sold the rings on eBay just to get rid of them. I can handle more than I used to.

I wish Jeremy could see me now. That thought comes out of nowhere, but once it comes, it's here to stay. If I'd been able to leave Eagle Valley sooner, maybe Jeremy and I would still be together.

Here come the 'if onlys.' If only I'd been braver. If only I'd been stronger. If only I'd tried harder.

Thinking like that gives me the urge to clean the house, scrub away everything I don't want to hear anymore and start fresh. Usually, coming home gives me peace like nothing else. It's not a testament to the past, like our house growing up, and it's not all about the life I'm living now, like Eliza and John's. It's a nice mix, I think. The house is over a hundred years old, and it used to belong to a quiet family that pretty much kept to themselves. Their stories have faded straight into the wooden beams, now. Since I had to do so much renovating and fixing up, just about everything in this house feels like me. The floor carries memories of Thor's first little tumbling steps when he was just a puppy, and the kitchen table I bought new and painted up holds the stories of all our quiet meals here.

Since I moved in just before Jeremy and I started dating, my house has lots of stories to tell about him, too. Not all of them are good to hear. I refinished the floors in the weeks after Jeremy left. The kitchen was next. I can still feel all the hurt I poured out when I put in the glass cabinet doors and painted the room. Even the entry table reminds me of the hours I spent analyzing the breakup while I sanded and shellacked.

Guess I can't get away from bad memories, no matter where I am.

Thor's following me around, so close that I'm actually tripping over him. "All right," I tell him. "I'll stop pacing. Let's find a project."

I take Thor down to my workshop in the basement. There's plenty to do. My laptop is charging down here, too. Maybe I'll jump online. I've got some inventory I need to get listed on my website.

That reminds me to take a look at Sylvie's website. "Antique and restored heirloom jewelry," it says. Tasteful photos of pendants, earrings, and bracelets march down the left side of the webpage. The ring I sold her this afternoon is already listed down at the bottom.

It's a decent website, nothing fancy. I hope her little business takes off. I think it'd be nice to run into her again. What was it she'd said? "If you have more pieces like this to sell, I'm happy to work with you." That was flattering, but I don't know how often I'll run across jewelry that nice in the future.

I take a look at the loose jewelry still scattered over my desk. After getting the rings appraised and sorting out the costume jewelry, all that's left are the worn-out pieces. I hate throwing out broken things. If all I have to do is replace a finding or mend a fastener, I can save a whole piece. Plus, jewelry gets broken in

some of the most interesting ways. Arguments, acci-
dents, snags and fits. Passionate lovemaking, too, but
those stories are a little embarrassing to overhear.
Makes me feel like a voyeur.

I pick up each piece with my bare hands, finding
each imperfection and the hum of its history with my
fingertips. There are a couple pieces of costume jewelry
that need to be brushed up with my gold paint pin,
and a watch with major missing links. This single earring could work if I take off the broken wire and add
the beading to the necklace, to replace the missing
pendant. Perfect. Two broken pieces that fit just right.

I guess that's what Jeremy and I were at the end.
Two broken people that didn't fit together anymore.
When we first met, he'd moved in with his parents to
help with the bed and breakfast. He didn't have a lot
of options. He has about the same story as most people
in our generation. He did all the right things, made
good grades and graduated on time, but the economy
tanked and took all the entry-level jobs with it. He
worked for only a year before his job was eliminated.
Then he was in a series of minimum wage jobs until
the last of that line disappeared too. At twenty-eight,
he moved to tiny Eagle Valley, Virginia, to live in the
basement of his parents' bed and breakfast and do
their bookkeeping.

Then he met me. That was supposed to be the fairy tale part. The it-all-worked-out-after-all part. He thought I was pretty and funny and smart. So what if I'd never left my hometown? He could understand being a late bloomer. And so what if he was back home with his parents? I could see him for who he was.

Thing is, Jeremy could be fixed. He could find another job. He could start over one more time. Me? Well, I didn't stop having spells. I didn't try to leave Eagle Valley. I didn't try to—what was that phrase he liked to use? Aim higher. I never aimed higher.

That's what happened, really. He fixed himself up. I stayed broken. He left, and I stayed.

"I'm not broken now," I say out loud. Thor startles. "Just talking to myself," I tell him.

Well, no need to get bogged down in all that. I run my index finger over the broken clasp of a gold brooch. This time I listen harder. Sure, I can hear all about the last time it was worn—that hasn't changed. There's more there than I thought, though. I could replace the brooch clasp, but it would look better if I made it into a pendant. The earrings are too gaudy, even for costumes, but I could add them to the clutch after I fix the clasp. *Where did I put that little clutch?*

It's hiding among another trove of to-be-restored treasures. I'm on a roll. I take a listen to the other things piled around it. The porcelain bookends I was going to restore would look even better in new colors, with the flowers painted brighter and bolder. The chair with the seat that needs re-caning would look perfect reupholstered entirely. Somewhere, I have a Victorian crazy quilt that couldn't be saved around the edges. Maybe instead of cutting and hemming it, I'll use it to recover the chair.

Thor is looking up at me with his chin resting on his paws. "Want to stay up late tonight, Thor?" I ask him. He wags his tail. I take that as a yes.

When I get back to the store on Tuesday, I have a load of new merchandise in my truck. I have the two wingback chairs whose legs I finally fixed, so those are ready to go right to the front of the store. The rest of my pieces are new projects that I started and finished last night. A lot of it is costume jewelry, accent pieces, and little statuettes. They're... different. I'm still not sure I like everything I did. It was exciting to do it, though. I haven't had a rush of inspiration like that in ages.

Thor trots in behind me, but stays in the stock room while I go back and forth to the truck to lug in more pieces. He's exhausted. I was up working until one o'clock this morning. Thor stayed by my side, loyal to the end, although he did creep closer and closer to the door as the night went on. Poor dog. What can I say? When inspiration strikes, it strikes.

I rearrange the front corner of the store so I have a little section for all my new pieces. I add a little placard that says, "Reclaimed History." Another idea that struck last night. No idea how well any of it will sell, since my reclaimed projects aren't strictly antique or vintage quality anymore. Guess I'll see.

I wonder what Janie will say when she sees my little addition. Janie likes things by the book, but then again, the little brooch I made from the necklace would look sweet with her usual costume for the Civil War Days. Maybe she'll like it.

I'm so busy admiring my handiwork that I barely notice Miranda Johns come in. Out of the corner of my eye, the first thing I see is how much she and Jeremy look alike. They have the same wavy brown hair, big green eyes, and long nose and ears.

"Good morning," Miranda says. "Just thought I'd stop by and see if you had any sales going on today."

I give her a long look. She knows I don't do sales. Miranda and Gordon have bought a lot of antiques from me. At least half the furniture in their bed and breakfast came from my store, and most of the paintings and trim, too.

"Why don't you look around and see what catches your eye," I say smoothly, "and then we'll see what we can do."

Miranda smiles and moves off to the front booth. She scans for treasures the way she always does—eye level first, then lower for the overlooked treasures, then up high for the nicest pieces. I taught her that. When Jeremy and I had just started dating, I used to go over and help Miranda put the finishing touches on their B&B. She wanted to decorate every room as a different era and asked me to help make sure she had everything accurate. Back then, I worked alongside her and wondered what it would be like to call her my mother-in-law.

It stings a little that Jeremy didn't stop by while he was in town over the weekend. Part of me is itching to find out more. Is he coming back this weekend? Did he think of coming by but worried it would be awkward? Was he just not thinking about me at all anymore? Maybe it's better not to know.

I sell a lamp and a tea set to a doddering out-of-town couple before Miranda reappears. She's holding a pitcher and bowl set. "How do you think this would look in the Green Room?" she asks, holding it up.

It would look historically inaccurate but pretty. The handle on that kind of pitcher wasn't made until the 1890s, and the Green Room caps off in the 1860s.

Nobody's going to know that but me, though, so I tell her I think it's perfect.

Six months since I broke up with her son, and it's still awkward when Miranda and I talk. Well, who am I kidding? It was awkward when Jeremy and I were dating, too. She drums her pearl-pink manicured nails on the counter while I ring up her purchase.

"I was wondering if I could ask a favor," she begins. "I wanted to start offering a tea service at the B&B in the afternoons—just a little something extra for guests when they're checking in. I was wondering if you could help me track down enough cups and saucers for the breakfast room."

"Don't you have cups and saucers?" I ask before I catch myself. As if I can afford to turn down work.

"Just the plain ones that come with the regular dishes. I saw a picture in a magazine of a B&B that had a different china cup and saucer for each place setting, and a teapot and creamer and sugar bowl at each table. I thought that would be fun."

"Of course," I say, recovering. "Come by later in the week, and we'll make up a list of what you want and the price points."

"I'll be by Thursday," Miranda says, obviously pleased. I feel a little warmer to her while I finish wrapping her pitcher and bowl. She hasn't offered me work in a long time.

"I'm not holding it against you, you know," she says. For one sickening moment, I think she's talking about Jeremy. *She's not holding it against me that I broke up with her son? How kind.* Then she lowers her voice and continues. "Sometimes our families act in ways we don't expect. Losing the view means as much to your business as it does ours."

It's an olive branch. A big one. For a minute, I wonder what it would be like if Miranda and I were on the same side.

Too bad I'll never know.

"Eagle Valley doesn't need a mountain view to make it special," I say stoutly. "Besides, what else could Mama and Daddy do? You know what it's like, being retired."

"Of course," Miranda says hastily. "I can't even imagine if Gordon was ill."

But she can imagine, and she imagines she could do it better. I hear all about it when I take her crisply-folded dollar bills and catch her hand. She'd hire an in-home nurse, for example. That couldn't be too expensive. They'd sell the bed and breakfast, if it came to that, but to a nice older couple that would cherish it the way they had.

Things do tend to work out better in our imaginations.

I take my time driving to Mama and Daddy's house after work. Thor is trying to run from one end of the seat to the other, so I have to keep an arm up to block him from running straight into my lap.

"Settle down, Thor!" I tell him sternly, but he just gives me a sloppy dog kiss on the cheek.

Mama and Daddy are actually out on the porch when I pull up. Mama gives us a small wave, but Daddy doesn't seem to notice. The pit of my stomach sinks. *Please, don't let this be another bad day.*

When I come around and let Thor out, though, Daddy lights up. "There's that dog," I hear him say. I get Thor's tennis ball from the glove compartment and bring them both up to the porch.

"Hey, buddy," Daddy says. He reaches for Thor and scratches both his ears. Thor is instantly calm. He even lays his big wet chin on Daddy's knee. "Hey, buddy."

"Want to play fetch with him?" I say. Daddy takes the tennis ball I offer, but he doesn't throw it. He holds it in one hand while Thor gnaws away. I've never seen my dog so gentle.

Mama stands up quietly and motions me to follow her through the screen door, into the kitchen.

"He's having a hard day," Mama says.

"I'm sorry," I say. "Anything you need? Anything I can do?"

Mama sniffs and waves one hand, as if to brush my questions away. "I've got all our essentials packed," she says. "We'll be ready to move by the weekend. I've already called the home and let them know."

I look behind her, but the kitchen and laundry room look almost identical to when I was last here. "Where are the things you're taking?"

"I have little sticky notes on the furniture. John and Eliza will come up with the truck Friday and take the big things and get them arranged in the room for us. I was wondering if you could help on Friday morning, since you usually take it off..."

"I'll be here," I promise.

"Now, if there's anything you want, you let me know," Mama says. "Before Bryson comes in and starts getting the estate sale ready. Is there anything you want?"

I shake my head.

"Even little things," Mama says. "We're not taking much of the tools or the kitchen utensils, since the home will take care of that for us."

Mama already handed me all of Daddy's tools when I bought my house. I guess she doesn't remember now.

"I don't need anything," I say quickly.

Mama smiles and looks over my shoulder, out the screen door. Daddy is still holding the tennis ball for Thor. I can hear him saying, "Hey, buddy. Good boy. Good dog."

I look back at Mama, and it's unmistakable—there are little, unfallen tears in her eyes. "That's the most he's said all day."

12

I head straight down to my basement workspace when Thor and I get home from my parents'. I was hoping I'd feel the same spark as I did last night, maybe lose myself in some projects again. I don't. I pick up piece after piece and turn it over in my hands, hearing but not really listening.

"Come on, Thor," I say. I take my laptop upstairs and settle on the couch. Thor abandons me for his doggie bed. He stretches out, belly up, and promptly falls asleep.

I type in the web address for the Alzheimer's forum. I've visited so many times that I only have to type three letters before my computer automatically fills in the rest. I scan the recent posts for familiar screen names and updates on threads I've read before. It's strange how familiar these people feel, even though we've never spoken. I've never even posted, myself. I've just read.

The woman whose siblings are giving her so much trouble has an update. She told her brother she was going to start taking their mom to the senior center a few times a week. She copied and pasted the entire e-mail exchange between them. She poured out how hard it all was and how much she needed a break, and the brother wrote back—in all capital letters—that their mother should be taken care of by family, and that's what he was paying for. It went downhill pretty fast.

Another poster writes "Sensitive" in his thread title, and spends eight paragraphs detailing his father's last days. There are over a hundred comments on his post. People saying everything from "sorry for your loss" to sharing their own last-days stories.

This is where we could be with Daddy, I think. Maybe next month, maybe next year, maybe years from now.

My daddy, the one I grew up with, would hate being the way he is now. I hate that I see so much that's the same between the way Daddy is now and the stories on here. My daddy isn't really like this, I want to say. He's different.

I open a new thread and start writing. "New here," I type. "I've lurked for months but I'm a first-time poster." Then it all comes out, as fast as I can type. How long Daddy's been going downhill. How sometimes it feels like it happened slowly and sometimes it feels like it all changed overnight. How my parents have to move and I don't know what will happen next and they don't deserve this. None of us do. My eyes are stinging with tears when I click the button that says, "Post."

Thor wakes up and comes over to me when I start crying for real. I don't like to cry. Everything I'm trying to let out just rolls down my cheeks and soaks back into my skin. Thor licks my face and tries to climb on my chest, and then when I'm sobbing too loudly to stop, he whines and howls along. I finally let him on the couch, which will probably start a bad habit but I don't even care anymore. He wiggles in next to me and lays his big, sloppy chin on my stomach.

It's not really that bad, I try to tell myself. *It could be different for him. It might be years yet. They could find a cure...*

That's the worst thing about being me, I think. I can't lie to myself.

After a good, long cry, I feel like I've turned myself inside out. My cheeks are prickling with the feelings I usually bottle deep in my core. Thor looks worried, so I scratch his ears and under his chin.

"It's okay, Thor," I tell him. "I'm all better." He still follows right on my heels when I go to scrub my face, make myself a cup of green tea, turn the stereo on and play the Ramones. When I sit back on the couch to collect myself, he curls up against my feet.

It takes half a mug of green tea before I feel ready. I open my laptop again and look at my post. It already has two comments.

"Welcome to the forum," says the first. "Sorry we're 'meeting' this way. My mom moved in with us six months ago, but many others have had their loved ones go into nursing and assisted care. It's a hard road but just remember the changes you see are the disease, not your dad. Hang around here. We're all here to support each other. Hope you stick around."

The second comment says, "Glad you're here, although sorry for the reason. Hope the move goes smoothly for your parents. Ask any questions you have on here. I got a lot of help from some people here when I was having trouble dealing with other people drifting away, which it sounds like you're kind of going through too."

I don't know anything about these people—not where they live or what they look like or any of the ten thousand things I would hear if I could reach out and touch them. But they seem to understand me just fine.

I swig down the last sugary dregs of my tea. "Come on down, Thor," I say. I grab my laptop and head down to my workshop in the basement.

An hour in, I've stopped and started half-a-dozen projects. I feel hollow, useless. I've been waiting for some of that spark from last night. I want something to grab hold of me and show me what it wants to be made into. Nothing I touch tonight gives me a story I care about. All I hear is noise.

Instead, I keep turning to my laptop and refreshing the web page to see if anyone else has commented on my post. So far, I've had two more comments. One is a basic, "Sorry you're facing this, but glad you're here!" The other is longer. "I just joined myself, a few weeks ago. I wish I'd come here earlier! Everyone here knows exactly what you're going through. The best advice I've had so far is this: take care of your dad the way he is now, but also think of him the way he was before. That's who your dad really is, no matter what this disease does."

I take a look at my scattered workbench. Daddy would have had a lot to say about this, before he got sick. I close my eyes and wipe my hands off with a baby wipe, trying to clear out every story but mine.

Imagining isn't really my thing. There's always some other story, someone else's story, jockeying for my attention. Seems the more I try to focus and shut out everything else, the louder everything gets. I can hear the radiator kick on, the hum of the fluorescent lights, Thor snoring softly in his sleep.

I try again to picture my workbench and imagine my father walking in.

I feel him coming before he actually turns the corner. That's how Daddy is. He fills up a room before he even opens his mouth to speak. When Daddy shows up, people stop talking and look towards him.

"Geez, Arden," he says, stretching out his e's like they're made of elastic. "What kind of mess are you getting into down here?"

I feel the corners of my mouth pull into a smile. "Don't know for sure yet, Daddy. I've been working on some new stuff for the store."

"Don't you mean old stuff?" Daddy says, smirking.

He takes a tour around my little basement, hands clasped behind his back. I can tell he's itching to pick things up, but he doesn't. He knows how I am about that. He stops and looks at a footstool I've taken apart. One of the legs was missing when I got it, but I've been prying out the staples and taking off the uphol- stery. The soft wadding of the cushion is dripping all over the place. "What the hell happened here?" he asks. "Looks like it was in a bar fight."

"I'm fixing it up, Daddy," I say.

"Somebody better."

Even if it's only in my mind's eye, it feels so good to see Daddy again. I want to hug him. I want to wrap my arms around him and feel how whole and healthy he is. I take one step forward, and my daydream dis- appears.

Another hour passes with no new comments on my post. I haven't been able to imagine Daddy again, and even calling up a real memory feels muddled now.

Above my regular toolbox, I keep Daddy's old set of woodcarving tools. They've been there ever since Mama gave them to me, ages ago. I've been so careful not to take them out and look at them. I don't want to touch them too much, let my own hopes and dreams and ideas cover up Daddy's. Usually, it's enough just to look up at them, know they're in there, evidence of who Daddy used to be. Today, I guess I need proof.

Lightly, gently, I pluck the box from the shelf and open it on the workbench. I hear Mama's stories first, from the day she handed them to me. She tried so hard to put a brave face on it, acting like Daddy had just lost interest in woodcarving, and she thought I could use the tools for my work. Truthfully, Daddy had cut his finger pretty badly the night before.

Reach deeper, I tell myself. Listen harder. There it is—the warm, sweet scent of pine, and the delicious hum of early autumn evenings, just like this one. Daddy must have spent hours out in the barn, working on his carvings.

The fluorescent lights hum louder, and I feel a little dizzy. A premonition. Here it comes. I wait for it, but there's no vision. Just the feeling of the air getting thicker and the lights getting brighter and whiter. It's taking a while to build. Whatever this premonition is, it must be a doozy. I pack away Daddy's tools, quick and light as I can, and put them back on the shelf. I don't want to cover up what's left of his history, not too fast.

Thor whines a little and scoots closer to me. I guess he can tell I've got a vision on the way. I wait it out for a few minutes.

My vision dawns slowly, like I'm watching the sun rise over the mountains. It's all three of us sisters, standing by Tripp's dogwood tree in my parents' yard. I try to get a good look at our faces, see what we're doing, but the premonition is already fading. Sure enough, Lila Beth was right there with Eliza and me, and it wasn't even a holiday.

Thor presses his cold, wet nose on my hand. "Nothing to worry about, boy," I tell him. "Come on. Let's go upstairs." Better get to bed for the night and start over fresh tomorrow morning. I start closing windows on my web browser.

My email inbox shows two unread messages. I hover over the icon for a moment.

The first e-mail is from Lila Beth.

"Hi, Arden. Sorry it took me awhile to respond to you. Mama told me about the move and Eliza filled me in too. Are you sure you need me to come down this month? I thought I'd come down after they were settled and try to cheer Daddy up about being in the new place."

She went on to tell me about life at the office and her coworker in the next cubicle over who snapped his gum and everybody hated it but didn't want to squeal to Human Resources. She ended with her usual, "I love you-Lila B." Apparently, nobody up in D.C. calls her Lila Beth, just Lila.

Normally, I'd have taken that. She's an Easter-and-Christmas visitor, I'd remind myself. I wouldn't want to force her to be someone she's not. But not now, not after I saw her standing with me and Eliza in a vision. She's part of this story, whether she knows it yet or not.

The second e-mail is from Eliza. "Hey, Arden. I tried calling you earlier but didn't get an answer. Do you ever turn that thing on or is that one cell tower in Eagle Valley overloaded? Just kidding. I know Eagle Valley doesn't even have a cell tower. Anyway, John and I are going to move Mama and Daddy on Friday morning. I thought I might stay over into the weekend to keep you company, if you wanted. Does that work? Let me know." She punctuates her last sentence with a smiley face and ends with, "Love ya, sis!"

I start to e-mail Eliza back, but pick up my cell and call her instead. Is it too late to call? I don't even think about it until I've dialed. I glance at my laptop. 9:05. She's still awake.

Eliza picks up on the third ring. "So you do have your phone on," she says. "What's up? The twins went to bed hours ago, so I can talk."

"I went to see Mama and Daddy today," I say. "Daddy was having a rough day."

Eliza lets out her breath in a long, gusty sigh. "I'm sorry," she says. "I keep hoping this will be better after they've moved. After they're settled."

"I hope so," I say. "I'm so glad you're coming. I need you."

I need you. I never say things like that. I feel like I'm turned inside-out still, wearing my feelings for the world to see.

I can tell Eliza is a little taken aback. Her voice gets extra comforting, big-sisterly. "I'll be there," she says. "We'll do it together, and then it'll be over. They'll be settled. Mama will have more help with Daddy."

"Right," I say. I want to tell her more, spill out everything I'm thinking. Maybe she'd like that Alzheimer's forum too. For some reason, I feel like I need to pull back, put myself back together. Find a safer topic to talk about.

"Anything else new?"

"I got an e-mail from Lila Beth," I said. Now why did I say that? Lila Beth is hardly a safe topic with Eliza. I keep blabbering on anyway. "I think she wants to wait to come until after Mama and Daddy are settled."

"Honestly, Arden," Eliza says. "Sometimes you just have to take people for who they are, you know? If Lila Beth was going to come help, she would."

Eliza and Lila Beth are closer in age. They have more memories of each other growing up, unlike me, the tagalong third sister that showed up years later. I don't think I know Lila Beth better than Eliza does, exactly. I just know this story has Lila Beth in it, too.

"Anyway," says Eliza. "I'll be up on Friday for sure, and I'll see about staying this weekend too. Even if we don't get anything done. I don't figure we'll be going to too many Festival weekends once Mama and Daddy move."

"Guess not," I say. "See you."

I think about what Eliza said after we hang up. The part about taking people for who they are. I try to think about what I know about who Lila Beth is. Lila Beth is ambitious. Lila Beth is smart. Lila Beth loves us but doesn't see us much.

I guess I don't know Lila Beth all that well after all.

I click back to her e-mail and tap out a reply.

"Hi, Lila Beth,

I hope you get your HR thing straightened out with the gum-snapper. We're having a hard time here. I know you don't get a lot of time off work, but if you could swing coming up sometime in the next few weeks, it would really help. There's going to be an estate sale with everything leftover after they move. I hate going through stuff without you. I know it's short notice, but if there's any way you can come, we need you."

I think about adding the real reason—that if she comes later, it won't help Daddy feel better about moving because, dollars to doughnuts, he won't remember the move is permanent. Or even remember which of his daughters she is. Or remember how many daughters he has. The last time Lila Beth saw him was on Easter. Things haven't just gone downhill, they've gone down an avalanche.

I read over it again and delete the "I need you" at the end. Instead, I write, "We'd love to see you." There. I press "send" and close my laptop.

13

I wake up just before dawn on Thursday. The sky is still mostly dark with the first sunbeams peeking between the trees. Everything feels electric this morning. I feel like I have three extra quilts on the bed, the air's so heavy. Sure sign that there's another premonition coming.

Well, that's no surprise. Mama and Daddy are moving out tomorrow, leaving behind the farm–our farm–and moving into assisted living. No coming back from that. Things are bound to change.

Thor is annoyed with me for waking up so early. I scratch his ears as I step over him and pull on my bathrobe. He rolls his eyes, half-asleep, but wags his tail twice in a half-hearted "good morning." He's going to jump up into my bed as soon as I leave the room. I'd be more irritated, but who can blame him? It's freezing and the radiator is struggling to keep up.

I toast an English muffin and slather both halves with butter and peach preserves. *Comfort food,* I think, and put another English muffin in the toaster. I wouldn't mind some coffee, too, but I'll have to wait. If I run the coffeemaker and the toaster at the same time, it'll overload the circuit.

The preserves are so sweet they hurt my teeth. Perfect. I run through my mental to-do list. I'll have to put out extra stock in the store to get ready for Festival shoppers. Then this weekend we have the Mill Days. I'll put out all the quilts, rugs, and linens I have in the back. I have that spinning wheel I've been saving, too. That would be good right by the front door. A little display to draw customers in. Janie doesn't come today, so it's all me until closing. I have more inventory to list online, too.

And then there's tomorrow.

My second English muffin is done. I unplug the toaster and start the coffeemaker. It feels so orderly, making a pot of fresh coffee. I could do it in my sleep. Actually, I'm pretty sure I have a few times.

While it brews, I finish eating. Mama used to make breakfasts like this. "Something to stick to your ribs," she'd say, filling us up with Cream of Wheat with butter or blueberry muffins and jam.

"I don't want sticky ribs!" I used to pout. When I was little, I said it because I really didn't understand. When I was older, I kept saying it to make her laugh.

It's been a long time since I heard Mama laugh.

I add sugar and cream to my thermos before pouring in the coffee. I twist on the lid and give it a good shake. That's Daddy's trick. It used to make Mama nuts.

"Vaughn! What if you forgot to close the cap? We'd have coffee everywhere."

"I never forget," he'd say, holding his thermos out with one arm while he pulled Mama close with the other. The exaggerated kiss that came next would make Mama blush. "Vaughn! The children!" But she'd still be smiling ten minutes later.

I haven't seen Mama smile for a long time, either.

I decide to take my coffee out on the front porch and swing for a minute. Before I go, I poke my head into the bedroom to check on Thor. Sure enough, there he is, sprawled out on the bed. His jowls puff out slightly as he snores. *That dog is drooling all over my pillow.* I add laundry to my mental to-do list.

Outside, the air is sharp and cold. I burn my tongue on my coffee. Across the road, over the trees, I can see just the tops of the Blue Ridge rising in the background.

I wonder what it would be like to leave Eagle Valley. Permanently. I've never really considered it before, moving away. Well, that's a lie. I considered it for about three seconds, right before Jeremy and I broke up. I've replayed that conversation in my head a million times since then.

We were standing right here on this porch. Jeremy was by the steps, looking out at the mountains, and I was all the way over by the swing. Studying his profile. Studying him.

"It's a good job," he'd said. "Better than the one I had."

"So you're leaving?" I asked.

"Of course," Jeremy said. He looked at me strangely. "Have to move on sometime." There was a long pause, where he looked everywhere but straight at me. "I thought you might come with me." He starts backtracking almost immediately. "Not right away. I mean. I know you have stuff to do here. I don't expect you to just drop your business and sell your house like that. But... someday."

I'll come with you, I wanted to say. Even better, *I love you, too.* I tried to imagine myself as Mrs. Jeremy

Johns. Living in Richmond. Selling this house and taking my business with me.

But that future wouldn't come, no matter how hard I tried to picture it.

"I never saw myself anywhere but Eagle Valley."

He was silent for a long time. "So this is it for you?" he'd asked. "Eagle Valley for life?"

"What's wrong with that?"

Jeremy had stared off towards the trees, towards the mountains, just like I'm doing now. "I guess I thought you were different."

"Why do I have to be different?" I'd asked. Anger surged through my chest, white-hot. "I own my own business. I own my own home. Hell, I remodeled and fixed up this house myself. Why do I have to pick up and leave for you? Why can't you stay here for me?"

"This is what I've been working for!" Jeremy said. "Richmond is where the jobs are. What am I supposed to do? Do bookkeeping for my parents for the rest of my life? Be a househusband while you run the store?"

I felt so shaken I'd almost missed the part where he said 'husband.'

"What am I supposed to do?" I asked. "My business is here. My home is here, my family is here."

"I thought that's why you started the online store," Jeremy said. "Why can't you do that from Richmond?"

Why not?

Because I couldn't afford to fail. Because I couldn't afford to give it all up and break down before I even got to Richmond.

I had remembered the trip-that-wasn't to D.C. then, the way Lila Beth had looked at me when she had to turn around and drive me back to Eagle Valley. I couldn't stand to see Jeremy look at me that way. I had started shaking my head even before I said the words.

"I can't leave Eagle Valley," I'd said.

"I don't think you are choosing to stay here. I think you're too scared to do anything else."

I looked away from him and bit the insides of my cheeks to keep from crying. I shrugged. "You're the one that wants to leave."

"You're the one that's not coming."

I heard him crunch down the gravel driveway, heard his car door slam and the engine start. I didn't look up until I was sure he had rounded the corner.

It's just a fight, I'd told myself. *People say things they don't mean. We'll work through this.*

Then I had walked over to the place where he'd stood, brushed my fingers along the railing until I could fit each of my hands right where his had been. I listened.

It was over.

After pulling myself together and convincing Thor to get out of bed, I'm about ten minutes late opening the store. I feel like I'm moving through molasses today. The way this premonition is building, I can tell it's going to be a doozy.

Please don't let it be about Daddy, I think. *Or Mama. Please let the move go smoothly.*

Maybe it will be about my business. There's always that possibility. I had some good sales last weekend, and selling the ring in Roanoke helped, but it's going to take more than that to get my business back in shape. I've been hovering on the brink so long, I almost forget what it was like not to shuffle around expenses like a deck of cards.

Maybe it will be about Jeremy. Not sure how I feel about that. Some days, I feel like the shredded pieces of my heart have finally started knitting back together. Maybe it's best just to leave it be, let myself heal all the way. On the other hand, maybe seeing him again would be a good thing. Maybe we just met too soon, the last time. I've changed a bit since then.

Eliza would shake her head to know the little surge of hope I got from that thought. Well, no matter anyhow. I need to focus on today. There's a ton to do before the Mill Days this weekend.

I haven't been open five minutes when Golda pops in, carrying a take-out cup of coffee and a brown paper bag.

"Thought you'd need a little something to start your morning," she says. "Today's the day, isn't it?"

"Tomorrow," I say. I peek inside the bag—blueberry muffins. "Thanks, Golda."

"Anytime, sweetie," she says. "You know we're thinking about your mom and pop, too."

Tears sting the back of my eyes. Apparently, I am cursed to spend today in tears. Great.

"I moved my mama into a nursing home thirty years ago," Golda says. "You be good to yourself. And don't let any other nonsense," she waved behind her, vaguely, in the direction of Miss Paula's museum, "take up any space in your mind. You've got enough to deal with."

I wrap my hand around the cup, right where Golda's was and feel the truth of her story coming through. "I know."

"And if you need lunch today, you come on by. On the house."

"Thanks, Golda."

"And don't go nodding and saying thanks and then holing up in here, hiding from the world. If you disappear on me, I'll come find you. We take care of our own around here." As she turns to leave, she calls over her shoulder: "And tell that dog of yours I'm making him some extra bacon."

From the stock room, I hear Thor's pace pick up. He's scampering, pawing at the door. If there's one word that dog knows, it's 'bacon.'

Miranda Johns pops by just before noon. I'd forgotten she was supposed to come in today to talk about her order for mismatched china. Usually, I get people in here trying to dredge up a perfect match to their dishware. It's kind of funny to get a request to find mismatched stuff on purpose.

"Am I interrupting?" she asks. She peers up at me, perched on a stepstool and spritzing down the top shelves with spray cleaner.

"Not at all," I say. I strip off my rubber gloves and immediately wish I'd left them on. The future is pressing in. The sky is bluer and the air sharper than it was earlier this morning. I hope this premonition breaks before Festival. If it's going to be a big one, I can't be passing out while the store's full.

Miranda is prepared, as always. She's worked with me enough to know all the questions I'm going to ask. She has an itemized list: 50 teacups, 50 saucers, 10 teapots, 10 sugar bowls, 10 creamers. No more than 5 pieces of the same pattern. All items should be in "good vintage condition."

I take the paper from her and run my index finger down it like I'm reading the list, when really, I'm trying to pick up the stories she's left dusted all over the page. It's not easy, not now when I've got this premonition hanging over my head.

"When you list 'no more than 5 pieces of the same pattern,' does that include color? If I find pieces of red transferware and then more of the same pattern in blue, is that okay?"

Miranda hems and haws a bit. "If it's the same pattern but a different color, I guess that's okay. But not too much of that. I don't want the same pattern in every color, I want it to look eclectic."

"Let's say no more than eight pieces of the same pattern in different colors. No more than five of the same pattern and color."

"Perfect."

I type out a few numbers on my calculator with the tip of my fingernail. "Since we're looking for a variety, some of the pieces will probably come at a higher cost, and some will be on the lower end. I'm going to price the lot for the average value of the pieces." I write my price in blue ink on the bottom of her list. It's hard, since I'm trying to write without actually touching too much of the pen. *This is ridiculous*, I think, and grasp it like usual. Immediately, I'm flooded with the memory of the last time I wrote with this pen. I was signing a check for the rent. That wasn't so bad.

Miranda reads the number and immediately looks crestfallen. She chooses her words carefully. "Do you think I could talk you down on the price? Maybe a discount for returning customers?"

I don't do discounts. Miranda knows that. No haggling, bargaining, or negotiating of any kind. It wouldn't be fair. I can read people too well, even if they don't know it.

I can read Miranda, too. I heard it when I held the paper, felt it when I brushed by her hand just now. She's worried. Gordon has been going into overdrive, trying to replace every fixture that looks more "old" than "charming." They're talking about offering deeper discounts after Festival, maybe making up some new packages, like a "Romantic Getaway" or "Girl's Weekend." And Miranda's doing everything she can think of to freshen up the décor and keep things interesting.

Business is bad all over Eagle Valley. For Gordon and Miranda, this bed and breakfast is their retirement. It was the way they managed to afford leaving Gordon's stressful job as a lawyer, leave behind the long weeks of overtime and lonely nights at the office. If the bed and breakfast goes down, well, they don't know what they'll do.

I tap out the numbers on my calculator again, slowly.

"I can offer you 20% off," I say, finally. "I'll give you the 10% discount I have on Festival weekends, plus a 10% off discount for loyal customers."

Sometimes people need to negotiate. That's what Bryson would say when I was working for him and he was giving me another lecture on the fine art of haggling. "Sometimes folks need to feel a little give and take," he'd say. "If they want a firm price, they can go anywhere and buy new out of the box. They want something personal. Something unique. That goes for the price, too."

I still feel a little bad doing it. Truth is, the real reason I offered 20% off is that it's the highest Miranda can afford, and the absolute lowest I can do without doing it all for cost. I need to make a profit, too. But now I've gone and made it personal, and I'm thinking more about Miranda and Gordon and their retirement than I am about business.

The look in Miranda's eyes wipes away my doubt–almost. "Thanks, Arden," she says. "Thanks a million. I know you don't usually... I really appreciate it."

"Pleasure doing business," I say, even though it isn't, not really.

14

It isn't even eight o'clock on Friday morning when I get a call from Eliza.

"When are you coming?" she asks. Her voice is high and tight, like a violin string.

"Geez, Eliza," I say, trying to lighten the mood. "You're up awful early. Had you even seen a sunrise before?"

Joking around isn't going to work. Eliza's voice is still taut with stress. "It's not going well," she says.

"What do you mean?"

"Daddy's upset that John's loading up the furniture," she says. "He doesn't understand."

In the months since Daddy's decline, *he doesn't understand* can mean anything from *he's asked the same question five times* to *he's refusing to wear shoes.* "What should we do?" I ask.

I'm pretty sure all of Eagle Valley can hear the sigh Eliza lets out. "I think he needs a distraction, maybe? Something to take his mind off things. Maybe you can bring Thor. He likes Thor."

"Give me ten minutes," I say.

Thor is plenty happy to hop into the truck and take off for the hills. He hangs his head out the side window, lapping up the breeze like it's water. I'm glad someone's having fun today.

John and Eliza's van is in the driveway, doors wide open, with the bed frame half-in, half-out. John is standing all the way out by the shed. He gives me a slight wave, holding his lit cigarette in the other hand. John hasn't smoked since he and Eliza were dating.

"Vaughn." I hear Mama's voice before I'm even out of the truck. "Vaughn. Come back inside. It's cold."

Daddy is standing on the porch in his boxers and a tee-shirt. I look away for a minute. Even with the day-to-dayness of it all, sometimes it still hits me how wrong all of this is. The Daddy I knew, the one I grew up with, he should still be whistling and tending the trees like a modern-day Paul Bunyan.

I don't want this to be happening, I think desperately. *I don't want to be here.*

Then I remember Golda, from yesterday. *We take care of our own.*

I reach into the glove compartment and get Thor's tennis ball. It floods me with happier stories from happier times. I try to tune it out. Right now, I need to focus. Thor leaps up, dancing, trying to nip the ball away from me.

"Daddy," I call. "Daddy. Do you want to play with the dog?"

Daddy turns. He doesn't acknowledge me, so much, but he watches Thor prance and jump, waiting for the ball.

"There's that dog," he says, half to himself.

"Here he is," I agree. Thor is drooling now, eyes on the ball, half-frenzied.

"There's the buddy," Daddy says, louder. "Hey, buddy."

We make an odd spectacle, Thor watching the ball, Daddy watching Thor, everyone watching Daddy. I feel like the center of one tiny universe, and no idea what to do next.

John smokes. Mama looks blank. Eliza is nowhere to be seen. I guess it's up to me.

"Daddy," I say clearly. "Get dressed so you can play with the dog."

"Here, buddy," Daddy says again.

Mama seems to come back to life then. "Vaughn," she says, and I see a glimpse of the old Mama. The one who always knew what to say and how to get things done. "First get dressed. It's cold. Then we'll play with the dog."

Daddy turns and goes into the house. I feel like I can breathe again. Thor, unaware of anything except the ball I'm refusing to give him, barks softly and whimpers.

"In a minute, Thor," I tell him. "You're doing a good job. Good boy."

It feels like eons before Daddy emerges, wearing pants and shoes. *This could be normal,* I think. So Daddy's wearing loafers with jeans. I can pretend he's wearing work boots, like normal. Daddy's not talking much. That's okay. I can pretend he's just playing with Thor.

"Arden," says Mama. "Why don't you and Daddy take Thor out to the barn to throw the ball around?"

I nod, grateful Mama is back in charge. "Come on, Daddy," I say, and I'm relieved when he does.

I throw the ball for Thor, who springs after it like a shot. He brings it back, and I throw again. He fetches it half a dozen times before we make it back to the barn.

Maybe it's the sudden dark after coming in from the sunlight, but Daddy stumbles over the entrance to the barn. I reach out to catch him, and his stories hit me like a shock wave.

He's tired, I realize. His exhaustion runs deep through him, straight down to his core. I look at him again, carefully, and I see it in his eyes, too.

"Sit down here for a minute, Daddy," I say and guide him gently into a chair.

The chairs are left over from our Christmas tree selling days. I used to sit up here, at this wide farm table, carefully pouring apple cider into Dixie cups and separating molasses cookies into plastic bags. On regular days, Daddy would sit at this table after chores, working on his woodcarvings.

"What do you think of this, Arden?" he'd ask, showing me one of his newest creations. He especially liked making little animals. He'd carve palm-sized birds and badgers, rabbits and even a little dairy cow.

Daddy sinks into the chair now and puts a hand on the table like it's grounding him. I put my hand on the table, too, willing an old story, a normal story, to come through. If only it worked that way.

Thor brings the ball to me then, and I give it to Daddy.

"There's my buddy," he says. I can feel a little flicker of energy through the worn shoulders of his flannel shirt. "Good dog."

Thor takes the ball nimbly in his teeth. Daddy is starting a gentle game of tug of war, and Thor pulls it back just enough. After a few minutes, Thor drops the ball at Daddy's feet and wags his tail.

"Good boy," Daddy says. "Good dog."

If I turn my head just so, I can see John and Eliza loading the bedframe into their van, going back for the mattress and boxes. I settle in next to Daddy. We're good here. We're fine right where we are.

All told, Mama and Daddy are moved in before lunchtime. On the last trip, when they come back to get Daddy, I'm braced and ready for the premonition to hit. Just something, to make it feel final, finished, done.

Nothing comes. After a morning of playing with Thor, Daddy is ready for a nap, and all the fight's worn out of him. He goes into the car with Mama without question.

"Do you need John and I to come help?" Eliza asks Mama.

Mama shakes her head. "Let us just get in and get settled." She doesn't have to add that, once they get to the home, she'll have nurses to help her with Daddy. I'm pretty sure we're all thinking it.

Everyone waves goodbye while Mama buckles Daddy in. She throws a kiss towards the dogwood tree and then starts down the long driveway.

"Well," Eliza says. "I guess that's that."

She's trying to be strong, but her chin quivers as soon as she says it. John holds her, and she cries softly into his shoulder.

I wish I could do that. Just lean into someone, let them hold me. Thor gives me a sloppy lick on the hand and runs in lopsided circles around the yard.

"We should go pick up the boys," John says.

Eliza looks at me. Her eyes look small and red. "I don't want to leave you all alone," she says. "Do you want me to stay with you tonight?"

"I'll be fine. I've got Thor, and I'll be plenty busy with Festival this weekend. Go home to your boys."

Eliza's shoulders slump with gratitude, but she asks again, anyway. "Are you sure?"

"Positive. I'm going to head in to the store and get ready for tomorrow. Keep my mind off things."

"Call me," Eliza says, giving Thor a friendly scratch behind the ears. "Promise."

"I will." *I won't.*

"You take care, Arden," John says, half-swooping in for a hug before he remembers, just in time, that I don't like that. He gives me an awkward smile instead.

"You too. Thank you for all your help today," I say. "And take care of my sister."

"I always do," he says.

They settle into the van and start down the driveway with me following right behind. I blow one kiss towards Tripp's dogwood tree. John and Eliza's van kicks up a cloud of gray dust from the gravel. I toss glances into the rearview mirrors as the house recedes in the distance.

It's over.

15

Thor is so worn out that he falls asleep in the truck on our way back to Main Street. A quick glance at my dashboard clock shows that it's just after one. I'm officially late for opening the store. I try to muster up some guilt, but I can't. Not on a day like today.

I pull into my usual parking space behind the store. Nobody's here, waiting for the store to open. Nobody's on Main Street at all, really. It looks like a ghost town. I lean back in the seat and feel just how exhausted I am, right down to my bones. Reminds me of how Daddy felt this morning when we were sitting togeth-er. This must be how he feels every day. From here, I can just see around my store and across Main Street to Miss Paula's museum. The edge of her "Save Eagle Valley" banner is flapping in the breeze.

Something inside me snaps. I won't go in at all today. Probably won't have any customers to miss me, and if I do, who cares?

"Come on, Thor," I say more forcefully than I mean to. He looks up at me with a confused look, like, *What did I do?* "Sorry, sweetie," I say, scratching his ears. "I didn't mean to snap. Come on. Let's go for a walk." That cheers him up instantly. He hops right out of the truck when I come around and open his door.

We walk up Main Street, towards the church. I stop at the library. It's deserted, like everything else in Eagle Valley. I don't think anyone's here but Mr. Carson. *Perfect.* I could use a little time to myself.

The library is still housed in the manse, the little stone house next door to the church. The house was originally built for the pastor and his family to live in, but around the early 1900s, the wife of the pastor at the time decided to turn the front parlor into a lending library. Ten years later, the books officially overtook the house, and the pastor's family moved out and kept the library running. When the county finally got together and organized a public library system, Eagle Valley fought to keep their local branch in the manse. Miss Paula got it on the National Register of Historic

Places, and now there's a little brass plaque outside the house.

Mr. Carson's been the head librarian here since I can remember. He's had his eye on the museum just as long, not that Miss Paula will ever let go of it. He talks about the past with so much passion that when I was little, I thought he was like me. Then I listened to him talk for a while and realized everything he knows about the past came out of a book, just like everyone else. It makes me feel sad for him that he's wrong about a lot. I think it would really bother him if he knew.

Nobody calls out a "hello" when I open the door. I guess Mr. Carson is in the back. Thor and I head in and wander through the shelves. Thor, thank goodness, is well behaved in here. Mr. Carson has a soft spot for him. For me, too, actually.

The library is the first place where I read more about Cassandra. She saw the future, all right, just like Daddy said. Depending on which book you read, Apollo gave her the gift of prophecy, either as a curse for refusing to have sex with him, or as a thank you gift the morning after. Either way, she had the follow-up curse of never being believed, even though her visions were spot on. I wonder if the Greek gods really needed to go out of their way to make sure nobody would ever believe her prophecies. Seems like it just naturally goes with the territory. Most days, I don't even want to believe myself.

The door opens again, setting the jingle bells tied to the handle ringing. Thor and I look up, and it's none other than Miss Paula, headed straight for us.

"Arden," she says. "Why is your store still closed? Shouldn't you be open by now?"

I just look at her, trying to think of something to say back. My brain feels fried.

"According to your posted hours, you take Friday mornings off and open at noon. It's after one. I think I've made it clear in our meetings that we all need to be working extra hard to put our best foot forward this month and be available to our customers."

Last October, I was late opening the store more often than not. Miss Paula always needed me to help her fix her printer, or find out what was wrong with her e-mail, or explain why the brochures weren't printing right. I guess now that she's on the outs with my parents, she's found someone else to do favors for her.

What would have happened if Mama and Daddy had sold the farm to the Society? Would Miss Paula have been up this morning, helping us load their things into the truck? Would she have driven down with them to help get them settled or brought them dinner?

It doesn't matter, I guess. Daddy used to say that a fair-weather friend was worse than no friend at all.

"I've had a busy morning," I say.

"Leave her be, Paula," says a deep voice from behind us. Mr. Carson appears, holding a tall stack of dusty volumes. "Everyone on this street has opened late a time or two. Cut her a break."

Miss Paula looks surprised that she was overheard. She recovers quickly, I'll give her that. "If there's one thing I've learned this year, it's that nothing good comes from *cutting a break* for a McCrae."

"That's enough," Mr. Carson says. "Leave her be."

Miss Paula wavers for a moment, like she can't handle the shock of being told what to do. She turns on her heel and heads for the door. The bells jingle angrily behind her when the door slams closed.

"You okay, Arden?" Mr. Carson asks. I can tell without even touching him that he's remembering my last spell. The time I first got the vision of Eagle Valley, split in two.

"I'm fine." I nod. "Thanks." He keeps an eye on me, but goes back to the stacks.

For a minute, I'm tempted to try and find that Greek mythology book where I first read about Cassandra, years ago. I decide against it. Cassandra is just a myth, and besides, there are people out there who understand me just fine.

Thor wakes only long enough to come inside the house with me and fall back asleep at my feet. I log on to the Alzheimer's forum.

I scroll down the page, searching for stories of someone who feels like I do right now. I read a few threads on parents moving in to a nursing home and one on moving to hospice care. That leads me to a thread about sorting through a great-aunt's personal effects after she died.

"It feels so weird to be going through her things. There are so many things I don't even recognize, but obviously they were important to her. I feel weird getting rid of them, but I can't keep everything. I passed on what I recognized to other family members, but what am I supposed to do with the everyday stuff? She saved a whole bunch of movie ticket stubs from years and years ago. I can't even read half of them. But here she's saved them all this time. Makes you wonder why."

Finally, something I can understand. Some people actually do bring stuff like that to my shop. "It's so old, it must be worth something," they'll say, clutching on to a newspaper that's only worth recycling. But maybe it is worth something to the person that had it. I've held junk that tells stories about friendship and falling in love and all sorts of things. Can't exactly put a price tag on that, but I like to think it matters that I heard the story, at least.

A sharp tone sounds when my instant messenger pops up. I forgot I was even logged on. People hardly ever message me anyway.

"How's it going?" It's a gal from the Alzheimer's forum, one of the ones that commented on my first post. Her screen name is SarahSue81.

"My parents moved out this morning," I type back. I want to add something cheerful, something about knowing it's best for him or knowing it's time or just trying to move forward. But I can't lie to her, someone that knows this is just the beginning.

"That's tough," she writes back. "My mom moved out last month. I'm still exhausted."

"Where'd she move to?" I ask.

"Nursing home," she writes. "We held out as long as we could, but we're not enough anymore."

"It's so hard," I type back. Funny how much easier it is to type it instead of say it. With anyone I saw in person–Eliza, John, Mama–I'd be keeping a stiff upper lip, holding it together.

The instant messenger blinks to show SarahSue81 is typing a response.

"It is hard. It's still hard. I feel like I'm doing the wrong thing no matter what I do. The whole thing just sucks."

"That's it exactly," I type back. "I feel wrong for not pushing them to get more help sooner, but I feel wrong for having them go to assisted living now."

"Did they sell their house?" SarahSue types. "Didn't they live on a farm or something?"

"Christmas tree farm. We're going to have an estate sale in a few weeks. My sisters and I have to go through and take the things we want to keep, and then we'll have to help a little with tagging and pricing, too."

"That's rough. Probably good to get it all done at once, though. We're still going through and trying to sell some of my parents' things. At this point, I feel like I'm just trying to get rid of it. It's so sad. I used to think about these things and see them every day, and now it all just seems like clutter."

"Ugh," I type back. "I can't imagine."

"Well, send me a message if you need anything," SarahSue types. "I've got to go. These boards have saved my sanity when I was going through everything."

"Thanks," I type. The instant messenger shows that SarahSue has logged off.

Maybe that's what this hovering premonition is about–going through Mama and Daddy's things. From what I saw, they took the barest of essentials with them to their new place. No need for extra memories, I suppose.

I keep mine close at hand. I already have some of Daddy's little woodcarvings on a shelf in my dining room. I've held them so often now that they just retell my stories. The times I felt scared and sad and was looking for a little comfort. My favorite is a little owl he made for me when I was eight. It has big eyes and chiseled, ruffled feathers on its wings. I carried it with me in my backpack all through elementary school. It still smells a little like pencil shavings.

I tossed all of my Jeremy-related objects in a box at the bottom of the hall closet when we broke up. Everybody does this, I guess. I have the things you'd expect, like a dried rose from last year's Jitterbug and Jive, and a bracelet he gave me that Christmas. I also tossed in a pen he touched when he was last at my house, and the sweater I was wearing when we broke up. Things that carry my hurt right on the surface, ready to strike next time I touch them.

On the top shelf of my bedroom closet, I still have the duffel bag I packed for the trip-that-wasn't to D.C. with Lila Beth. I haven't unzipped it once since Lila Beth brought me back home, whispered an apology to Mama, and took off back for D.C. without me.

I look back at the Alzheimer's thread and reread the post about the woman sorting through her great-aunt's things. The last two lines jump out at me. *But here she's saved them all this time. Makes you wonder why.*

Why have I saved it all this time? Am I just going to leave it there, waiting, until I get old and someone else has to come clear out my house? What would they even find?

I glance at my computer then down at Thor. Why not. I get up and pull the bag down.

The duffel is ripe with memories from high school. It's bright blue and has an athletic company logo on it, proof positive that it came to me as a hand-me-down. Lila Beth is the only athlete in the family. She was on swim team for three years. I'd picked this bag for our trip, hoping it would give me some of her confidence. Didn't work, obviously.

I unzip the bag and plunge in both my bare hands. It's funny how I remembered most of the things inside exactly. There's a pair of my favorite jeans at the time, tight through the thighs and sprinkled with glitter. The glitter flaked off in the bag, just like it used to do when I wore them. I had a black top, too, with see-through sleeves and shoulders. Back when I put that outfit together, I thought I looked perfect for a trip to D.C. Just me and my oldest sister, exploring the city. Touring her old college. Going to places like the Washington Monument and the Lincoln Memorial and the National Mall. I'd never been anywhere that important, but the names rolled off my sixteen-year-old tongue like I'd seen them a thousand times.

Lila Beth drove me up with her after her Easter visit that year while I was still on Spring Break from high school. We would go up together, stay at her apartment, and I'd take the train back.

"You're sure you can take the train?" Mama had said over and over. She alternated this with asking, "You're sure you want to go?"

"Yes," I'd said to both questions. I'd never been on a train, either, but I was sure I could handle it. I felt terribly grown-up just to be asked. Just me and Lila Beth, off to D.C. to stay in her apartment and look at colleges. When I'd pictured that future, it felt electric.

"Arden's got this, Mama," Lila Beth had said just before we left. "She'll be fine."

Things started falling apart two hours into the car ride, before we even got past Harrisonburg. Everything was fine while we were driving up Interstate 81. Then it was time for lunch, but instead of going to a drive through or picking up something, Lila Beth took me into a Ruby Tuesday's and had us sit at a booth. I don't like restaurants so much. Even though everything's clean, I still know that dozens of other people have sat at this table and used these salt and pepper shakers and held this same menu. Freaks me out.

I still remember the look on Lila Beth's face when she saw me holding the menu through the napkin clenched in my hands.

"Arden, stop," she'd whispered urgently as the waitress came over. "You don't have to act like the thing's diseased."

I don't think it's diseased, I wanted to say, but I couldn't tell her the real problem, either. It's hard enough deciding between the pasta and the soup without hearing traces of all the stories other customers had left behind. Apparently, lots of people dither between choosing something healthy or indulging.

I still have the cloth napkin in my duffel bag. I pull it out and wrap my hands around that moment, of being sixteen and so horribly, desperately weird. I don't normally run around stealing napkins from restaurants, but in this case, well, it kind of had to come with me. No matter how many times Lila Beth raised her eyebrows or whispered to me, I couldn't let it go. The longer I sat there, the louder and heavier all the stories on the table and bench felt, and the more I got the feeling of a premonition on its way.

Not here, I remember thinking. *Not now.* Not when I was out with Lila Beth. But still it came, pressing closer and sharper and darn near taking all the air out of the room.

By the time dessert rolled around, Lila Beth was looking more worried than irritated. "Arden, what's wrong? Is something going on?" she'd ask every few minutes.

"I'm okay," I'd say and try taking a sip of water through my paper-covered straw.

"You're white as a sheet," Lila Beth insisted. "Tell me what's going on."

That's when the premonition came, dropping in on me like a hailstorm. I saw myself back in my bedroom at home, staring through the window as Lila Beth drove away in her little yellow Honda. As she drove, I saw grass cover up the gravel road behind her, growing over. *She's never going to want to come back,* I'd thought desperately.

When the premonition was over, Lila Beth was staring at me, wide-eyed. I buried my face in the napkin, breathing in the starchy air and wondering if it was possible to suffocate on premonitions and embarrassment. By the time I pulled my face back out, Lila Beth had already paid the check, left a tip, and gathered her purse.

"Come on, now," she said in a voice two notches too high. She tried to guide me to the car without actually touching me. She hovered her hands a few inches over my shoulders as we walked.

"I'm okay," I insisted. "I really am. Sometimes it just happens. I'm okay. I'm sorry, Lila Beth. I'll pay you back for the lunch."

"I shouldn't have done this," said Lila Beth. "I'm sorry. I'll take you home."

She turned the car back the way we came instead of heading farther down the highway.

"Please, Lila Beth," I'd said. "I promise I can do it."

"Another time," Lila Beth had said. And I didn't need any premonitions to know that was a lie.

16

On Saturday morning, I'm at my store before anyone else on Main Street. It feels ghostly quiet, walking from the back alley to my storefront with Thor. The sun is just peeking up from behind the church, to the east of town. To the west, towards my parents' farm and the mountains, everything is coated in early morning shadows.

My premonition is going to break today. I'm sure of it. I was up most of the night, trying to catch my breath while the crisp, cool air stretched over me like a sheet of cellophane.

I think Thor feels it too. Instead of running to the stockroom, like usual, Thor stays close by my side, winding around my knees until I almost trip over him.

Well, premonition or no, it's a Festival weekend, and the Mill Days at that. We're sure to have a good turnout today, so I need to get prepped and ready for customers. I move most of the quilts I have in stock up to the front, right by the door. I stack them in fluffy armfuls over a few bushel baskets and benches. The others I scatter over the little vignettes I've set up through the store to draw people in. I pull the spinning wheel closer to the front and move back my typewriters and globes to make room. When it's done, it looks about the way I like—set up like little vintage rooms. Perfect.

I turn a critical eye to the front of my store. It has to look extra-inviting and fully stocked to draw in customers. Most people who come this weekend for the Mill Days will spend most of their time at the other end of Main Street. The local Quilter's Guild sets up a quilt show in the field down by the mill, and there are usually some craft demonstrations. I think this year it's candle-making and pottery. We always have vendors selling kettle corn and hot dogs and beer down there, too.

On the whole, the Mill Days have a better turnout than the Founding Days. Our mill is still in working order, but we only open it for tours and a demonstration during this one weekend every year. Used to be we gave tours year-round. When the economy took a hit, people ran out of money to spend on things like historic mill tours and the Historical Society ran out of money to keep it running. It's on the list of things we'll start back up again when things get better. If things get better.

The bells on my front door jangle, and Thor and I both jump. *It's too early for anyone else to be here,* I think, panicked.

It's Eliza. "Hello!" she calls, stretching out her o's the way Daddy used to. I wonder if she realizes she does that.

"Eliza!" I say, just catching my breath. I wait to see if this is it, the moment my premonition will break. Nope. Whatever vision's about to come, it's bigger than a surprise visit from my sister. I shiver.

Eliza stops suddenly, giving me a once over. "Did I scare you? I didn't mean to. John offered to take the boys to the Hoffenmeier's birthday party, so I figured that gave me the day to come up and see my sister."

"Hoffenmeier? Didn't their youngest bite Wyatt a couple weeks back?"

"That's the one. She said sorry and shared her trains, though, so they're friends now." Eliza heads back to the stock room to drop her tote bag. Thor rushes over to greet her and sniffs the bag. She thinks better of it, puts the tote up on the table and scratches Thor's ears.

"Where did you park? You know you're going to be blocked in until closing if you come this early." I peer over her shoulder, checking to see if she parallel parked on Main Street. Miss Paula would have a fit. Parking on Main Street is strictly against the town ordinances.

"I stopped by your house first. When you weren't there, I parked in your driveway and walked into town. Hope you don't mind."

I glance down at her red ballerina flats. "You walked here from my house?"

"My love for you knows no bounds." She makes a show of flexing her toes. "So. What can I do to help?"

"I've got everything pretty well set up," I say. "I need help pricing a few things, though."

"Show me what to do," Eliza says. She's a quick learner, my sister, and before I know it, she's spent close to an hour tying on price tags and marking down inventory. I take a moment to log online and upload some pictures and product descriptions to my online store.

Since she got settled in doing price tags, Eliza hasn't been talking much this morning. She'll make the occasional comment about how the sewing machine looks like it's in good condition (it isn't) or that a hat and scarf set look like they're straight from the Roaring Twenties (they are). Mostly, though, she seems lost in thought. I don't reach over and try to hear any of her stories, not right now. I know what she's thinking about, and I don't need to dwell on it myself.

"What are these?" she asks. She's finished with the regular inventory and spotted some of my new reclaimed history pieces. One is a little evening bag made from the good parts of a silk scarf. I also have a few earring and pendant sets and a button necklace that I'm not sure I like. In the back somewhere, I have some throw pillows made with pretty handkerchiefs. Nothing I could keep on my couch, thanks to Thor, but I imagine someone would like them.

"I've been working on some projects," I tell her. "Trying to make new things out of the remnants, you know?"

Eliza runs her fingers over the button necklace. "You made all of these?" She shakes her head. "I shouldn't be surprised. You're so creative."

"Thanks," I say, taken aback by the unexpected compliment. "I'm not sure how to price any of it. I guess I'm too close to it to be objective."

"I'm not," Eliza says. "Let me have a go at it."

We work side by side with Thor darting between our chairs. Silly dog. Sitting here with Eliza reminds me of when we used to set up for Christmas tree sales or helped Mama make dinner. I'd sit on one side, carefully tying bows around a wreath or analyzing how many pasta noodles to add to the pot. Eliza would work faster, checking off the number of molasses cookies she bagged for sale or tossing salad so hard some of it escaped the bowl.

I steal another glance at Eliza, at her profile bent over the desk, cross-referencing the price tags she just wrote with the inventory log. The furrow between her brows makes her look just like Mama.

"Finished," Eliza declares, slamming her pen down. She was always doing that when we were growing up. Announcing she was done with her chores the way some people would announce their coronation.

I take a glance over her price tags. "That's too high," I say immediately. "Eliza. Nobody is going to pay that much."

"How do you know?" Eliza says. "That's what I'd pay."

"This is amateur," I insist. "It's crafty and it's imperfect. You've priced it like I'm an artist."

"That's because you are," Eliza says. "Here, I'll prove it to you." She pulls out her wallet and counts out exact change for the button necklace.

"Half that," I say.

"I thought you didn't negotiate," Eliza says.

"I'm turning over a new leaf."

"Turn it back."

Finally, I take the money and slide the button necklace across the work desk to her. Each folded bill holds a lifetime of stories. Millions of transactions for coffee and newspapers and clothes. The stories I hear loudest of all are the ones Eliza left behind.

She thinks I sell myself short.

She thinks I've got more to offer than dealing other people's antiques.

She's happy to see me doing something new.

She believes in me.

Eliza is fastening her new necklace, admiring herself in an antique shaving mirror. "Pleasure doing business," I say.

I can tell Janie is surprised when she comes in, just before it's time to open. I guess she got wind that I wasn't around yesterday, and Janie's smart enough to figure out why. When she walks in, Eliza and I are organizing the just-tagged merchandise. Eliza's putting things out of order on purpose, just to get my goat. I'm pretending I'm angrier than I really am, just to make her laugh. We're both giggling when we hear Janie's awkward throat-clearing.

"Hey," she says, like it's a question instead of a greeting. "I just came to help with the store today."

"Aren't you sweet," gushes Eliza before I get a chance to say anything. "You must be Jamie."

"Janie," I mutter.

"Janie. I'm Arden's sister, Eliza. I just dropped by for the day."

"The one that lives in Roanoke?" Janie says, looking from one of us to the other. "I could tell you were family. You look a lot alike."

"Thank you," Eliza says, even though she's prettier than I am. I'm no slouch, but our Davison and McCrae genes combined a little more elegantly for her than for me.

Eliza stays and helps the rest of the day. It's needed. More people than I expected are leaving the mill and strolling through Main Street. I'm glad I thought to feature quilts in the store today. I've sold five by lunch, and two more customers are sidling up to an Ohio Star quilt I have spread out over a bed.

By noon, we've all worked up a bit of a sweat. Things have sold so fast I haven't been able to keep track on my mental calculator. That's a good sign, if ever there was one.

"Why don't I watch the store while you two go and get something?" Janie says. "Eat some lunch. I don't mind. I'll give Thor his kibble when he wakes up."

I consider telling her no, thanks, but suddenly the idea of lunch with my sister sounds so much better than the warm Coke and sandwich waiting for me in the back room. And Thor is snoring so peacefully there in the stockroom. He loves Janie. A little one-on-one time with her would be good for him. "Thanks," I say. "Are you sure?"

Janie moves in behind the counter. "No problem," she says. "Take as long as you want. I'll be here."

It's been at least five years since I walked through Festival with Eliza. She brought John when they first got married, but then the twins came and I guess pushing a double stroller over charmingly uneven brick sidewalks isn't much fun. We wind our way down to the mill, where the quilt show is still in full swing and the water wheel is churning through the creek. Used to be that this part of town always had that churning sound in the background. Since we've had to keep it off except for Festival weekend, the noise takes getting used to again.

Eliza gets a hot dog and a soda. There aren't a lot of vegetarian options at the booths, so I settle for two large pretzels. We find a hay bale and sit side-by-side, eating our food and watching the quilts wave on the clotheslines.

When we were little, Eliza and I were usually picked to be white glove girls at the quilt show. Eliza tried to be all show-offy about it, naming all the quilt patterns and flipping the back of the quilt even when no one asked. I liked it. Through the thin cotton gloves, all I could feel about the quilt was a sense of warmth or sweetness, not so many details about the quilter or the fabric or everyone who'd slept under it.

Being the oldest, Lila Beth was usually pressed into service at the ticket booth. Sometimes she defected, though, and left the ticket booth to hang out with Eliza and me. She'd duck behind the quilts and pop out at us to make us scream, and then we'd try to run and hide too. The long clotheslines of fluttering quilts made for a good maze.

"I think that one looks like you," says Eliza, pointing out a scrap quilt. From here, the pieces look tiny—maybe just an inch square. Whoever made it arranged the pieces to look like diamonds working their way out. A diamond of white surrounded by a diamond of patchwork surrounded by white surrounded by patchwork.

"I have one like that," I tell her. "But just plain patchwork. No white blocks in between."

"Maybe that's what I was thinking of," Eliza says distractedly. I watch her from the side of my eye. She's looking down at her lunch, picking at the hot dog bun, but not really eating.

I sidle over a little on our hay bale, brush my arm against hers just for a second. The intensity of Eliza's stories give me a jolt. I make myself catch my breath, reach over for my soda so I can brush up against her arm again.

She misses Lila Beth. I feel it more than think it. It's like I pulled a little bit of Eliza's yearning straight off of her and wear it on my own skin for a minute. For just a second, I see through her eyes. The middle sister playing big sister. Nobody to help her through parenting our parents.

"You okay?" Eliza asks. "You look like something's on your mind."

I feel my cheeks flush a minute. I've been so caught up trying to read her I didn't realize she was trying to read me.

"Just thinking about Lila Beth," I say.

Eliza fixes me with a look. "No use trying to figure people out, Arden," she says. "She'll come when she's ready." The implied *if* hangs heavily on the end of her words.

"I just meant..." I fish around for the words I want, but come up short. "I'm always here for you, too, you know?"

"Of course you are!" Eliza says. "But I don't want you worrying about me. I'm here to help you. You're right in the thick of it, dealing with Festival and the store on top of everything."

I try to come up with a response to that. The sun glints off her new button necklace, and suddenly the air gets colder, crisper. I start to feel a bit of a tingle. It's happening. Here comes my vision.

It's a short one, but intense. It's Jeremy, holding me in both his arms and looking at me intently. He kisses me, and for a second–just one second–I feel whole and beautiful and new.

Then the vision is over, just as abruptly as it started. Eliza is looking at me with eyes wide.

"Arden?" she asks. "You just turned white as a ghost. Are you okay? I shouldn't have mentioned everything that was going on. I'm so sorry. I meant to come here and help take your mind off things, and here I am bringing it up. I'm sorry. Arden? Please say something."

"Well, I would if I could get a word in edgewise," I say. "I just got a little overwhelmed for a minute. I must be hungrier than I thought." The whole time, my body feels electrified while my brain tries to catch up with what I just saw. *Jeremy. Jeremy's coming back. Jeremy still loves me.*

No, he doesn't, I think rationally. That was wishful thinking, nothing else. As if he'd show back up again after all this time. As if I'd let him. That can't have been a real vision.

But the air is softer and warmer and easier to breathe, now. I take deep, easy breaths and marvel at how good it feels.

"Drink something," Eliza orders. "And finish eating that pretzel. That's not enough after how hard you've been working all day. Sure you don't want anything else? What about a soda? I'll get you a soda."

A voice from behind interrupts us, making my heart skip two beats and do a backflip to boot. "Arden?"

It's Jeremy.

Eliza looks from him to me and back then declares, "I'll go get you that soda you wanted. Anything else?" I shake my head. Jeremy and I both watch her walk away.

He sits down on Eliza's part of the hay bale, "How's it going?" he says.

"Fine," I say. "You?"

He shrugs. "I'm back for this weekend and next. Helping my parents and all."

Sitting next to each other makes me remember how tall he is, how my head comes just up to his shoulder. I have to lean my head back to talk to him, which makes me feel like we're about to kiss. My stomach flutters.

The vision was real. He's back and he's here and he's talking to me and he still loves me. I know it. I know he does.

He's wearing sunglasses, which hide his eyes and reflect me. Two little Ardens, one peering out of each lens. We look like deer caught in headlights. I resist the urge to smooth my hair.

"Well, I'll be around," I say.

"I was counting on it," he says. He looks towards the food stand and checks to see if Eliza is watching. She is, but suddenly becomes absorbed in reading the ingredient label. "It's been too long," Jeremy says. "Let's catch up sometime."

"Sure," I say. "Why not?"

"Tomorrow," Jeremy says. "Are you free tomorrow?"

This is new. When we were dating, Jeremy liked to leave his plans soft. "Well, I'm working most of the day," I say.

"You have to eat dinner sometime. What do you think?"

We're meeting for dinner now? Jeremy was more the lunch-or-coffee type, at least towards the end. "Won't that make you late driving back to Richmond?"

"I don't mind."

I wish I could see his eyes behind those sunglasses and get a feel for what he's thinking. I consider brushing my knee up against his. I almost have heart palpitations at the thought. Too soon.

I shrug. It would feel so good to say, "No, sorry, that ship's sailed. I'm different now. I've moved on."

But then I see that vision again, and feel how inevitable it is. Like a wave washing right over me. I'm going to see him again. We're going to get back together. Maybe he doesn't deserve a second chance. Maybe I don't. But it's happening, either way.

"Sure, dinner or whatever," I say. "That'd be nice."

17

There's an envelope on the floor of my shop the next morning, like someone just slid it under the door. I recognize the yellow paper peeking through the envelope immediately. I used to be in charge of printing and folding them, back when I was in the good graces of Miss Paula and the Historical Society.

I can hear the fingerprints all over the envelope. Power, self-righteousness, fear, resentment. This is Miss Paula's doing, 100%.

The yellow paper has been folded crisply into thirds. I could recite most of these words from memory, but they still make me cold when I read them.

Dear Eagle Valley Main Street Shop Owner,

As a representative of the Eagle Valley Historical Society, it is my duty to inform you that you are at risk of non-compliance with three Eagle Valley Historic District Ordinances, to wit:

Section 2, Article 1, Subsection B *All businesses on the Eagle Valley Historic Main Street shall remain open no less than forty hours per week, during the times posted by the business and approved by the Society.*

Section 4, Article 2, Subsection A *All business owners on the Eagle Valley Historic Main Street shall make a reasonable effort to attend all Historical Society meetings. Failure to attend two meetings consecutively may result in punitive action, to include loss of voting privileges.*

Section 5, Article 1 *All businesses on the Eagle Valley Historic Main Street shall uphold the mission and purpose of the Eagle Valley Living History Days through participation in events as directed by the Society.*

Eagle Valley's Historic District is a precious reminder of Virginia's rich heritage and historic significance. As a shop owner on our Historic Main Street, your compliance with all Historic District and Town ordinances are essential to maintaining our historic integrity and public dignity.

Please regard this letter as a friendly reminder. Continued disregard for these ordinances will result in fines of no less than $500 per infraction, to be donated to the Eagle Valley Historical Society fund for the continued maintenance and beautification of our historic district.

Sincerely,

Paula Abernathy

I have to read the last sentence more than once to let it really sink in. $500 per infraction. Time was that I could afford a $500 fine, maybe even several. That hasn't been the case for a while now. I guess this is the fallout for not opening my store on Friday. I don't think I've missed a meeting, though. I'll have to double check. And that third ordinance, well, I know what that means. There's a reason that language is so vague in the books. I can't get away with refusing to hand out pamphlets or choosing not to support the fundraiser.

One more infraction, one more early closing or late opening, and I'm finished. No more storefront on Main Street. I look around at my store, like I'm seeing it for the last time.

Thor whines, leaps up and bats his front paws in the air. At this point, I think my dog can sense a premonition coming on before I can. I sit, right there on the floor, right up against the footprints I haven't mopped up and the dirt people dragged in. No wonder I feel shaky.

It's a quick one. No build up, really, or maybe it doesn't feel like much since the vision about Jeremy took so long to get here. The air feels sharp and the lights get bright. Then I see it, just as clear as if it's happening right now.

I'm driving. I don't recognize the road, but it's empty. Buildings and houses I don't know are on either side. Thor's in the seat of the truck right next to me, licking the passenger's side window and wagging his tail. I don't feel scared, for once, even though I don't know where I am. It's the feeling I get that strikes me more than anything. No knots in my stomach, no tension in my shoulders. I can breathe so easily, stretch one arm out across the other seat and drive with just one hand on the steering wheel.

Peace.

And I'm back, sitting on the floor of my store, holding Miss Paula's letter in one hand and my giant dog pinning me down and licking my face. For once, after a premonition, I feel calm.

It's going to be all right. I feel it. There're a thousand reasons why things shouldn't be all right, why I should be falling apart over slowly losing my father and my business and my town. Why I should be in pieces over the idea of dinner with Jeremy, the same Jeremy who wrecked my heart the last time he took it for a spin. But I just know, the way I know about a good sale or a good story. It's going to be all right.

Jeremy swings by fifteen minutes before closing time. I've got a few straggling customers that need my attention, so he walks around the store, hands clasped behind his back, studying pieces like he's actually interested.

When the last one leaves, it's just Jeremy and I with about ten feet and a few stacks of well-priced merchandise between us. Feels like miles.

It's a strange thing, knowing what's going to happen before it does. If I was a regular person, I'd be wondering how our dinner tonight will go, whether I still like him as much as I think I do, and whether he still likes me too. Thanks to yesterday's vision, I know how it'll go, or at least, I know we're going to kiss. That's promising.

I hear my jingle bells chime on the front door, and my heart makes an unexpected leap. I look over, but nobody's there. Jeremy didn't seem to hear anything, but he's looking at me with a furrowed brow. I remember that look. Whenever I would startle or turn white before a vision, he'd look at me like he didn't know what was the matter. Well, I guess that's fair, since he didn't know. Bless his heart.

What did I hear? *Maybe it was the wind,* I reason, but the leaves on the trees outside are still. Could it be a premonition? I look up and down the street outside, but I don't see anyone.

"So, you about ready to go?" Jeremy asks.

My chest feels tighter and it's getting harder to breathe. I nod.

The jingle bells chime again, and I have to reach out and steady myself on the counter. *Nerves,* I think, until a familiar voice calls, "Yoohoo! Arden?"

It's Miss Paula. She does a double-take when she sees Jeremy. The knot in my chest gets tighter.

"Well! Your parents told me you were in town. It is just so good to see you," Miss Paula says, coming over and throwing her arms right around him. Jeremy waits a few seconds before he gives her an awkward shoulder pat. Miss Paula pulls back but keeps a hand on each of his shoulders, looking him over like it's been decades instead of months. I see a thick stack of "Save Eagle Valley!" pamphlets sticking out of her pocketbook, and my blood runs cold.

"I know how much your parents appreciated your help this weekend. There's just so much to do for Festival, and I hear they've been packed! Guests in every room. Isn't that something? It was so good of you to drive all the way here to give them a hand." Miss Paula turns to me. "Don't you think, Arden? Isn't he a sweetheart?"

Yes. Yes, I do. I'm starting to see stars. *Please don't let me pass out.*

"I was just stopping by with a little Historical Society business," Miss Paula says. "Here are some of the pamphlets we talked about at the meeting. Make sure each of your customers gets one, especially on these Festival weekends. Let me know if you need more." She lays them on the counter, like it's no big deal, business as usual, and flashes another smile at Jeremy. "So how long will it take you to drive all the way back to Richmond from here?"

I'm going to slip under. I want to shut my eyes and just get it over with, have my spell.

No, I decide. Not this time.

The hard knot in my chest pops loose, and I stand up straight.

"Take these back," I say. Jeremy was talking, I think, but I didn't hear and don't care. Miss Paula turns back, her mouth open, like I've slapped her or something. Good. "I'm not giving these to anyone. Take them back."

Miss Paula flicks her eyes to Jeremy then back at me. "Arden," she says with a little smile. Like she's indulging a child. "Obviously this feels very personal to you, but you are a shop on Main Street and this is Historical Society business. Don't you think you're being a little overdramatic?"

"No," I say. "I think you are." I don't just feel free, I feel giddy. I pick up the pamphlets off the counter and hand them back to her.

Miss Paula's cheeks turn pink under her face powder. "I'd hardly call the most critical mission of the Historical Society *overdramatic*," she says. "Saving the farm for the historic district is crucial to the continued preservation of Historic Main Street—"

"I've heard the spiel," I tell her. I'm still standing there with the pamphlets in my hand, like I'm brandishing them at her.

Miss Paula twitches her mouth and gives a little sigh. "I just don't understand why you and your parents had to make this into such a crisis," she says. "This could have been so simple. If they would have just sold the land to us directly, we wouldn't need to do any of this. But they didn't, so now we're in a bind, and we're just doing what we have to do to protect what's ours."

"I imagine my parents would say the same." I could have left it there, but there's just something about Miss Paula's big fake-sorry face and Jeremy's eyes getting wider and wider and the air getting thin and bright that makes me keep going. "And if you're in a bind, you can remember that Mama and Daddy offered to sell to the Historical Society first. If the farm meant that much to you, you should have bought it then."

Miss Paula isn't just flushed any more, she's red. "I made a *very fair offer*," she says. I almost expect her to stamp her foot with each word. "Your parents know how tight the budget is for the Society. I explained it to them. I said this was the best we could do. I just expected a little cooperation, a little understanding."

"And you know my parents need the money for Daddy," I say. "They couldn't take a low offer."

Miss Paula flings her arms out in exasperation. "And we didn't have the money to offer more."

"You seem pretty set on raising it now," I say coldly.

Miss Paula snatches the pamphlets out of my hand and slams them on the counter. "Just remember that you're a store on Historic Main Street," she says. "That doesn't change, no matter who your parents are. There will be consequences for going against the Society." She turns on her heel and walks out. The trace her fingers made across my palm told her story. She's betting. She thinks I'll run after her and apologize for talking back. She knows I got her letter this morning. She's hoping she can scare me back in line.

Well, it's not going to happen. I feel out of control and in control at the same time. Maybe more in control than I've ever felt.

The bells clang shrilly when the door slams behind Miss Paula. Jeremy's eyes are wider than ever. "Um. Wow," he says.

"So. Dinner?" I ask. I'm being flippant, with a devil-may-care attitude. So this is how it happens. This is when Jeremy's smile spreads slowly across his face. When he starts looking at me like he sees someone new, someone special. I'm so full and lit up inside I feel like I might bubble over.

"Sure," Jeremy says. "Thought I'd take you to Golda's. I remember you like it there."

"Golda's is fine," I say. What he remembers is that Golda's is the only place I ever went to eat out. Well, used to be. The way I'm feeling now, maybe I could go out somewhere else. Roanoke or Richmond or Rome, if I wanted to. "I'll meet you there. I have to take Thor home."

"Can't he come along?" asks Jeremy, and darned if he doesn't melt my heart, just like that. Being as Thor was one of my post-breakup changes, Jeremy's never met him before. I guess any man who can include my dog on a dinner out deserves a second chance from me.

Thor runs in circles around us as we walk across the street. If he was on a leash, he'd probably tie Jeremy and I together, like this is some kind of cute little romantic comedy.

"Arden!" says Golda before I'm halfway through the door. "I knew you'd be stopping in. You didn't come get your lunch Thursday, and then when you weren't here at all Friday, I said to myself, 'She'll come by. When she's ready, Arden will come by.'" She stops dead in her tracks when she sees Jeremy walk in behind me.

"Hey, Golda," says Jeremy, like it's been only days since she last saw us together.

Bless Golda's heart, she recovers fast. "Well, hey, Jeremy," she says. "Nice to see you here." I'm relieved she left off the *again.*

"Back at you," Jeremy says, shooting her a lopsided smile. He's trying to be extra-charming, and it's working.

Golda waves for us to sit and brings over two menus—sure signs that we're getting special treatment. Jeremy chooses the smallest table alongside the wall, away from the exhausted Eagle Valley store owners and the straggling visitors. We've got about half an hour between Main Street closing down and the beginning of tonight's ghost tour. Most people are down by the mill already, getting their candles and awaiting the story of poor Gracie Gray.

"I like your hair," Jeremy says. Back when we dated, my hair was long, almost down to my elbows. In my post-breakup haircut, I'd gone short, and my wavy hair had sprung up in coils. It's taken six months for me to grow it back past my shoulders.

It's taken six months for me to face Jeremy again, too, but I try not to dwell on that.

"Thanks," I say. I should return a compliment, I know, but all the ones I can think of sound cheesy. "So how've you been?"

"Busy," he says, and rambles for a bit about his new job, his apartment, and his coworkers. On the surface, I'm smiling and saying *oh really?* and *mm-hmm* in all the right places, while the rest of my mind compares Jeremy-now with Jeremy-then. He sounds more relaxed, for sure. The tight undercurrent of worry is gone from his voice, now that he has a job. Is he happier? I study his eyes, his posture, and whether he dimples when he smiles.

Jeremy stops talking suddenly and studies me right back. "I've been talking about me this whole time," he says. "How are you? How's business?"

"I'm going under," I say matter-of-factly. Golda chooses this moment to appear and take our orders.

She even writes them down, which may or may not improve her chances of getting it right. I order a tomato and avocado sandwich on sourdough bread with a cup of her broccoli and cheese soup. Jeremy orders a grilled cheese sandwich. I see he remembers Golda's specialty.

When she leaves, it's just us again, puzzling each other out. "I didn't expect that," he says. "I'm sorry to hear it." I can practically see the wheels turning in his head. "Is it because of your parents selling the farm? Or because of Paula?"

"Basically," I say, and give him a run-down of the letter I got today.

He whistles through his teeth. "Harsh," he says. "I guess there aren't any loopholes."

"Nope."

That makes Jeremy pause. "You seem pretty okay with the whole thing."

As if I could possibly be okay with any of this, I think, but strangely, I do feel better than I did yesterday. I get a little glimpse of my vision again, feel the breeze against my cheek, even. *Freedom.*

I shrug. "I guess I saw it coming. It didn't feel like much of a surprise."

Jeremy nods. "I could see that," he says, and I can tell by the way he looks at me that he's remembering my little spat with Miss Paula. "What are you going to do next?"

"Beats me!" I say glibly, as if it's all some big game to me. Like I don't have a care in the world.

"Wow, Arden," says Jeremy. "You've sure changed."

"Good way or bad?"

He smiles. "We'll see."

Golda brings us our food. A grilled cheese and to-mato sandwich for Jeremy and an avocado sandwich for me. At least she got my soup right. She puts a lit-tle plate of bacon and a side of scrambled eggs on the floor for Thor.

"He gets his own plate?" Jeremy asks.

"Thor's a special customer here," Golda says. "Just like his mama."

There's the tiniest hint of a warning in her words, and Jeremy looks down, properly abashed.

Please don't say it, I think.

He says it. "I'm really sorry for how I left things between us."

Great. I feel like we're embarking on part two of our breakup conversation. I notice that the avocado on my sandwich has tiny brown spots on it and put it down.

"Things happen," I say, trying to stay nonchalant. My newly-bubbling confidence is starting to crash.

"Things shouldn't have happened that way," Jeremy says.

I pretend to check on Thor, who's slurping greedily at his dinner. "It had to," I say, keeping my eyes on Thor. "You needed a job, and Richmond is where you needed to be."

"I took it out on you," says Jeremy. "I haven't been able to stop thinking about it."

He doesn't say anything else, and I can't help it. I look up at him.

Jeremy meets my eyes, straight on. "I'm sorry."

So that's how it happens, right when my parents leave, when my business starts its death spiral, and I finally start to manage my life instead of letting it manage me. Right when everything changes, Jeremy Johns comes back to town and rips the scabs off my heart.

After dinner, we go for a walk down Main Street. It's dark out now, with the street lamps glowing and the icicle lights over the shops lighting the sidewalk. Thor trots a half-pace behind us, like he's giving us privacy.

We can see the ghost tour starting down by the mill. "What's the story for the mill girl again?" Jeremy asks. "Drowned, right?"

"Supposedly," I say. "Story goes that Gracie Gray was working at the mill and sending the money back to her widowed mother. Had to quit school and start working when she was just sixteen. All the boys liked her, so none of the girls did—guess you know how that goes."

In the light of the streetlamp, I can see Jeremy's white teeth when he smiles. "So what, one of them pushed her?"

"No-o," I say. "All they say is that one morning, Gracie was found floating in the water by the mill wheel, dead. Everybody had a theory. Spurned lover, jealous mill girl, maybe a thief after the money she was saving for her mama. Nobody ever solved the mystery."

"What do you think happened?" Jeremy asks, like he's really interested. He's walking closer now. Almost hand in hand, but he hasn't reached for it yet.

"None of them," I say. "There never was a Gracie Gray."

Jeremy laughs. "And how do you know that?"

"I looked it up in the library, back when I was a teenager. The whole story is garbage. The only person they ever found floating in the creek was Tim Buxton. He did have a daughter named Gracie, but she'd already married and moved away by the time of the drowning."

"So how did he die?" asks Jeremy.

"He had five kids, lost his job and drank too much. One night, he stumbled out of the house drunk as a skunk and didn't come back. They found him in the creek the next morning."

"What made you go and look all that up?" He's not sarcastic, just curious.

"I just wondered. Figured it wasn't possible that a town this small had that many ghosts." Truth is, of all the ghost stories, the one about Gracie Gray creeped me out the most. I couldn't stand to come near the mill when I was little, before I found out the truth. I'd wear my white gloves and flip over the quilts for the quilt show out in the field, but no chance I'd go inside the mill or anywhere near the creek. I finally looked it up just to give me some peace of mind.

"It's cool you found out the truth," Jeremy says. "Even if it wasn't that exciting."

We're getting close to the end of the sidewalk now. Across the street and down a ways, we can see every-one gathered around Mr. Carson, their faces lit up in the dark by their candles. Mr. Carson is intoning the story in his deepest voice. I can't hear the words, but the tone sends shivers down my spine.

In all the time Eagle Valley's spent mourning a girl that never existed, over a fate that never happened, they've all forgotten Tim Buxton and the life he lived.

Not that Tim's life makes a good story. But it's still a life, and he's more a part of Eagle Valley than made-up Gracie Gray could ever be.

I look out past the mill, at the shadows of the fields that used to be my parents' farm. Sooner than not, it'll be a neighborhood. Everything we're living through now is going to be somebody's trite little story about Eagle Valley history. Someday. I wonder what they'll say about my parents, if anyone even remembers the farm at all. I wonder if anyone will even care that Eagle Valley once had a historic district, if we lose our status the way Miss Paula says we will. If anyone bothers to tell the story at all, they might get all our names wrong or mess up the timeline or forget the point entirely. Sure hope there's someone around to set the record straight, if it comes to that. If not, I hope they make my part interesting, at least.

"What are you thinking about?" Jeremy asks.

"Just," I look past his shoulders, at the mill. "Everything's changing."

"I hope so," says Jeremy. And I guess things have changed, finally, because that's when we have our first together-again kiss.

18

Kissing Jeremy sets me spinning, pulling me out of my head and deep into his thoughts. I feel free again, being close like this. Skin to skin and holding both his shoulders like I might lose myself completely if I let go. There is so much Jeremy has to tell me. I can feel every one of his stories racing along his skin, under my fingertips, between our lips.

It's me, I realize, dazedly. Every single one of his thoughts are about me. I see glimpses of myself through Jeremy's eyes. My hands are soft, and the freckles across my nose look like stardust, not sunspots. My hair is a little redder and a lot curlier than usual, but he sees it as vibrant, not unruly. My eyes are deep and he might just fall into them if I let him. I look beautiful.

Kissing him, I feel beautiful, too.

"Walk you back?" asks Jeremy. I nod, even though I don't want to say good night, not yet. Thor is already ahead of us, glancing back every now and again to be sure we're following and not kissing again. We walk up the sidewalk, hand in hand, our stories passing between our palms.

When we get to my truck, he kisses me one more time. Thor, tired of waiting, hops up to his seat.

"See you next weekend?" I ask.

"I can do better than that," he says. "I'll call you tomorrow." I don't have to wonder if he means it. He doesn't want to be leaving now, and that's a fact. I wrap my arms around him more tightly, and he pulls me in close.

"You've sure changed," I tease.

"Good way or bad?"

"I guess we'll see."

He does call. He calls Sunday night, just to let me know he got back to Richmond. Sends a text on Monday morning, too. "I miss you already," it said.

It might be silly, getting this excited over a text, but it sure keeps me smiling throughout the Monday morning meeting. Miss Paula's icy stares and her pointed references about fundraising and supporting the Society's mission bounce right off me. Instead of fretting over my store and the town, I daydream about Jeremy all the way home.

How can this happen, that we can pick things up again so easily? I walk down to my basement workshop, but keep my phone nearby just in case he texts again.

I have a few half-finished projects that need tending. The earring and pendant sets that Eliza priced sold over the weekend, which was a nice surprise. Even if my storefront is going to close, I need to keep earning and making money until the bitter end.

I use needle nose pliers and tweezers to adjust a string of beads onto a tiny wire. It's perfect, just about. I love seeing how these broken parts can come together and make something new. I move on to my next project. I have a gorgeous little cameo that popped straight out of its setting. With a little finagling, I've managed to get it reset, this time on a lighter, brighter chain. The new setting is perfect. It's more discreet, not the heavy, ornate feel of the original.

My favorite thing about the cameo is the hair. Usually, necklaces like this have a profile of a lady with neatly done hair, a proper bun or a little updo. This cameo has a woman with flyaways and curls draping over her shoulders. *She looks like Cassandra,* I think. Looking out into the future, and ready to take on the world.

I fasten the cameo around my neck. The chain sings, shiny and slippery and whispering stories against my skin. It feels just right.

Thor is annoyed with me. He follows me around the house with his toys, and trots off in a sulk when I don't focus on our game of tug-of-war. I'm lucky he's so forgiving. When I jangle my truck keys, he comes running, instantly friendly again.

"We're going for a ride!" I tell him. He's so excited I'm afraid he's going to have an honest-to-goodness fit. We have a ways to go today. I'm dropping him off with Eliza and the boys once we get to Roanoke, and then I've got to see Bryson and see about some of the tea sets I need for Miranda.

I roll down both windows in the truck for a cross-breeze. The air is a touch too cool for that, but I know it'll make Thor happy and I'm feeling pretty charitable this morning. It doesn't even sting when we roll down

Main Street, past Miss Paula's banner on the museum and over the hill towards my parents' empty house. Former house.

After we drive out of Eagle Valley, it's nothing but fields and mountains and open road until we hit the highway. It is pretty here. If there aren't any other cars, I can kind of forget there are other people at all. Feels like the whole world is just me and Thor, driving with the mountains by our side and the sun rising just ahead. I flash back to the vision I had yesterday. Peace. I could live like this.

The drive is long enough that my knees cramp up by the time we get to Eliza's. She's on the phone and waves me in. Ian and Wyatt come tripping out the door, calling for Thor. Almost as an afterthought, they acknowledge Auntie Arden.

"Sorry," Eliza mouths.

"It's okay," I say. Thor and the boys have already descended on the backyard, ready for some rough and tumble play.

Eliza says her goodbyes and clicks the phone off. "Can you come in for a few minutes?" she asks.

"I wish I could," I say. "Maybe when I get back. Thanks for watching him."

"Are you kidding?" Eliza asks. "He's a sweetheart. And speaking of sweethearts..." She raises her eyebrows at me.

"I am too? Aw, thanks, sis."

Eliza rolls her eyes. "Someone hasn't filled me in on a certain date last night."

"I don't kiss and tell," I say smugly.

Eliza isn't thrilled that Jeremy popped back into my life. I can tell that. But she's trying to be support-ive and trying even harder to be happy for me. I love that about her.

"Gotta go," I tell her. I glance out back, where Ian and Wyatt are tumbling with Thor. "Give the boys a kiss for me."

It's a short drive to the antique mall, just past the jewelry store, actually. I wonder if Mr. Harris is back today, or if Sylvie is still running the show. I feel a little swell of pride as I drive past. I'm not just han-dling my life, I'm running it. Feels good.

The antique mall is a long, low building with a big parking lot and a wheelchair ramp at one end of the porch. It's not so far outside Roanoke—from the edge of the parking lot, you can just see the star on Mill Mountain. I bet at night, when the stars are all lit up, you'd be able to see it from here, clear as anything.

The booths inside are big, and I've been around Sadie and Bryson long enough to know business is usually steady. They actually own two adjoining booths in the corner, so their space is pretty big. The booths are more Sadie's thing. She has a lot of health problems, so decorating the booths and keeping up with sales is just about all she has energy for these days. Bryson uses this spot as his home base for arranging estate sales and coordinating auctions. Most of the time, he's all over Virginia and North Carolina, doing auctions, making sales, and hauling back the best stuff to their house. Bryson will be here this morning, though. He'll be just back from an auction in Danville this past weekend.

Sadie sees me first as I wind my way back to their spot. "Hey, Arden!" she calls out. "Here for Bryson? He's out back."

"I'm here for both of you," I say, leaning down and giving her an air kiss on the cheek. I'm careful to avoid tripping on her little green oxygen tank. I can hear it clicking as it delivers a stream of air up through the tubes that loop over her ears and under her nose. "How're you feeling?"

"Oh, you know. Ups and downs," she says. "How's your pop?"

"Ups and downs," I tell her.

"Who you talking to?" Bryson calls out. "Sadie?" He appears down the hallway, coming up from the back loading dock. He grins when he sees me. "I thought you said you'd be by this week. How's your pops?"

"Okay," I say. "They just moved in."

"Ah," Bryson says. He waits a beat. "And how are you doing?"

"Can't complain." I'm good and ready to change the subject, though. "So I came about the estate sale, but I've got some other business, too."

Sadie laughs. "That's Arden," she says. "What was I just telling you, Bryson? Wasn't I just saying that? Arden just gets right down to business. That's right. That's Arden."

"Sure is," says Bryson. "That's you all over. What've you got?"

"I'm looking for some teacups and saucers. About 50 sets, all different patterns and colors. I need at least ten teapots and sugar bowls and creamers, too. Have you got anything?"

"I don't know if I've got 50," says Bryson, scratching his bald head. "I might. Any pattern, you said?"

"Any pattern. Actually, she wants as much variety as she can get." I unfold the list Miranda wrote out for me. "It's for that bed and breakfast in town. She wants mismatched place settings for their teatime."

"Ah, it's that mother-in-law again," says Bryson. "Mother-in-law-to-be, I mean. How are things going with that young man of yours?"

"Bryson," Sadie hisses, shooting him a look. She gives me an apologetic smile.

"It's okay," I say. "Actually, Jeremy and I just got back together."

"Well, isn't that something," Bryson says, grinning like it's the best news he's heard all day. Which is a pretty good save, considering he forgot we'd even broken up.

"Now we'll have to get you your tea sets," Sadie says. "Make sure you get in good with his mama."

It's probably too late for that, but I have to appreciate the gesture.

"I'll take a look," Bryson says. "Anything else?"

"Just the estate sale," I tell him.

"I got you your postcards printed up," Bryson says. "Are you putting an ad in the paper?"

"I don't think so," I say. "With it being the last weekend of Festival, I think we'll have plenty of traffic."

"That's good thinking," says Sadie. "Good timing."

I doubt Miss Paula would agree, but it's working out for us all right.

"My boys and I can get started tagging the Monday before. You and your sisters are helping, right?"

"Sure are," I say, even though only Eliza has agreed so far. I should e-mail Lila Beth again. "We'll get it done."

"Of course you will," Sadie says. "Never saw a family who got things done like the McCraes."

Bryson disappears into the back to look over his stock for the tea cups and saucers. Sadie's happy to keep talking to me.

"So how are things really going?" Sadie asks.

"What do you mean?"

Sadie chuckles, long and low. "Arden, I lived in Eagle Valley most of my life, and I worked in that store from when I was eighteen until we sold it to you. If I know anything, and I believe I do, things are getting pretty ugly about now."

"It hasn't been good," I confess. Sadie keeps her gaze steady, which makes it easier for me to spill it all. I start with Miss Paula's fundraisers, and end with the letter and my run-in with her over the brochures yesterday. I stop short of telling Sadie about my visions. Out of anybody I know, Sadie would probably be the least surprised. She says her great aunt had "the sight," whatever that means, so I think she'd be okay with knowing about me.

"So I'm guessing you're going to close," Sadie says. "Well, it's a darn shame. You're so good at what you do."

"How did you know that?" I ask. "I didn't say I was closing."

"Didn't say you weren't, either, and that was enough for me."

I feel sad, talking about this with Sadie. Makes it feel more real than when I was telling Jeremy.

"I just don't understand how it all fell apart so quickly," I say. "A month ago, Mama and Miss Paula were the best of friends. I don't know how you go from being that close to launching a full-out campaign that quickly."

Sadie shakes her head. "Don't you know how your mama and Miss Paula got to be friends?"

"They both wanted to restore the town, right?" I say. Truth is, I never looked that deep into it.

"Before that," Sadie says. She settles in and gets comfortable, letting her oxygen tank deliver two clicks before she gets started. "Right around the time your mama and daddy lost Tripp, Paula moved back to town. Now, Paula and your daddy grew up in Eagle Valley, but your mother moved there when she married your father. Paula went the other way around. When she got married to a local boy–Stan, I think he was called–they both high-tailed it to the big city. She wasn't going to be stuck in a place like Eagle Valley for life, no sir."

"Why'd she come back?" I ask. It's hard for me to picture Miss Paula as a young bride, anxious to shake Eagle Valley's dust off her boots.

"The marriage was a bust. Paula tried to hang in there, too long, I think, but he cheated more times than she could forgive. So home she came to Eagle Valley, and that's when she met your mama. They clicked, though who knows why. If they'd met at a different time, they probably wouldn't have. But your mother was so broken up over losing Tripp and Paula was so broken up over her marriage, I guess they had that in common. They were both trying like hell to cover up how bad they were hurting."

I feel unexpected tears stinging my eyes. "I guess I could see that."

"Well, they were a good team. Paula was good at shaking things up, getting people's attention. Your mama was the quiet one. She was behind the scenes, doing the legwork and making it happen. They balanced each other, I guess you'd say. Paula drew your mother out, and she reined Paula in."

Yin and yang, Daddy used to call them. Maybe they were unlikely friends, but it worked. Until now, I guess.

"The way I see it," Sadie continues. "For your mama, the Historical Society and Festival helped her keep on moving. It was a good distraction. Got her out of bed and putting one foot in front of the other. For Paula, running the Historical Society became her life. When the chips fell, they both chose what was most important to them. For your mama, it was your daddy, pure and simple. For Paula, it's the town."

Bryson reappears with a big box and a stack of postcards. "I've got 40 sets of the cups and saucers," he says. "All ten teapots but only five each of the sugar bowls and creamers. Is that enough for you? Think you can come up with the rest on your own?"

"Sure can," I tell him. "Thanks, Bryson." I pay him, and he hands me a receipt along with a stack of postcards. They're professional-quality, printed up with the pictures I sent him on thick, glossy paper. Some of Mama and Daddy's best furniture is featured on the front, and information about the sale and a little map to the house is on the back. "Think you have enough time to get these mailed? Or do you want me to do it?"

"I'll do that," I promise. "I'll take care of getting the word out." I give Sadie a goodbye squeeze and feel how much she hurts for me. "Thank you," I say, leaning down. "Thank you for telling me."

Bryson walks me out and helps me load the truck. "That young man of yours," he starts.

"Jeremy."

"Make sure he treats you right," he says. "Man lets you go once, it's a damn shame. If he does it twice, he's a damn fool."

"No complaints here," I tell him. He smiles and waves at me while I back up and start down the road. *Jeremy's not going to let me go again,* I think.

Then I remember my vision. Me and Thor, heading down the highway, the whole world wide open just for us.

Just for us. Jeremy wasn't anywhere in sight.

I figure I should stop in and see Mama and Daddy, seeing as I'm already here in Roanoke. It's strange how much I hate the idea of going. I guess with me, seeing really is believing.

It's only ten minutes from the antique mall to the nursing home. *Assisted living*, I think automatically, but there's hardly a point in trying to dress it up with different words. When I turn into the parking lot, I feel like I'm pulling up to a hotel. A nice hotel with flowering plants on either side of the doorway and weedless gardens around the outside. But still, it's not home.

The inside smells like the unlikely combination of Lysol and begonias. There's a group sitting in little clusters in a front sitting-room area. Some of them look up, as if maybe I'm the visitor they've been expecting. Some ignore me and keep playing checkers or talking. Some just stare straight ahead.

I feel lost for a moment before I see a front desk up ahead. "I'm here to see my parents, in the Alzheimer's wing," I tell the girl. She looks close to my age with a nametag that says Franny.

"Sure," she says. "Can I have their names?"

"Vaughn and Dorothy McCrae."

"Our new residents in 12B." She smiles. "You'll want to go down the long hallway, take your third left, and that'll take you to the breezeway. Cross through to get to our memory care building. You'll see the room numbers over the door."

That's a fair difference from letting myself in the kitchen door. I thank her, focus on remembering her directions and not touching anything. That works until I have to find a way to knock on the door. I think for a second before I pull my coat sleeve over my fist and knock. It's muffled, but it works.

"Hello?" Mama calls, and then opens the door. "Arden! What a nice surprise."

Does Mama sound...happy? Not chipper, exactly, but her shoulders are hanging loosely and there's a lot less strain behind her smile.

"You look pretty good for someone who's just moved," I tell her.

"Come in and sit down," she says. I'd ask where, but there aren't many choices. Their room is organized like a little studio apartment. The kitchen table and chairs are by the front, and then the sofa and two easy chairs make a little sitting area to the left side. On the right side, there's a bed, two dressers, and a steamer trunk beside the bathroom.

Daddy is propped up on the sofa, asleep. He's dressed, which is a relief. He has a green sweater over a white collared polo, gray sweatpants, and navy blue slippers. I know I've seen him wear those clothes before, but they look huge on him now. Like the clothes are wearing him instead of the other way around. He's sitting with his head tilted back, snoring softly. Next to him is a picture album.

"I took all the pictures that we had along the staircase and put them in an album for him," Mama says. "So he can look through whenever he wants, but we put it away if it gets to be too much."

I sit gingerly beside him, afraid to wake him up. He snores on, completely undisturbed. Mama takes one of the easy chairs and lowers herself into it with a sigh.

The picture album lays open to Lila Beth's senior picture. She looks a lot like Eliza and Mama. "Have you heard from her?" I ask, indicating the picture.

"I called her to give her our new address and phone number. She seems to be doing well. Do you two talk much these days? She'll be down for Christmas. I guess she'll stay with Eliza and John, since we don't have a guest room here."

Has Mama always been this talkative? Or did caring for Daddy wear her down just as slowly as the

Alzheimer's took over his body? I can't remember the last time I saw her lean back when she sits, like she is now.

"The nurses here are phenomenal," she gushes. "So considerate. If your father needs help, I just push a button and down the hall they come. Not right away, you understand, not if they're busy with another patient. But someone does come along. After they get your father settled in for the night, I have a chance to stay up and read for a bit. I'm halfway through this one already." She holds up a novel that's set during the Revolutionary War. I gave it to her for her birthday two years ago.

"Glad you like it!" I say. "What part are you at?"

"The Patriot family is storming through the town, trying to find where the traitor is hiding. I was just picking it up again when I heard you knocking. Are you reading anything these days?"

"Me? No," I say. I remember back when I lived at home, and Daddy and Mama and I would trade novels with each other after we'd finished them. I'd read them through with gloves on, then after I was done, I'd pick it up again and overhear their thoughts as they were reading. I happen to know that Daddy skips over paragraphs with too much description, and Mama has a habit of snacking while she reads.

When was the last time I'd sat down and picked up a book?

"I've been busy," I tell her. "Did you know Jeremy's been coming into town again?"

"Is he?" Mama asks. "Has he been making time for you?"

"We had a date on Sunday," I tell her. "He said he'll be back up next weekend, too."

"He will if he has the sense God gave a rock," Mama says with unaccustomed venom. I can't think of a response to that. She sees me staring and goes back to her usual gentle tone. "I was sorry to see him go when he went off to Richmond. Jobs are a dime a dozen, but if you have someone special, you should hang on to them."

"Jobs aren't a dime a dozen anymore, Mama," I say, suddenly irritated. "People are struggling these days. People have been struggling."

Mama gives me a long stare, as if she's just realized something. "How's your store?"

I've already told Jeremy and Sadie. Might as well make it three for three. "I'm going under."

Mama purses her lips. "Tell me honestly, Arden. Is it because of Paula?"

"No."

She raises an eyebrow.

"The campaign didn't help," I say. "But I've been just managing for a long time. If it hadn't been the campaign, it would have been something else."

"I wondered," Mama said. "Isn't there something we can do? What if you sold some of our old furniture, instead of putting it through the estate sale?"

"No, Mama. No. That's kind. The business is over, though. It would take much more than a good sale to turn it around at this point." As if I could profit from my parents' things when Daddy needs so much.

"Just you keep it in mind," Mama says. "I told you and your sisters to take what you'd like before the sale. You are going to go through it, aren't you? You and Eliza, at least?"

"Yes, Mama," I say.

There's a knock at the door. "Mrs. McCrae?" calls an unfamiliar voice. A nurse, I assume. "We have Mr. McCrae's twelve o'clock medication."

"I should get going," I say. "I need to pick up Thor from Eliza's. I stopped by Bryson's place on my way here." Actually, I stopped here on my way back, but I'm not putting it like that.

"Thanks for stopping by, sweetheart," Mama says. "You take care of yourself."

"You too," I say, looking at her and Daddy both. "You too."

19

The rest of the week, I start the slow business of getting ready to close. Even without paying Miss Paula's
fines, the numbers are in, and they're not pretty. I
could squeeze by another month, maybe two. But why
bother? Festival will be over next month, so there's
hardly a point staying open. I'd rather leave before I'm
actually bleeding money.

In the evenings, I work on my new projects and
wait for Jeremy to call. He does, every night. After
that, I hop on the Alzheimer's forums. I've started to
look for certain screen names and check for updates on
different stories. The woman whose brother got so an-

gry that she took their mom to an adult day care center hasn't cooled off, but one of their sisters visited and took her side. That's something, I suppose.

On Thursday, SarahSue81 sends me a private message. "I've been thinking about you," it says. "The days after the big move, I felt so strange. Kind of relieved and kind of numb. Someone on these forums reached out to me back then, so I'm paying it forward, I guess. Just know that if you need somebody, I'm here."

Relieved and numb. That's exactly it. I didn't want Mama and Daddy back in their farmhouse, trying to manage. I wouldn't wish that kind of living on anybody. But I do feel strange now that they're gone. I walk around town and rustle around the shop like I'm all thumbs. I suppose some of that could be blamed on my love life, but it's more like I don't know how to live in Eagle Valley without my parents.

I sit at the computer, trying to puzzle out something to type. The phone rings. It's Jeremy.

"Am I calling too late?" he asks. It's adorable that he thinks I have something to get up early for.

"I have Friday mornings off," I remind him.

"Right, right," he says. "I'm just getting home. Had to go to my boss's house for a dinner party."

Based on what Jeremy's told me about his boss, I can't imagine that was any fun. "I'm sorry. Was it awful?"

"I swear he's different around his wife. He pulls out her chair for her, helps with the dishes, asks her to tell everyone about her day, the whole nine yards."

"This is the same guy who's had sixteen reports to Human Resources?"

"Same guy."

"Wow."

"Some of the guys brought their girlfriends, and Rhonda brought her fiancé," he says. "I wish you'd been there with me."

I try to imagine that. I've never been to a dinner party before. Closest I got was a holiday party at Eliza's with her in-laws and some of the neighbors. I guess the Eagle Valley Legends gala my parents used to throw would count, but they didn't serve a lot of food. Mostly punch and finger foods.

"I've never been to a dinner party," I say.

"Some of them are kind of fun," Jeremy says. "Not ones for work, generally, but my friends have thrown pretty good ones."

"Maybe I'll meet them someday."

"I'd like that," Jeremy says. "I think they'd like you."

"What's not to like?"

"Exactly. So, am I meeting you this weekend?"

"You better be."

"I have to babysit the bed and breakfast for my parents on Saturday night, but I'm free Sunday afternoon."

"Where are your parents going?"

"Some kind of Historical Society meeting." He pauses. "Did you forget? I figured you'd be going too."

"I don't remember anything about it. I'll check my e-mail." My heart starts beating faster. Had I not gotten a meeting notice? Were they voting to run the last McCrae out of town or something?

Calm down, I tell myself. More than likely, I just skimmed past the e-mail. Now that Miss Paula is on the outs with me, I've had to learn to keep the town schedule straight without her calling with a dozen reminders.

"So Sunday," I say, forcing my voice to be brighter, stronger. "What do you say? Hiking? Lunch?"

"Both. Make it a picnic."

My phone beeps, signaling that someone else is trying to call. Eliza.

"My sister's calling," I say.

"I'll let you go. Talk to you tomorrow," Jeremy says. "Good night."

"Night," I say distractedly and click over to Eliza. "Is everything okay?" I ask before she has a chance.

"Everything's fine! I was just about to leave a message. Who were you talking to?"

"Jeremy," I say.

"And you got off the phone for little old me? I'm flattered."

"Why'd you call, Eliza?"

"I'm just trying to get a time together to go do the estate stuff before Bryson and his guys get in there and we start tagging. Mama mentioned it again Tuesday, but I forgot."

"She said something to me on Monday, too. It completely slipped my mind." I reach up and run my hand through my hair. "When do you want to do it?"

"Does tomorrow morning work? Since you have off? Or do you want to wait until next Monday? It's up to you. John's mother can watch the twins either day."

"Monday," I say. I don't have anything special to do tomorrow, but I'm in no hurry to go through my parents' house. "Do you know what you're going to take?"

Eliza lists everything slowly, like she's embarrassed to have thought of it. "I'd like to have Grandmother's china, if you don't want it," she says. "And maybe the silver to match."

"No problem here," I say. "Do you think Lila Beth wants it?"

Eliza snorts. "I doubt it. Have you even heard from her?"

"Not yet," I admit. "I wish we were doing this with her."

"Don't count on it, Arden." Eliza waits a beat. "Was Jeremy going to call you back? I don't mean to keep you all night."

"Yeah," I say. Not that I think he'll call again tonight, but I suddenly feel ready to be alone.

When she hangs up, though, I stay planted at my computer instead of going up to bed. I open up a message box to send back a private message to SarahSue81.

"Thanks for reaching out to me ☺ This is such a strange time. I don't really know what to do with myself. How did you handle your mom's things? We're having a friend of mine coordinate an estate sale, but my sisters and I are supposed to go through and take what we want before that happens. One of my sisters is close, but the other lives upstate. I've e-mailed her, but I don't know if she understands everything that's going on, and I don't think she's going to come down any time soon. What do you think I should do?"

SarahSue81 is online. I can tell from the way the message window blinks. She sends me a reply five minutes later.

"It's hard to try and keep everyone in the family in the loop, isn't it? Sadly, I was the only one that was left to handle my mom's affairs. Nobody else stepped up no matter what I said. I don't know if it would work or what the dynamics are in your family, but if you think your sister who lives upstate doesn't really get what's going on, I think you should keep trying, for her sake as well as yours. If you think she knows but doesn't want to be involved, I wouldn't push it. Does that make sense? Maybe run it by your nearby sister and see what she thinks?"

I know full well what Eliza thinks. As far as she's concerned, Lila Beth has written us off, and we might as well write her off too. I don't think that's all there is to it. And it's not like Lila Beth has never tried to be involved, even after she moved upstate. I remember the trip-that-wasn't that she tried to take me on.

Maybe that's why. Maybe Lila Beth stopped coming down so much because of me. I feel a pang of guilt, which surges into something stronger. Bravery, maybe. Well, no matter what she may have thought of me back then, I've changed. It's time to write Lila Beth another e-mail.

Hi Lila Beth,

Mama and Daddy are settled in to their new place. Mama looked a lot more relaxed when I saw her, so I think it was a good move for them. There's still stuff to handle here, though. My friend Bryson is doing the estate sale. We're supposed to go through and get what we want to keep in the family before they come in and start tagging everything. Eliza and I really need your help with that. I know you might not think you want anything, but I feel bad making decisions about what to keep or sell without you. If there's any way you can come down in the next week, it would mean a lot to me.

Do you remember Jeremy? We're back together again. That's a nice change in the middle of all this other stuff going on. What about you? What's going on in your life?

I love you.

Arden.

I reread it. I never talk to Lila Beth like that. Never put it all out in the open. Then again, maybe that's what I need to do. I press send.

There's no reply from Lila Beth when I wake up on Friday morning. Not that I should expect one, I guess. Maybe Eliza is right. Maybe she just doesn't want to be involved.

I remember the vision I had of us three sisters standing shoulder-to-shoulder beside Tripp's dogwood tree. Lila Beth is part of this story. I've got to keep trying.

Thinking of not wanting to be involved reminds me of the Historical Society meeting Jeremy mentioned his parents going to. I don't want to go, but I suppose I should, if only to avoid the fine. I search through my old e-mails, the stack of mail on my counter, everything. No mention of any kind of meeting Saturday night. *I must have misplaced it,* I reason, even as a sense of foreboding washes over me. There's another premonition coming. Great.

But it doesn't come right away, so I decide to take matters into my own hands. I have about 50 cup and saucer sets for Miranda Johns, and it's high time I deliver them.

I leave Thor at home for this one. He's sleeping on my bed, so hopefully he'll stay there while I'm out. I'm not about to subject Miranda to a dog in her treasured bed and breakfast. More to the point, I'm not about to subject Thor to Miranda.

Friday mornings at the Johns' bed and breakfast look just about the way you'd imagine a quirky inn on the English countryside. The tea service is out, newspapers are folded, and there's even a plate of hot scones and fresh whipped butter on the buffet. The whole dining room is dressed in chintz and aggressively floral wallpaper.

"Arden!" Miranda says, rushing out to greet me when she sees the big box in my hands. "Come on in to the office. Let me help you carry that."

Carrying a heavy box with Miranda is like a three-legged race. We have to turn sideways and waddle through the kitchen, where the smell of omelets and hash browns makes my mouth water. I'm relieved to kick the office door shut behind us and set the box down on her desk.

"These are perfect!" Miranda exclaims, unwrapping each cup and saucer in turn. "Exactly what I was going for. Arden, you're a mind reader."

I give her a vague smile. "I'm glad you like them. I think they'll add a nice touch to your breakfast room."

"Perfect," Miranda purrs again. When she's checked them all over for chips, she goes to the little lockbox under her desk for the checkbook. I wait until the check is in my hand before I bring up my real reason for visiting.

"Jeremy mentioned he'd be in town this weekend," I say conversationally.

"Yes. He mentioned you two were seeing each other again," Miranda says. The lack of "I'm so glad you're back together" is obvious.

"We'll probably see each other Sunday. He mentioned he was inn-sitting while you and Gordon had a Historical Society meeting?" I try to keep my tone light and politely curious. Miranda's face says just about everything I need to know.

"Oh! Yes, that is Saturday night, isn't it? Jeremy's so good to come and watch the B&B for us."

"Do you mind telling me what time it is? I looked all over, but I don't think I got a notice."

There it is. I feel like I've been slapped up both sides of the head when this premonition comes through. *I wasn't invited.* "Oh, you didn't?" Miranda says, eyes wide. "Are you sure? Maybe you misplaced it."

"That's probably it," I agree. I can feel my cheeks burning, but I forge ahead anyway. "But since I'm here, can you remind me what it's about? I hate to show up unprepared."

"Oh, you know," Miranda says. "I think Paula wanted to go over some...budget concerns."

"The budget for Festival, you mean?" I ask. My voice sounds way too high. So much for trying to sound innocent. I'm a bad actress and I know it. Miranda is too, though, so I don't worry too much about it.

Miranda laughs uncomfortably, shifting her weight from one foot to the other. When she sees I haven't budged, she drops her smile down a notch. "I really hate to get in the middle of things."

"It's town business," I say. "You're hardly in the middle. We both work on Main Street." For now.

"Paula's nowhere near her goal to buy back the farm from the developer," she says. "She had to get at least halfway in order to qualify for a matching grant from one of the foundations she knows. We're not even close."

"Oh."

"She just wanted to have a meeting of the minds to think of some other fundraising ideas. Maybe she didn't reach out to you so you wouldn't feel uncomfortable."

"I'm sure," I say.

"It's not personal, you know. Like you said, it's town business."

"Of course." I say. "Well, thanks for keeping me in the loop! It's a pleasure doing business with you."

"You too," Miranda says. She watches me all the way out the door.

20

Civil War weekend begins exactly the same way it always has, ever since I took over the antique store. By the time I pull up, I already have two customers waiting outside the door, dressed head-to-toe in their 1860s-era finest. It's not until I'm close enough to greet them that I see a grouchy-looking woman in hoop skirts standing behind them with her arms folded.

This little group has been here awhile. I graze my wrist along the brick storefront and touch one finger to the door handle. That tells me everything I need to know. They're in desperate search of period-appropriate buttons, because one of the gentleman reenactors forgot to mend his when they fell off. He's silently blaming his wife, the lady in the hoop skirts, for forgetting to remind him. She's seething from the implication. It's not her job to remind her husband to fix his costume. He should feel lucky she agreed to come along at all.

After picking up all that, I feel fairly dizzy. I try to unlock the front doors and lead them to the front counter without touching anything else.

"I'm sorry to trouble you with something so trifling," says the gentleman reenactor. He's already in character, using his 19th century manners even though I'm in modern clothes. I bring out all my button jars from the back room. I'm not sorting through them, but they can have at it.

"No trouble at all. Buttons are twenty-five cents apiece," I say.

The buttonless man peruses the selection with the trained eye of a fine jeweler. "What about these?" he asks, holding up two.

"It looks farby," says the other reenactor. The wife looks irritated. I'm guessing she's heard them arguing about period-accurate pieces one too many times.

"Well, what do you expect on such short notice?" huffs the buttonless reenactor.

"Nobody will notice," says the woman in hoop skirts. "Please, can we go? We've been driving for hours. I want breakfast."

I wrap the buttons in newspaper and tuck them into the bag with an estate sale postcard and the receipt. "Pleasure doing business," I say with a smile. "If you're hungry, Golda's Diner is just across the street. Tell Golda I sent you. She makes the best pancakes in town." She also makes the only pancakes in town, unless you're staying at the Johns' bed and breakfast. A little flattery helps Golda remember to measure the pancake batter, though.

The men tip their caps at me and follow the lady in hoop skirts out the door.

Normally, our reenactors come pretty well-prepared. We aren't any kind of big name in the reenactment circuit. We didn't have any Civil War battles near Eagle Valley, so there aren't any battlefield reenactments. Instead, we host a town-hall meeting where the townspeople debate whether to send an envoy to Wheeling, asking to join the Reformed Government of Virginia. Then, there's an ice cream social down by the mill in the evening, before the ghost tour kicks off. On Sunday, there's a hymn sing and a service project, hosted by the Eagle Valley Presbyterian Women.

The Civil War days are actually one of our biggest weekends. Lots of Civil War buffs come in from all over the state, some even farther. I don't mind the reenactors, and I sure don't mind the extra revenue they drum up. Funny as it sounds, most of them are trying for a little piece of what I feel every day. They want to walk in someone else's footsteps, try to feel how people felt long ago and live how they lived. Some of them are trying to understand family members that died long before they were born. Some of them just like history, and they're after that feeling of losing themselves and being in someone else's world. Living history, we call it.

That's me all over–today and every other day. I'm living history. Come to think of it, I guess Daddy is too.

People in modern clothes aren't allowed at the town hall meeting. Ruins the atmosphere. A couple years back, Russ figured out how to set up a web cam that wasn't noticeable, and I helped him get it to stream live online. It's not great quality or anything, but it's cool to watch. It helps put the non-reenactors in the mood to buy antiques, which is even better. I put the live stream up on my laptop screen and let it play while customers mill around the store.

The theme of the debate is whether to remain with Virginia, which had joined the Confederacy, or to appeal to join the Restored Government of Virginia. We all know what happened from there. The western counties split off and joined the Union as West Virginia, and our county stayed with Virginia and the Confederacy. It's kind of hard to get into the debate when I already know what's going to happen. I can tell a few of the reenactors are having trouble getting into it, too, when the debate first gets going. They fidget with their clothes and look each other over, trying to find farby costumes or insincere reenactors.

Historical Society members who aren't running a store are expected to attend, dressed to period perfection and ready to lead the debate. Mr. Carson plays the mayor. Miss Paula plays his outspoken wife, since she can't be the mayor herself, not in the 1860s. Cliff sits in the midst of the townspeople, wringing his hat. His job is to argue for staying with the Confederacy. Pastor Drew, also sitting with the townspeople, is in charge of leading the argument for the Union.

Janie rolls into the store just as the debate is getting started. "Hey, Miss Arden," she says. "Who's winning this year?"

"If Mr. Carson gets his way, they'll settle on sending an envoy to Wheeling and asking to rejoin the Union."

"Has it ever gone that way?"

"A couple times. Usually people vote to stay put because of the trade routes."

"You'd think they'd want to join up with the Union. I would've."

I recite Miss Paula's credo of living history automatically. "It's not about how we think things should have gone. It's about trying to portray things as we think they would have gone."

"Right, right."

I change tracks. Time to get down to business. "So, today, we want to direct customers to the Civil War era artifacts. The biggest pieces are on either side of the door, but there's a bigger display towards the back, too."

"So everyone has to walk through the rest of the store," Janie says, nodding. She's a natural. I'm going to hate telling her that the store will have to close. She'll have to find another part-time gig, but I'm not worried for her. People like Janie always land on their feet.

"And when you're ringing people up, put one of these into the bag, along with their receipt." I point to the stack of postcards advertising my parents' estate sale. Janie raises her eyebrows a little, but nods again without comment.

On the monitor's small screen, I can see Miss Paula's face coming into shaky focus. "Husband, shall we start the debate?"

Mr. Carson looks annoyed and gives his gavel a few extra bangs. "The meeting will come to order."

The debate starts, haltingly. Cliff gives his argument as if he's memorized it from the script. Pastor Drew counters too quickly, and a handful of reenactors look nervous about jumping in. Even without being in the room, I feel like I can sense Miss Paula's growing desperation to get things on track. She starts piping up, feeding people lines.

"Husband, I cannot help but be concerned about this new government."

"Husband, perhaps we should ask the local townspeople what they think."

"Husband, what about our trade partners down the river? Might not the change in government affect our farms and businesses?"

"Silence, wife," Mr. Carson says tersely. Janie and I both burst into snickers. Some of the customers are smirking, too.

"That was classic," Janie says, clearing her throat.

"That's not even the best one. A couple years back, someone referred to the western counties as 'West Virginia' and Miss Paula turned red."

"How'd they recover from that one?"

"I think Mr. Carson just acted all confused and guessed that the person meant western Virginia. Got everyone back on track."

"Nice."

We're interrupted by an older couple, looking to haggle. The wife's been watching the live stream of the proceedings while the husband's been studying the Civil War artifacts.

"Excuse me," the husband begins. "What's your best price for these two coins if I buy them together?"

On the live stream, I can hear voices getting heated. I feel the air getting thicker, heavier, the lights getting brighter. There's a premonition coming. No. Not now.

I smile gamely for the husband. "My best price is what's written on the tag."

"We must have order!" Mr. Carson says over the live stream. He's slipped into his naturally high, reedy voice. He corrects quickly, and goes back to his usual fake-deep voice. "I will not have this town being split up. Look at what's happened to our country."

"So you do support the Union!" shouts a reenactor I don't recognize. "As long as Eagle Valley is part of Virginia, we are part of the Confederacy."

"Virginia's government has reformed," another shouts. "The state is rejoining the Union, and we need to go with them. The government that joined the Confederacy is in error. Will you go down with a sinking ship?"

Miss Paula chooses this moment to rise from her seat, surveying the hysteria with a practiced calm. "I will speak," she tells Mr. Carson, and addresses the room. "I was born in Eagle Valley, and I will die here. We need to stand together and preserve what's ours. I won't see our town split in two."

I know she's just performing for the webcam, but I feel like Miss Paula's looking straight at me.

"Excuse me? Miss?" asks the husband. He's looking at me intently. "What if I buy these three together? Could I talk you into a discount then?"

I try to smile and ignore the burst of applause that's just erupted on the live stream. Behind the customer's shoulder, I can see Main Street out the store window. I see the fault line again, erupting down the center of the town and splitting it in two. Here it comes.

"Miss?"

I feel like the fault line is running straight through me. I reach blindly for the countertop, and everything goes black.

I come to on the floor, looking up at Janie and the two customers. The store is unnaturally quiet, and someone's turned down the volume on the live stream, too. Or maybe it's just me. I can hear blood rushing through my ears.

"I'm afraid she doesn't negotiate very well," Janie says, trying to brush it off with a joke. It works. Everyone laughs, relieved, and the couple hurriedly buys two of the coins. Full price.

Thor has escaped the stockroom. He's pouncing on me and licking my face, even though I'm trying to stand up and make like I'm okay and nothing happened. Janie takes the opportunity to order me to stay sitting for a few minutes. I keep sneaking glances out the store window. There's no fault line. No divide. It was just the premonition.

One silver-haired customer whips out a bottle of water from her sizeable handbag and gives it to me.

"Are you diabetic?" she asks. "I am. I've got some snacks if you need them."

"Oh, no. Thank you," I say. "Just got a little overheated. I skipped breakfast, is all." I hope Janie doesn't remember the yogurt and banana that I devoured half an hour ago.

"You can't go skipping breakfast," the customer says disapprovingly. "Diabetic or not. Ain't nothing so important you need to be skipping meals. And look at you, skinny as all get out. You need to eat more."

"Yes, ma'am," I say meekly. She leaves me a granola bar, despite my protests, and buys a teapot before she leaves.

Janie insists on manning the register while I drink the water and assure Thor that I'm all right. By then, pretty much all the customers who witnessed my blackout have left, so I feel like I can get on my feet and pretend nothing happened.

Janie, wisely, acts like everything's fine, even though her curiosity and worry are crawling on her every handprint. She waits until we're closing before she speaks up. "You sure you're okay, Miss Arden?"

"Like I said. I skipped breakfast."

"No, you didn't." She hesitates. "It's okay, Miss Arden. I know you've got a lot on your mind."

She meets my gaze head on. She knows. Not about my premonitions. Practical Janie would never believe anything so strange. She already figured out that the store is going to close. She's just waiting for me to tell her, make it official.

"I have been under some stress," I allow. Then, finally, "I'm going to have to close the store."

Janie tries to act surprised. "Even with the Festival? I know things have been...tight...but I thought that Festival would help."

"Not this year," I say. "I'm sorry, Janie. I wish I could say there's a chance things could recover, but this is the end."

"When?" Janie asks.

"November," I say. There it is. The thought that's been rolling around in my head since last week. I'll get through Festival, and then I'll close. Funny, it doesn't seem quite as scary now that I've said it out loud.

"Wow," Janie says. "That's fast."

"In a way. But it's been a long time coming."

"Miss Arden?" Janie fidgets. I can tell she's walking that fine line. She's old enough to speak her mind, but young enough to worry about respecting her elders. Bless her heart. She thinks I'm her elder.

Finally, she decides to ask. "Is it because of the farm? And Miss Paula?"

"Not exactly," I say. "If all this hadn't happened, it would have been something else. Times are tough."

Janie lets it go at that. She gathers her backpack and gives Thor a good scratch behind the ears before she goes. Just as she gets to the door, she says, "I'll help. When you have to pack up the store. I'll come help you."

I fight back my impulse to say no, that's okay, I've got it. I swallow twice and say, "Thanks. I may just take you up on that."

When Thor and I get ready to leave the store on Saturday evening, the ghost tour has already started. This one's a love story, or it should have been. It's about a young couple, Samuel and Martha. They grew up together and thought they'd marry, which is about the way everybody met their future husband and wife in Eagle Valley back then. They came of age during the Civil War. Samuel tried to convince Martha to move with him across the Blue Ridge, to the part of Virginia that called itself the Restored Government of Virginia.

"My father will never allow it," Martha had said.

"Then come away with me," Samuel had implored. "We'll elope and make a new life together."

"If my family can't be part of it, I don't want anything to do with it," she'd said. These words have been repeated in Eagle Valley through at least four generations worth of weddings now. Mothers and fathers of the bride are particularly quick to mention poor, heartbroken Martha, and her devotion to her family, whenever wedding planning gets tense.

Story goes that Samuel was struck dumb and died the day after he crossed the mountains for Western Virginia, and she wasted away, dying of a broken heart. Samuel was actually struck by lightning, and

Martha died of diphtheria, not heartbreak. End result is the same, though. They both died alone.

I've never liked this ghost story, but I really hated it after Jeremy and I broke up. I gave into a fantasy that Jeremy and I were the new Samuel and Martha, doomed to loveless lives because neither of us was brave enough to stay with the other. I try to put it out of my head. We aren't repeating history. This is new, what Jeremy and I have.

I wonder if that's true, or if I'm just trying to convince myself.

I pull out my cell phone and hit Jeremy's name on speed dial. It rings through to voice mail. Of course. He's probably tending a guest or fetching extra down pillows. Lucky him.

Across Main Street, the town hall is all lit up. Practically everyone else in town is inside, planning new and better strategies to buy back my parents' farm. There's only one more weekend of Festival to go. If they can't make up the money quick, the developer will keep the land. Instead of a view of the mountains, Main Street will look out onto a sprawling neighborhood of tasteful, modest homes.

Would it really be so bad? I try to imagine it. Without a premonition to guide me, my mind's eye is cloudy. Sometimes, I picture the hills dotted with a few tiny dollhouses. Other times, I see mansions sprawled out, towering over the mountains. I look again, look hard at my parents' house and imagine two or three more where the farm is now. Then I picture ten, twenty. Maybe even thirty.

Well, it might not be ideal, but who can promise things will stay perfect? Not the McCraes, that's for sure.

Thor is sticking close by my knees. He's extra protective this afternoon, watching, waiting to see if I'll black out again. I pull his leash a little closer and take some time to walk back up Main Street to the church.

Back when Jeremy and I were together the first time, I thought we'd get married here. Now there was something that was easy to imagine. I guess when there's a future you want to see, it's pretty easy to dream it up. I must have walked myself down that aisle a hundred times in my mind. I pictured us having a storybook Eagle Valley wedding, settling into my house, and living out our lives here.

Maybe I'll end up with Jeremy after all–maybe–but we won't be staying around Eagle Valley.

I walk up to the doorway and pull Thor even closer so he doesn't wander inside. I try to picture it again, see myself as a bride. I have to stop and start my day-dream again a dozen times. Miss Paula sure won't be the wedding coordinator, which is probably a good thing. When I picture Eliza and Lila Beth as my bridesmaids, I see Eliza glaring at Jeremy and Lila Beth checking her phone. Neither of them look good in peach.

Daddy won't be able to walk me down the aisle, I realize. No lifting of the veil, no shaking Jeremy's hand and warning him to be good to his daughter. Another might-have-been family moment gone.

Thor settles himself on the front steps, keeping watch over me. I lean against the doorframe and stretch both my bare hands on the cold stone. Just once, I'd like to pull out a story of the future that I want to hear.

No future comes, only millions of snippets from past stories. Seems that most of Eagle Valley has come through here at some point or another. Most people actually attend, but the ones that don't, like our family, still come for the funerals and weddings and holidays. Always have, always will.

"We're open on Sundays, too, you know," says a voice behind me. "You're welcome to join us."

It's Pastor Drew. He's wearing regular-person clothes: corduroy pants and a green sweater. I'm relieved to see him out of his Civil War costume. Even though he couldn't see me on the other end of the webcam, I'd like to leave that whole fainting spell behind me.

"I think people would be more comfortable if I didn't," I say.

Pastor Drew looks me over. His eyes don't look judging, just kind. "Would you like to come in?" he asks, gesturing inside, towards the pews. I throw a glance back at Thor.

"He can come too," Pastor Drew says. "We just blessed the animals here a few weeks back."

Thor comes with us, but I stop him from climbing up on the pew beside me. He curls up in the aisle instead, his nose quivering.

"May I?" Pastor Drew asks, gesturing to the pew. I nod, and he slides in and sits next to me.

I like that he is comfortable in silence. The sun is streaming through the stained glass windows at the altar.

"What's troubling you, Arden?" he asks.

I don't answer him. Everybody in Eagle Valley knows what's troubling me.

Pastor Drew seems to realize this and sighs. He uncrosses his legs and crosses them the other way. "You don't have to carry this alone."

I picture telling him. Telling him that I can see the future, actually, and it's not pretty. I will be alone. "I think I do."

I grip the back of the pew in front of me. Press my fingers and palms hard against the polished wood. I listen through the hymns and prayers that come up first to the ones underneath. The stories that were never quite said out loud but rise up anyway from the places they've been buried. I listen until I'm not quite sure where I end and the pew begins, until this church and I are both vessels, pouring our stories from one of us to the other and back.

When I lift my hands again, I can breathe full and deep for the first time. I look over at Pastor Drew, and notice his head bowed forward and his eyes closed. At first I think he's sleeping, until I look closer and see his lips moving ever so slightly in silent prayer. When he opens his eyes, he looks the way I feel. More empty and more full at the same time.

"Are you at peace?" he asks.

Peace. The word feels like the first step into the pond on a hot day. It shocks me at first, and then I ease into it with arms open.

"Yes," I say. "I'm at peace."

21

Sunday is pretty well deserted on Main Street. Most everyone is at the church for the hymn-sing. Afterwards, they'll do a service project. It's usually packing medical supplies to send overseas or making care packages for hospice programs. It's supposed to be in remembrance of the time when the Eagle Valley Presbyterian congregation pulled together to send supplies to Civil War soldiers. They didn't, actually, but I suppose it's as good a reason as any for a service project.

I tell myself that I would go, if it wasn't just me at the shop. Janie goes to church with her parents every

Sunday. That's not entirely true, though. The Eagle Valley Historical Society makes allowances for stores to be closed on Sunday, if the owners want to go to church. I just don't.

Jeremy doesn't either, because he drops in the store right after the church bells ring. There isn't another soul to be seen on Main Street anywhere. I take a minute to look at him, framed in the glass doorway, smiling the way he used to.

"Hey, you," he says. I even get a hello kiss. A long one.

"So I've got an idea," he says. "Want to hear it?"

"Sure," I say.

"You have off on Mondays, right? Why don't you let me take you to Richmond? Just for a little daytrip. I'll drive you up, show you around then bring you straight back home."

I freeze. "Tomorrow?" I hedge. "Tomorrow I'm supposed to work with Eliza on my parents' house."

"Oh," Jeremy says. "Right. Well, another time then."

I can't say anything. In the long silence that follows, Jeremy does.

"There isn't going to be another time, is there?"

"I can't go with you." I don't feel panicked at all, strangely. It's just true. I wait for a familiar knot of fear, a little anxiety. Nothing comes. I just feel sure and certain of the future I'm walking into.

Jeremy runs a hand through his hair, making it bristle. "I thought you wanted to leave Eagle Valley."

"I do. I am. Just, not now."

"What are you waiting for?" Jeremy asks. "Your family isn't here anymore. Your business is closing. There's nothing keeping you in Eagle Valley but you."

"I'm not ready to leave."

"Arden, come on. I heard you fainted yesterday."

That surprises me. "You did?"

"This place is going to tear you apart. I get that it's your home, but if you aren't going to help yourself, I don't know what to do."

"Who says I'm not helping myself?" I demand. "Why are my only options Richmond or Eagle Valley?"

"Where else are you going to go?"

"Wherever I want," I spit.

"And where is that?" Jeremy says. "Arden, we broke up last time because you wouldn't leave this place. I thought things were different now. I thought you'd changed."

"I did change," I say. "Guess I didn't change into the person you wanted me to be."

"So this is it," Jeremy says. "Eagle Valley for life."

"I didn't say that," I say. "I said not Richmond, not right now."

Jeremy's face softens immediately. "Oh."

I'm too far away to touch him and see what he means by that. "What?"

"This is all still new to you, isn't it? What's it been, a month? How long have you known your parents were moving?"

I try to count backwards in my head. "They got the notice about the room...three weeks ago, I think."

"And here I am pushing you to move and find a new place on top of everything else. I'm sorry."

I'm sorry. Words he rarely said to me when we were first together. I savor them and sink back into the words he offers now. Maybe he does understand.

"It has been fast," I say. "It's all been so fast."

Jeremy crosses the store and wraps his arms around me. I think about how Eliza falls into John's arms. I try leaning in, seeing what it's like to let someone take the weight off me for a change.

It doesn't work. I feel like everything I'm trying to pour out just bounces off him and back to me. I hear his thoughts loud and clear, though.

"Take all the time you need," Jeremy says. "Whenever you're ready, give me a call. Don't worry about this until after everything's settled with your parents' house."

It's all right there. He's ready to be patient. He'll let me say my goodbyes and come to grips with leaving. Then he'll drive me to Richmond and I'll see that I'm meant to be there, meant to be with him. There will be a wedding, in Eagle Valley, if I still want that. Then I'll move in with him. I'll run my online business and I can have the spare room to be my workshop until we need it for a nursery. He's got it all planned out. He's just waiting for me to see it.

Except it's not the future I want. I don't want to trade a life of living up to Eagle Valley's standards for a life of living up to Jeremy's dreams.

"I can't," I say.

Jeremy pulls back. He's angry. I feel it before I hear it in his voice and see it in his eyes.

"Then what is it?" he says. "You want time, I'm ready to wait as long as it takes. You want to think, I'm giving you something to think about."

"I'm not ready," I say.

"Not ready to move or not ready for me?"

I can't make myself answer. I'm biting the insides of my cheeks to keep from crying.

Jeremy crosses back to the front of the store and barely even glances back.

"You're going," I say. It comes out flat.

Jeremy turns and looks at me with darkened eyes. "You're the one that's not coming." His words sound biting. A perfect echo of my words during our first breakup. *You're the one that's leaving.*

"No," I say. Simple, clear. Like my heart isn't breaking down familiar fault lines. "I'm not coming."

"Well, if you ask me, you did the right thing," Eliza says.

A full twenty-four hours after my second break-up with Jeremy, and I can barely believe I'm holding strong. I barely registered anything that was said at this morning's meeting. If anyone mentioned the meeting on Saturday, I didn't even notice. I was too busy avoiding looks from Miss Paula and trying not to think about Jeremy.

I spilled it all to Eliza the second she pulled up to Mama and Daddy's house. Ex-house.

"Jeremy just wanted different things from you," Eliza continues. "I don't blame either of you for having a hard time letting go. You just didn't have what it took to make it long-term."

I know she can't help it, but the wedding ring flashing on her left hand isn't making me feel better. "Thanks a lot."

"I mean... You know what I mean. I'm sorry, Arden. I really am."

"Let's just do this," I say, opening the screen door to the kitchen. I can feel Eliza weighing her words, deciding, finally, to drop the subject. I'm grateful.

Eliza has a memo pad and a pen. Always prepared, that one. "Okay. Kitchen," she says. "Anything you want to keep in here?"

I shake my head. "Avocado green isn't really my color."

Eliza giggles. "Really? No seventies throwbacks for you?"

"No, really. You can have them."

"Actually, the estate sale can have them," Eliza says. "Okay. Next: dining room."

"You want Grandmother's china, right? And the silver?"

"If it's okay with you," Eliza says. "And you can borrow it whenever you want."

"For all those fancy dinner parties I throw?" As soon as it's out of my mouth, I think back to talking with Jeremy last week. Was it only last week we were joking about dinner parties and life together?

Eliza registers the look on my face. "Are you okay, Arden?"

"Yeah," I say. "Come on. Let's get it packed up."

It's mechanical after a time. We pack up the china with a foam protector in between each plate. Mama would be proud. The silver is still in the felt-lined box, neat and orderly like little tin soldiers. Eliza declines to take the glassware. I don't want it, either. No matter how well they've been washed, I feel strange drinking out of glasses that have been used hundreds of times before.

Neither of us wants any of the front parlor furniture. Family history or not, it's too uncomfortable to keep. The family room is all utilitarian. Nothing really valuable, except for the memories. We each take an armful of quilts and afghans that Mama kept on the quilt rack. These quilts are full of good memories–some of our best. When I was little, I used to dig my fingers through the loose knit of the afghan and remember the stories Daddy had told the night before. The basket quilt is the biggest, and it was the best for building forts. The Flying Geese quilt is starting to wear through along the edges. It was never that pretty–it was made from scraps of curtain and upholstery fabric–but it's nice and warm. Mama and Lila Beth used to spread it out on the porch and play cards.

"Maybe Lila Beth wants some of these," I say uncertainly. "I'll text her."

"If it makes you feel better," Eliza says. She watches while I tap out a short message. If she notices that I hold a tissue over the keys while I type, she doesn't mention it.

The stairs sound hollow under our feet when we make our way up to the second floor. We both pass by Mama and Daddy's room. Their bedroom looks bare with the bed and dresser gone.

"Anything in here?" Eliza asks, peering down the hallway to where our rooms used to be. Lila Beth's and Eliza's were both converted into guest rooms, even though we don't know many people outside of town. My old room is kind of a storage room now. It was the nursery for all four of us kids. It's not really big enough to be anything else, but by the time I came along, we were out of other bedrooms. I didn't mind. I always thought it was a cozy little spot, nestled in between two eaves.

I put a hand out and touch the rose-covered wallpaper. One of my first memories is Mama changing out this wallpaper. It had been yellow ducks since before Tripp was born. I could feel in every seam how it hurt Mama to take it down. But I had wanted a big girl room, like my sisters, and she made it happen. For me.

"Arden?" Eliza asks.

"Just remembering," I say.

Everything we didn't have room for in the rest of the house is stacked neatly in this room. When I moved out, Mama took up knitting for a time before Daddy started to go downhill. There are three baskets of yarn and knitting needles in the corner.

"I wonder why she didn't take those with her," Eliza says.

"I don't think she liked knitting as much as she thought she would," I say. There are more unspoken cusswords on those knitting needles than almost anything else in the house.

Tripp's memory box is gone, I notice. Of course they took that. The little dining set that belonged to Mama's parents is gone too. Now that I think of it, I remember seeing it in their new apartment.

"Arden?" Eliza asks gently. "Do you want anything?"

I take one last, long drink of the room—my room—before I turn and flick off the light. "No," I tell her. "Nothing."

Outside, the wind is starting to whip up. I guess the developers will mow over the Christmas trees. Mama didn't lease out the tree farm to anyone else to tend this year. They were leaving, and there was no money for it, anyway. Maybe someone will think to cut down some of the good ones and use them for Christmas. It'd be nice for someone to enjoy the farm, one last time.

We take a peek into the barn. It still smells like pine. In the corner of the barn, I see the table where Daddy and I sat just a week ago when we moved them out. Past the table is the green trashcan that held all of Daddy's blocks of wood. It's nearly half full.

"Wait," I say, stopping Eliza in her tracks. "I want something."

"What is it?" she asks. She follows my gaze to the wood. "Oh, Arden."

I dig both hands into the bin and pull out block after block. In some of them, I can feel clear handprints of Daddy's from when he was younger and stronger and tackled the world head-on. When a tree didn't sell, he'd chop it up. This side of the barn almost always had pieces of white pine left to dry for months, even years. He had enough pieces of dried wood to keep him busy woodcarving through retirement, if he'd ever had one.

"Arden," Eliza says. She's hovering, trying not to touch my shoulder or pull me away. "Arden. Talk to me, please."

"This is what I want."

"Some of Daddy's wood blocks? That's sweet, honey. He'd love that."

"All of them."

Eliza looks doubtful. "All of them? It's a big can..." She stops herself. "I'll help you carry them."

It takes a long time and a lot of shuffling for us to ease the can out of the barn and out to my truck. I use my bungee cords to fasten the lid of the can on top and more cords to fix the can in the bed of my truck.

"I think I have a splinter," Eliza says, examining her hands.

"Where?" I ask, but Eliza is already bushing her hands together.

"It's just a tiny one. I'll take care of it when I get home." She looks at me instead. "Are you okay? Need anything else?"

"No," I say. "I don't even know what I'm going to do with all this."

"You're going to make something," Eliza says matter-of-factly. "You have that look on your face."

"What look?"

"The one you get when you're about to spend all day at the craft table. Remember the paper dolls you used to make?"

"I did?"

"You were really little. Every so often, Mama would ask if anyone had seen you, and you'd be off in a corner somewhere, drawing."

"Really?" I wonder why I don't remember this.

"You made little clothes for your stuffed animals, too. Remember? You had the best dressed teddy bears in Eagle Valley."

"That's right," I say. "I do remember that."

"You've always been so artistic," Eliza says. "I can't draw my way out of a box, and Lila Beth can't either. You were always making something." She turns and looks back up at the house. "This is it," she says.

A cold, sharp wind shakes the branches of Tripp's dogwood tree. It stings my cheeks and makes Eliza pull her jacket collar up. "We should go," I say, and she nods.

I drop everything off at home before going back to town to get Thor. It takes longer than I want to hoist the can down the basement stairs. Feels anticlimactic, huffing and puffing and slamming the can into the corner of my workspace. I'll revisit those memories later. For now, I've got to get my dog.

Cliff is giving Thor a good belly rub when I come in. "Well, he sure looks like he missed me," I say. "Did he even notice I was gone?"

"Course he did!" says Golda from behind the counter.

"Until she fed him," says Cliff. Thor finally notices me and gets up to greet me. He takes a good whiff of my jeans and boots. I smell like pine. That dog is going to be attached to me all night.

"How are you holding up?" asks Golda with a sympathetic grimace.

"Can't complain," I say.

"No, really," Golda says. "How are you?"

I guess she's in the mood to hear complaints. "Wouldn't mind some warmer weather," I say. "Eliza and I about froze to death towards the end."

"Sure, sure," says Golda. "Want some dinner?" She's already cutting slices of potato bread for my favorite tomato and avocado sandwich.

"How's the store?" Cliff asks, taking a long, noisy slurp from his coffee. I'm guessing it's not his first dose of caffeine today. He gets pretty worn down as Festival goes on. Dealing with tourists takes a lot out of him.

"It's all right." I decide to come out with it. "I'll probably be closing up shop before the end of the year. November, actually."

There is actual shock on both Cliff and Golda's faces.

"Why?" asks Golda. Her hands are hovering in mid-air over the tomatoes.

Somehow it was easier telling Bryson and Mama, even Janie. I don't know if I'm ready to deal with questions yet. Should've thought about that before I went and opened my mouth.

"The online business is really just doing better," I say. "Running the store is... not as good for sales as the Internet has been lately."

Cliff seems to accept this. "They say that's how things are going," he says. "Everything online, easier to get it shipped to you than to pay for the gas to run around searching for what you want."

"And you'll still be around," Golda says. "You've got that nice house all fixed up and Thor to keep you on your toes. It might even be kind of relaxing to take a break from keeping up a storefront. Less drama, that's for sure."

"We'll see," I say. "Maybe I'll end up moving or maybe I'll stay."

"I hope you don't have to move," says Golda, cutting chunks of tomato and piling them on top of the avocado. "I hope there's a way you can stay."

"We'll see what happens."

Golda wraps up the sandwich in a wilted wax paper bag. I try to pay, and she waves me off.

"Don't let them run you out," says Golda. "That's all I got to say. You don't have to go anywhere."

22

I may not have been in the loop about Saturday night's Historical Society meeting, but I hear tell of it all over town. Not everybody went. Golda and Cliff didn't, and Russ stayed away too, to Felicia's dismay. Miranda and Gordon Johns were there, and so was Felicia. It was evenly split.

Truth is, a lot of people like Eagle Valley–love it, even. But people these days don't have money to buy a farm just to keep an unspoiled view. Not the Main Street store owners, not the townspeople, and not the visitors.

The Society came up with a couple last-ditch ideas, not that they'll do any good. Miss Paula promised to host a big gala on Halloween if they were able to raise the rest of the money. Now that Mama and Daddy won't be hosting their Eagle Valley Legends gala, I guess Miss Paula feels like she needs to fill the gap. I wonder what she'll do instead if they can't raise the funds. When they can't raise the funds.

They're going to drum up donation attempts, too. They vetoed adding "Save Eagle Valley" coin jars to the counters of stores on Main Street–too tacky–but store owners are now invited to ask, "Would you like to add a donation to the Save Eagle Valley fund?" after every transaction. During the Jitterbug and Jive, they'll pass the hat a few times, discreetly, of course.

They also voted unanimously for cracking down on Main Street store owners and collecting fines for infractions. That means my letter came, Tuesday morning, right into my post office box.

Dear Eagle Valley Main Street Shop Owner,

As a representative of the Eagle Valley Historical Society, it is my duty to inform you that you have been found non-compliant with the following Eagle Valley Historic District Ordinances, to wit:

Section 5, Article 1 *All businesses on the Eagle Valley Historic Main Street shall uphold the mission and purpose of the Eagle Valley Living History Days through participation in events as directed by the Society.*

Section 5, Article 2 *No business on the Eagle Valley Historic Main Street shall engage in advertisement, lobbying, or other support of businesses, events, or causes that are not specifically endorsed by the Eagle Valley Historical Society.*

Eagle Valley's Historic District is a precious reminder of Virginia's rich heritage and historic significance. As a shop owner on our Historic Main Street, your compliance with all Historic District and Town ordinances are essential to maintaining our historic integrity and public dignity.

As noted in our previous communication, your continued disregard for Historical Society ordinances will result in fines of no less than $500 per infraction, to be donated to the Eagle Valley Historical Society fund for the continued maintenance and beautification of our historic district. Your immediate donation of $1,000 would be appreciated.

Sincerely,
Paula Abernathy

I keep the letter folded up in my coat pocket. A thousand dollars. I expected this, even played it up myself. Hadn't I refused to put out Miss Paula's brochures? Hadn't I decided to pass out postcards for the estate sale? I know those ordinances as well as anybody.

It's not that I didn't know it was coming. It's just worse, now that this hovering future has closed in. All day, I think about how to balance the budget. If I sell this dining set plus the dishware, I can get that much money. If I sell everything on this shelf or everything in the vignette with the bedroom set, that could cover it.

It won't happen that way. It's been too long since I've had a big sale, and I'm already stretched thin just from paying the rent for the store. I'll have to pay the fine from my own money.

One thing is sure–Miss Paula might appreciate my immediate payment, but I'm pretty sure I have thirty days to pay. On lunch break, I get my copy of Eagle Valley Historical Society ordinances.

When I get back home after work, I unfold the letter and leave it on my entry table. I'm not doing anything about that just yet. I need some time to think.

What I need, actually, is time to clean. Everywhere I go in this house, I can feel leftover stories of Jeremy. There are my handprints on the counter or the wall where I tried to steady my sweating palms while we talked on the phone. There's the section of the floor I paced up and down when I was waiting for Jeremy to call me back. And there's the millions of places where I remembered and relived the moments when Jeremy kissed me one more time. One last time.

Thor is lying in his dog bed, for once. It's the only place safe from me once I start scrubbing and washing. Half an hour of swishing the mop over the wood floors, and I'm rid of the footsteps I made when I first came home after breaking up with Jeremy the second time. I practically wear the protective coating off my phone from cleaning off memories of our every conversation.

When I'm done, my knuckles are cracked and bleeding, and my knees are raw. Still, my mind keeps replaying our last conversation, our last kiss, how he saw me the last time. I did the right thing by breaking it off. I know I did. Trouble is, I can't scrub him straight out of my heart.

Thor is concerned. He's mincing across the clean floors, following me through the house.

"Things are going to change around here, Thor," I tell him. "Think you can handle me working from home?"

Thor rubs the top of his head on my leg.

"We'll hang out all day. I can let you outside to play whenever you want."

Even the word 'outside' isn't cheering him up.

"It'll be all right," I tell him reassuringly. "I promise I'll do something besides clean. I'll be online more, but you don't mind that, do you? Snuggling with me while I do some work?"

Thor looks a little happier at that.

"I'll cheer up. Come on. Let's go make something."

It's funny how trying to act happier can actually make me feel a little happier. In the basement, my workbench is covered with paints and scrap pieces of plywood and paper. I already feel better.

Eliza is right. I did spend a lot of time doing arts and crafts when I was little. I remember the watercolor paintings I did when I was seven, the origami phase I went through in middle school, and the constant drawing and doodling. Why did I stop? How did I get so caught up in retelling other peoples' stories that I forgot to tell mine?

I still don't know what I'm going to do with the wood I collected yesterday. It's still standing in the corner, scenting the air with a homey pine scent. For a minute, I think about digging through, finding more pieces that tell the story of my father when he was younger and stronger. Happier.

Instead, I reach for a pack of my air-dry clay. Usually, I take little pieces of it to repair a broken teacup handle or fill in a spot on a vase. The last time I used it, I had to make a new nose for a porcelain man, sitting on a bookend. I take out the whole block of clay, unwrap it and work it with my hands.

It feels almost greedy, using all-new materials instead of reusing and refurbishing. The clay feels smooth and clean against my skin. I knead it until all the bubbles are out and every bit of it sounds like me.

It's an eagle. Not the same tall, imposing eagle that's painted over the town's welcome sign. It's a new one, smaller, with a perfectly shaped beak and large eyes. Its wings are spread out, like it's just landed or is just about to take off. I use the eye of a darning needle to press each feather, working around and around until both wings are covered.

I perch the bird on a dowel rod and a crumpled paper towel to dry. It's a little better than an amateur attempt. I haven't sculpted anything like this for years. Since high school, maybe. The neck is a little long for an eagle, and the head is too flat. I like it. With some practice, I could get better. Maybe a lot better.

When the store closes, I'll have to move everything I haven't sold into this basement. It's going to be crowded down here for awhile. Maybe I can take some of the larger pieces to Bryson and have him sell them for me. I'd have to give him a cut of the commission, but it's better than trying to sell big pieces of furniture online. Everyone wants stuff like that delivered, and it's a hassle to drive and a bigger hassle to ship.

I make myself focus on the one good premonition I had. Thor and me, driving down the road, free and ready to take on the world. It can happen. It's going to happen. I just have to believe it.

I think back on the letter, and what I found in the town ordinances. I know exactly what I have to do.

Miss Paula looks startled to see me in person. I'm sure I don't look too friendly, myself.

"Arden," she says. "Can I assume you've brought your donation?"

"You can assume I have a question about your letter," I say flatly.

Miss Paula half-smiles. "I think the letter very clearly states our position on the town ordinances…"

"It left out some important points," I say. "For example, I think you'll find that my meeting attendance was directly impacted by the Historical Society's failure to notify all business owners in time."

Miss Paula's brow furrows. She wasn't expecting that one. "I don't think the letter said anything about missing a meeting. The first one did, but not the second."

"Why wasn't I informed of the meeting?" I ask.

"We assumed you wouldn't be interested."

"I see," I say. "But doesn't that conflict with the Eagle Valley ordinances? Shouldn't every Main Street store owner be given due notice of every meeting?"

"Well," Miss Paula says, licking her lips nervously. "Under most circumstances, of course. However, I'm sure you'll agree that..."

"Section 4, Article 2, Subsection B," I recite. "*All business owners on the Eagle Valley Historic Main Street shall be given reasonable notice and expectation to attend all Historical Society meetings.*"

Miss Paula looks startled. "And you'll notice that we didn't fine you for missing a meeting because you–" She catches herself, realizing what's happening as she says the words. "Because you weren't notified."

"No, I wasn't," I say. "When can I expect to be notified of the next Historical Society meeting? I'd like the opportunity to present my grievance to the board and file for appropriate compensation."

"Arden," Miss Paula says. She suddenly looks smaller and older than I remember. "Arden. Please. This town has been through so much. Why are you pulling this now?"

I grit my teeth at that. "I'm not pulling anything. I just want the opportunity to be compensated by the Historical Society for this oversight."

Miss Paula sighs, long and low. "Okay. We can admit that we both made mistakes. If you'll drop the issue of the meeting, I can drop one of the fines. Just pay $500 instead of $1,000."

She's negotiating. She knows how I hate to haggle, but on the flip side, I know how much she loves it. How much she needs it, really. That's what Bryson used to say, "Some people feel like they need a special deal, just for them." That's Miss Paula right there.

"No. I'm sure if it was brought to the board, I'd be compensated more than that. What does it say about our town if we..."

"All right!" Miss Paula says. "Fine! You don't have to pay. Forget the whole thing ever happened." She's working herself into a fury. I can feel my heartbeat racing now. I can make it better if I apologize. Soften my tone, say I overreacted, and say I want to leave on good terms.

"I'd like it in writing," I say instead.

Miss Paula pecks at her keyboard like she's going to break it. In a few minutes, I hear her old printer starting up. And there it is, on official Eagle Valley letterhead. Arden McCrae can please disregard the previous two letters. The issue has been resolved and the letters were sent in error.

"Thank you," I say. *This could be my last conversation with her,* I think. If I move away, it probably will be. This month has been so strange, trying to interact with Miss Paula as anything other than "Mama's best friend." I try to picture her as a young divorcee, coming back to Eagle Valley to start fresh. How much she's poured into this town, lived through it, even.

"I may not have said this before," Miss Paula says. In a personal, not professional, voice. "I truly am sorry for your father's illness."

I wait to see if there's more to that apology. There isn't. "Thank you."

"I've heard some talk around town that you'll be closing your store," Miss Paula says. "Are you planning to move closer to your parents?"

"I'm not sure yet," I say. "I'm going to concentrate on my online business for a while."

That surprises Miss Paula. There goes her easy explanation: *Of course Arden had to close the store. Her father is very ill. I'm sure she wants to spend as much time with them as possible.*

"Well," she says finally. "I certainly wish you all the best."

I try to see her as the woman that came back to Eagle Valley, broken and looking for something to make her whole again. The woman that's scared of losing it all again, having to start over and find a new passion. The woman that's hurting.

"You too, Miss Paula," I say softly. "I hope you find what you're looking for."

I walk down Main Street and turn towards home while the wind whips all around me. *The winds of change,* I think, like a romantic.

I've had more premonitions in the last month than I have in a long time. Years, probably. I hope they're slowing down now. There've been enough changes to knock us all in a tizzy for a while. It'll take some time before we settle out again. But settle we will. There will be new routines, new traditions.

There's just one more change I need to make. When I get home, I open up my computer and type out an e-mail.

Dear Lila Beth,

A lot of things have changed since I e-mailed you last. Eliza and I went through the house and took everything we thought should be kept in the family. I saved some of the quilts and afghans for you. Did you get my text? Soon we'll have to help Bryson and his crew with tagging everything. The estate sale is Halloween weekend.

Mama and Daddy are pretty well settled in to their new place. I've been to see them. I think I told you about that. I can't get away as much now because I need to wrap up my sales at the store. I'm going to be closing my storefront and focusing on the online business. Jeremy and I aren't together anymore, either.

Hope you're doing well up there in D.C. Sure do miss you.

Love,

Arden

23

The last weekend of Festival is devoted to World War
II. It's my favorite.   Everyone turns out for the Saturday Night Jitterbug and Jive. The elders, the ones
who remember, come dressed to the nines and preen at
the front tables. Our town's one surviving World War
II veteran, Mr. Toms, wears his uniform every year
without fail.

A girl from the high school choir is dressed in perfect costume, down to the pin curls and liquid stock-
ings. She opens with a charming rendition of "The
White Cliffs of Dover" as the lights dim.

When she's done, the audience bursts into applause. The girl nods and curtsies. She knows she's good. Miss Paula practically has to push her off the stage.

"Good evening, and welcome to Eagle Valley's Jitterbug and Jive!" Miss Paula beams, and everyone applauds again. She introduces a long list of people that have been just indispensable this evening, just really top-notch. The high school marching band, the high school choir, the Eagle Valley floral society for the beautiful arrangements, and the Eagle Valley Presbyterian Women for their help with set-up and clean-up. People start clearing their throats and shifting a little in their seats as the list starts dragging on.

"As always, we're collecting for the Wounded Warriors Project at the door. And please, don't forget to make a donation to our town's special fundraising event this year. Help us keep Eagle Valley as a historic preservation site!"

Last year—actually, the last five years—donations from the Jitterbug and Jive were all sent to the Wounded Warriors Project. Feels tasteless to be splitting proceeds this year. By the weight of the silence in the room, I'm guessing I'm not the only one who thinks so.

Miss Paula thanks us again and the music starts up. The choir girl who opened is back with two other girls and a guy on trumpet to sing "Boogie Woogie Bugle Boy of Company B."

It takes about two minutes before Mr. Toms eases himself to a full stand and puts out a hand for his wife. He always likes to start out the dancing, and as much as Mrs. Toms blushes and mumbles about it, I don't think she minds the attention one bit. Everyone takes the cue to make their way out to the dance floor, except the seniors with troublesome hip replacements and the single people. Like me.

Last year, Jeremy actually came and danced with me. Nothing fancy, but he could do a respectable East Coast swing. I remember focusing on each step: triple step, triple step, rock step, triple step, triple step. Then I couldn't help but focus on Jeremy's hand on the small of my back, and the strong feeling of his left hand enclosing my right.

He was imagining us dancing years later–just like I was. Only in his imagination, we were in a big ball-room in New York, listening to a live band, not some small-town high school choir. We were living the life. On top of the world.

I'd stumbled, and Jeremy laughed. I remember him thinking I was nervous, thinking about how much he liked me. I was nervous because I was hoping he'd never stop.

This year, I have nothing to do but watch the seniors dancing toward the front edge of the snap-together tiles of parquet floor. The music segues into a recording of "It's Been a Long, Long Time." For a second, I wonder if someone's altering the track just to mock me.

Mr. and Mrs. Toms are planted front and center. They're barely keeping time with the music, but they're swaying and rock stepping with their eyes locked on each other. My parents will never dance like that. I can't even imagine what Daddy will be like a year from now. Will he remember Mama's name? Remember that she's his wife?

I'm starting to wish I hadn't come. The other non-dancers are chatting easily at their tables or circling the buffet for appetizers. Everyone is conveniently too involved in other conversations to be the first one to talk to me, the only McCrae that had the nerve to show up. I wonder if it would cause more talk to slip out now or stay until the end.

"You call this a party?" asks a voice behind me.

It's Lila Beth.

I'm so surprised to see her that it takes me a full thirty seconds before I jump up to say hi. She gives me the air-hug she's become accustomed to since the disastrous trip to D.C.

"When did you get in?" I ask and immediately wish I'd started with everything else I'm thinking. *I'm so glad you're here. I missed you. How long are you staying?*

"A few hours ago," she says. "I started driving this morning. I checked in on Mama and Daddy first, but Daddy's sleeping, and when you didn't pick up your cell, I figured you were here."

"I'm so glad you came," I manage. Lila Beth looks surprised and pleased.

"I took the week off work." She pauses, like she's a little embarrassed. "I came to help you and Eliza with the tagging for the estate sale."

"Stay with me," I say so impulsively that we both stop to see if I mean it. "Please. I have a guest room that's almost never been used, and it'll be easier on you than staying all the way out in Roanoke."

"I don't want to trouble you," she says hesitantly.

"No trouble."

"Thank you," Lila Beth says a little formally.

I take a last sip of sweet tea–too much lemon, not enough sugar–and get my clutch. "Let's head on home then," I say. "I've been here long enough."

Lila Beth needs no convincing. She hasn't even taken off her jacket since she came in.

"Donate to save Eagle Valley?" asks a bright-eyed teenager by the door. "Help keep Eagle Valley a historic preservation site."

"I'm a little busy trying to preserve my parents," Lila Beth says crisply, ushering me out the door.

It's good to have Lila Beth back.

Outside, people are already preparing for the ghost tour. Lila Beth stops dead for a minute when she hears the first mournful cries, "My son, my son, come back to me."

The ghost story for this weekend is one of the worst. It's the story of Mrs. Underbridge. Back during the war, she started calling out her son's name at the oddest times. Middle of the night, during breakfast, on her way to the store. She'd turn white, look into the distance, and call out to her son. Doctors were called. Neighbors and friends were concerned. Everyone assured her that the war was nearly over, the boys would be home soon, and then her son would be back to her.

Nothing worked. For two weeks Mrs. Underbridge grew more erratic, claiming to see her son all over town. She disappeared for good on the day the telegram arrived. Her son had died two weeks before—the first time Mrs. Underbridge cried his name.

Lila Beth gives an involuntary shiver. She bumps elbows with me, jerks away and quickly mutters, "Sorry!"

"It's okay," I tell her. It's enough. She's remembering the same thing I am.

The only fight I ever remember Mama and Miss Paula having—before now, anyway—is about that ghost story. Eliza and Lila Beth were at home still, and we'd all been in the kitchen folding pamphlets and tearing tickets for the next Festival weekend. I guess I was about seven or eight, which would've made my sisters in their teens.

Miss Paula had come by, as usual, blustering on about the last-minute calamities that had dropped in her lap.

The woman assigned to play Mrs. Underbridge on the ghost tour caught bronchitis, and Miss Paula was hunting up substitutes. I wasn't really listening, but I saw Lila Beth stop folding and Eliza blink her eyes at me and glance upstairs. We quietly drifted upstairs when Mama and Miss Paula started to fight in the kitchen.

Lila Beth had started talking about something loudly–asking me if I wanted to play Barbies with her, I think. Definitely a sign she was trying to distract me. I could still hear some of the things being said downstairs.

"How can you even ask me to play that part?" Mama had said.

"Dottie, it's just a ghost story. The town needs you."

"The town does not need me. You need me to make your ghost tour a success."

"And you're my best friend. You've walked right beside me through every part of restoring Eagle Valley, from starting Festival to revitalizing Main Street. I need you again. Please."

"If you were the friend I thought you were, you never would have asked. Not for that."

Lila Beth and Eliza had both started talking then, each trying to be louder and more cheerful than the other. I'm not sure exactly how that argument got resolved. Miss Paula left, and Mama went to her room for a long time before emerging to get dinner ready. None of us ever mentioned it. If I recall right, Miss Paula played the role of Mrs. Underbridge herself, and the next time we saw her, it seemed like nothing had happened. At any rate, if there was anything going on, I wasn't listening. After all, what kid wants to get mixed up in their parents' business?

At first, having Lila Beth stay is like having an extra-polite houseguest. She asks for a glass of water, whether it's okay to turn down the volume on the TV, and if she can help set the table for dinner. Thor is the only one who seems oblivious to the awkwardness. On her first night, he finds the Italian loafers she kicked off and gnaws on them with delight. For her sake, I'm horrified and offer to pay for them. For my sake, she says of course not and pretends not to care.

Our first real conversation doesn't come until after dinner. "Daddy's changed a lot since Easter," Lila Beth says.

I nod.

"I know you tried to tell me in your e-mails," she says. That's Lila Beth all over, just diving right into a conversation like that. "I really wasn't expecting him to be so different. I thought Alzheimer's took years."

"Everybody's different, I guess," I say. "It happened kind of fast and kind of slow at the same time. Like we didn't notice from one day to the next, but then suddenly it just seems like everything's different."

"And the house?" she asks. "How long did you know about that?"

"Mama just told me right before Festival started," I say. "All at once. They got a spot at the assisted living place, they found a buyer for the house, and they were moving out by the middle of October."

"That's Mama," says Lila Beth. I look at her questioningly. "It's just like her to take charge like that," she explains. "She sees a problem and she's got it handled before anyone else even notices something's wrong."

"I like that about her," I say.

"I didn't mean it as a bad thing."

Thor comes into the room, dragging his half-chewed bone and depositing it at Lila Beth's feet. She picks it up between two fingers and flings it gently across the room. Thor bounds after it and brings it back. This time, he spits it right into her lap.

"Thor," I say. "Come on. Play with me. Auntie Lila Beth has had a long day."

"He's just making friends," says Lila Beth. "We could go outside and throw it around. I don't want him tearing up your house while we play."

I decide not to explain about the chewed-up living room, since there's not much to explain anyway. We go out on the front porch, and Lila Beth alternates between throwing the bone and his tennis ball into the yard. Thor is so happy he's snorting and drooling as he runs.

Lila Beth looks around. I'm sure she's mentally comparing it to the way it looked last Easter when she dropped by for a short, tense visit. "So I see you painted the house. What color do you call this? Purple? Gray?"

"Lilac," I say.

She nods. "It's pretty. Different."

"Thanks. When I did it, I kind of expected there to be more of a reaction. Russ— you remember Russ, from the hardware store—he wasn't too keen on it. But then the farm sold and I guess that took up everyone's attention."

"A lot's changed," Lila Beth says. "More than I thought. So what's next for you?"

I seem to be destined to have all my what–happens–next conversations on this porch. "I'm not sure," I say. "I can keep the Internet shop running for a bit, pour some more energy into that and see if it'll be enough."

"Your Main Street store is really closing?"

"Really," I tell her.

"Just because of the farm selling?" Lila Beth asks. "I saw Paula's campaign everywhere, but I can't believe she shut you down."

"She didn't shut me down," I say. "It was more like the straw that broke the camel's back. Everyone on Main Street's been struggling the last few years."

"Wow," Lila Beth says. "I never thought of Eagle Valley being hit by the recession, exactly."

"Believe it," I say.

Lila Beth shakes her head. Thor brings his tennis ball back to her and drops it on her foot. She throws the ball and his bone at the same time, sending him running in a frenzy of excitement.

"I think I'll have another store someday," I say. "Not here, but maybe down at Bryson and Sadie's place. I might rent this house out, get something closer to Roanoke. Get a little extra income that way."

"You're thinking of moving?" she asks. She says it like I'd suggested moving to the moon.

"It's a possibility."

Lila Beth still looks shocked, but I have to give her credit for trying to recover. "Who's going to rent a purple house?"

"Lilac." I grin. "Someone who likes to be a little different, I suppose."

Thor brings back the ball and she tosses it gently, letting it bounce across the front yard. Thor tears after it.

She shakes her head. "I guess I just never thought of you leaving Eagle Valley."

The memory of our failed trip to D.C. hangs between us. We both look towards Thor, watch him trying to pick up the bone and the tennis ball at the same time.

"I've always felt bad about what happened when we went on that trip," says Lila Beth.

I feel the heat rising to my face. "It's not your fault."

"I always thought you were the way you were because Mama and Daddy sheltered you," Lila Beth says. "Giving in to you on the touching thing and growing up in this tiny town. I guess I just thought if I got you out for a bit, let you into the real world, it wouldn't scare you so much."

"I agreed to go," I remind her. "I wanted to give it a try."

"I pushed you," Lila Beth corrects me.

"You were trying to help," I say. My face is on fire, thinking about how everyone stared at me in the restaurant, and how Lila Beth had to turn around and drive me all the way back to Eagle Valley. "I always felt bad that I ruined the trip."

Lila Beth sighs. "I hate to say it," she says. "But that was the first time I really understood that you couldn't help it."

I decide to let Lila Beth downstairs to see my workspace. She looks impressed with some of the jewelry, and then I show her the wood I collected from the barn.

"What are you going to make out of these?" she asks.

"I don't know yet," I say. Then I show her the little eagle I made out of clay. He's dried now, and I can see every mistake even better now that a few days have passed.

"It's perfect," Lila Beth breathes. Normally I'd let something like that go. I'd assume it was an exaggeration, just a compliment to be nice. But with Lila Beth, I have to know for sure. I reach over and brush her arm lightly with just my fingertips.

She means it. She thinks it's perfect, and she's amazed that I can do that with just my hands and some tools. The feathers look so real, and his wings look ready to take off in flight. She's impressed, all right.

Lila Beth looks over to me when I pull my hand back. "I didn't know you could do that," she says. "Are you...getting better?"

I shrug. "Some days are better than others," I say. Which is true no matter who you are. Lila Beth might understand my business and my art and maybe even my whatever-that-was with Jeremy, but no way is she going to understand that I hear things by touch.

Lila Beth looks back to the eagle. "Are you going to make more?" she asks.

"Maybe later," I say. "We should get to bed if we're going to help Bryson with the tagging tomorrow."

24

Eliza meets Lila Beth and I at the farmhouse on Monday morning. Bryson's already there with his sons, tagging and pricing. I brought three thermoses of hot coffee. If my premonition last night is right, we'll need it.

"Thanks, Arden!" Eliza says extra cheerfully. She takes a thermos and takes a big, long gulp, probably scalding her tongue. Then she turns. "Hello, Lila Beth."

If the frost hadn't already come, it would have from the chill Eliza's giving off.

"Hey, Eliza," Lila Beth says. "How are the boys?"

"They're fine," Eliza says. I can feel the tension bubbling, like magma beneath a volcano.

"Let's get inside," I say. "I don't want to leave Thor with Golda all day."

We walk single-file through the kitchen and down the hall to the family room. Eliza passes out copies of the pricing sheet Bryson drew up and a roll of stickers. Lila Beth takes out three coasters for our coffees. Got to save the to-be-sold furniture from drink rings, I guess.

Once we start working, the only sounds are from Eliza ruffling the pages of the pricing sheet and Lila Beth's marker squeaking as it marks the price tags. I feel like I'm about to crawl straight out of my skin.

"Daddy used to love these," Eliza says, running her hands along a row of Tom Clancy books. She sighs a little melodramatically as she fixes a sticker on each spine.

The silence is broken. "How much should I price this for?" Lila Beth asks. She's been working through the furniture, and she's stopped at Daddy's recliner. It's well-worn, and it looks it.

I take a glance down the pricing sheet. "Does that count as good condition?" I ask. "Or fair?"

"Daddy would say it was perfect," Eliza says.

"He'd have said it was priceless!" I add.

"Stop doing that," Lila Beth says suddenly. We both turn to her.

"Stop doing what?" asks Eliza.

"Talking about him like he's dead," says Lila Beth. "He's sick, not dead."

"Have you even seen him yet?" Eliza asks. If eyes could shoot daggers, Lila Beth would be in trouble.

"I stopped by Mama and Daddy's first," Lila Beth says coolly, "and then I came to Eagle Valley."

"I just don't think you can waltz in here..." Eliza starts.

"Nobody's waltzing, and we need to keep pricing," I say.

It's just as well Bryson picks this moment to pop in. "How's it coming in here, girls?"

"Fine," we say in a chorus. Same voice, three totally different tones.

"Dang, if you three ain't sisters." Bryson chuckles and moves on to the next room.

Our family might not be the chattiest, but when there's dead silence, there's trouble. Eliza smacks stickers on the rest of the books. Lila Beth rifles through the pages of Bryson's price list, but I doubt she's really reading anything.

"Y'all want to talk this out?" I ask.

"Stay out of it, Arden," says Lila Beth.

"Don't snap at her!" snaps Eliza.

"The both of you are driving me nuts," I say severely. "Can we please just drop it? Whatever it is?"

Of course I know what it is. The whole Commonwealth of Virginia could probably tell, if they could see the looks my sisters are shooting at each other. Hearing the stories they leave in their wake just gives it a little extra punch.

Eliza stepped into the big-sister role when Lila Beth took up and left for D.C., and she's not about to go back to being the middle child, not now when Lila Beth decides to show up at the eleventh hour. Lila Beth would just like a certain someone to see the irony in being annoyed that she's not around much if they just wish she'd leave. I make up an excuse to start scrubbing at the furniture with Clorox wipes. Nobody's going to want to buy this stuff if it's been angried all over by my sisters.

"I'm going to see Mama and Daddy on my way back," Eliza says. "Anybody want to come?" Her tone is a little warmer, a little sheepish. She's still mad as all get out, but she's decided to be the bigger person. For now.

"I can head in. Arden?"

"I'll come, but I can't bring Thor. I'll have to be quick."

"Let's split up so we can finish early, then," Eliza says, and we're all grateful for an excuse to scatter to different rooms of the house and tag in peace.

Mama looks like we could knock her over with a feather when the three of us show up. "Well, if it isn't my girls," she says. "All my girls. Come on in. Anything to drink?"

Sweet tea, we answer. After the morning we've had, we could all use some sweetening up.

Daddy is in the living room section of the apartment, rifling through his crossword puzzles. He picks one up and flips through the pages, licking his fingers to turn the page every so often. After awhile, he puts it down and picks up another.

There was a time when Daddy would spend every Sunday morning doing the crossword in the paper. When he started to go, Mama bought him books of crosswords to help keep his mind sharp. I haven't seen him pick up a pencil and write in a while. I'm still glad he has his books.

"Vaughn, our girls are here," Mama says a notch louder. "Won't you say hi?"

"Hey," Daddy says, glancing up. "Hey, now."

"Hey, Daddy," Eliza says. She's dropped her dukes now that we're in the room with Daddy. Gives us some perspective, I guess.

"We had a recital here in the visitor's room last night," Mama says. "A big middle school group. Reminds me of when you were in the band, Eliza."

"Were they any good?" Lila Beth asks.

Mama makes a little face. "Well, they sure tried."

"Sounds like they keep you pretty busy here," Lila Beth says. "Didn't you all have a craft night earlier this week?"

"Well, yes, but we didn't go to that. We're not too big on crafts these days."

Daddy interjects. "Hey. Hey, now! Look at this." We all stop to see what it is he's looking at. He keeps flipping through the pages.

Lila Beth clears her throat. "Speaking of crafts, you should see what Arden's been working on," Lila Beth says. "It's amazing."

Eliza turns on me. "What are you working on? Why haven't I seen it?"

"I just started it," I say. "And it's not that amazing. I'm just messing around."

"If that's what messing around looks like, you should mess around more," Lila Beth says.

"You should come by," I tell Eliza. "If you can, I mean. Lila Beth and I are just hanging out."

"I'll have to ask John if he minds taking the boys for a night," Eliza says a little stiffly. "But maybe. If I can."

"I can't tell you how nice it is to see you three together," Mama says. "Mind if I get a picture?"

We shuffle into our usual arrangement. Lila Beth and I on either end, Eliza in the middle. I can't imagine how convincing our smiles are. Since Mama is still using a film camera—she's the last holdout to switch to digital¬¬—I guess no one will know until she gets the film developed.

It doesn't take long before Daddy drifts off into a restless sleep, and Mama looks tired around the edges, too. We turn to go. Lila Beth is making arrangements with Mama to come down and visit again, so I catch Eliza by the shoulder, just as she's about to stalk off to her car. "Wait," I tell her.

The stories I catch off her sleeve could be a novel on their own. She smiles and tries to look like she's okay, but the raging jealousy almost singes my skin right off.

"Thank you," I tell her. "You've always been there for me." Even though I know she can't sense things like I do, I hope that she can hear in my voice how much I mean it. Judging by the way her shoulders loosen up, she does.

By the time we get back to Eagle Valley to pick up Thor, I'm too exhausted to think about cooking. Lila Beth orders two of Golda's personal pizzas before I have time to warn her. They're already cold by the time we get home. Figures, since Golda barely warmed them over in the convection oven. She saw a little oven like hers go up in flames once, and now she treats pizza-making like a dance with the devil.

Lila Beth still manages to finish hers, cutting it up in neat squares with a fork and knife. I pick around the edges. Golda's pizza sauce is homemade, all right, but there's enough garlic to keep vampires away for miles.

"So you're closing this weekend?" Lila Beth asks.

"Yep. I need to be all moved out before November first."

"Is somebody actually lined up to rent it next?"

"Not yet," I say. Not for a while, I happen to know. Since I've stopped hearing my own future in the store, all I've sensed lately is dust.

It's the beginning of the end Miss Paula's been so afraid of. If she'd been paying attention, she would have seen it coming long before my parents sold the farm. Festival was big this year, but not big enough.

It's nowhere near what it was when Eagle Valley first started the Living History Days.

I think back to our last conversations together. Maybe she did see it coming. Maybe that's why she's been fighting so hard.

"I'm heading down to the basement to work for a bit," I say when I can't choke down another bite of pizza. "Want to come?"

"Sure," says Lila Beth. I don't figure she'll stay long. It's cold down there, and Thor likes to hog the space heater.

I pick out some of the wood blocks from the can in the corner. The smell of pine fills the basement. I hold each one in turn, wondering what I can make from it. Waiting to see if it will tell me what it wants to be.

Lila Beth watches over my shoulder for a minute before she turns and pretends to be interested in the stock I have stacked against the wall.

"Is this most of it?" she asks. "Or do you have a lot more to move out of your shop?"

I snort. "That's barely a quarter of it. Bryson's going to take the furniture pieces for me, but anything I can haul in my pickup is going to end up here."

"And you have to be out by Saturday?"

"Yep. Halloween," I say.

Lila Beth looks around again, like she's trying to picture where everything will fit. "I'll stay and help you," she says.

"Are you sure?" I ask. "What about...work and everything?"

"Family first," Lila Beth says. She gives me a hesitant smile that looks just like Mama's.

"If you're sure you don't mind," I say. "I'd love the help."

I settle on a small, flat block of wood. I can feel Daddy's old self shining through so clearly here. I pull out his tools and whittle a rough shape, narrowing here, squaring off there.

Lila Beth watches me intently. "You do that just like Daddy did," she says.

"I hope so," I say. It's a small piece, so before I know it, I'm switching tools, carving the basic shape.

"It's a flower," Lila Beth says. "Amazing."

She watches in silence while I sand, polish, and carve little notches and divots. The final product is smooth and clean, just right to hold in the palm of a hand.

"It's a dogwood flower," Lila Beth says.

I nod. "For Daddy."

"He'll love it."

I stand up and stretch. Thor takes this as his cue to head back up the stairs, so I flick off the space heater. "Come on. Let's watch some TV before bed."

We settle into the couch, only inches between our elbows. We haven't sat that close for years. Maybe ever.

"So have you decided if you're staying here or renting it out?" Lila Beth asks.

"Both. I'll put out a for-rent sign and live here for as long as it takes to get in a good renter. Then I'll see what's best for Thor and me."

"Still thinking of Roanoke?"

"Makes sense. Most everyone I know lives there, unless they live here."

"I don't think you have to move," Lila Beth says slowly. "Not if you don't want to. Things are tense, I can see that, but people will get used to it. You've got some good friends here. You don't have to give up everything all at once."

"We'll see," I say. "Even if everybody else in town was comfortable with me staying around, I don't know if I'm comfortable here anymore. Not like I was."

"I could see that," Lila Beth says.

I look at her sideways, trying to find that note of truth that's hovering between us. "Is that why you moved away? Because you weren't happy?"

Lila Beth weaves her fingers through the loose knit of the afghan, just like I used to. "It's not that I don't think it's a nice life," says Lila Beth. "I just always knew it wasn't my kind of life. Eagle Valley just makes me feel like... I don't know. Not good enough. Like I never fit in and never will."

"But everyone loves you," I said.

"Being loved is different from belonging," says Lila Beth. "I never really belonged here."

Sometimes you can hear something your whole life, and never really listen. I always thought Lila Beth was uncomfortable here because we weren't her kind of people. Turns out, she was uncomfortable because she knew she wasn't our kind of people.

"But you like where you are now," I say.

"It's perfect for me. There's always something going on. I spend a lot of time at the museums, actually. The exhibits are always changing."

"I didn't know you liked history."

"I like it," Lila Beth says. "I wouldn't devote the whole month of October to reliving it, necessarily. But I like it."

I grin at that.

"I don't think you would like D.C., though," Lila Beth says.

My cheeks burn. "Because I'm weird," I say softly. "Because I don't like busy places and lots of people. Because—"

"Not what I meant," Lila Beth interrupts. "You're different from other people, but you're different in a good way. You do your own thing, your own way. You wouldn't like being boxed in to anything."

"Sometimes I feel like I am boxed in," I say.

"Not the way you would be in a city. Doing the 9-to-5 thing, following the crowd. Trying to fit in with what everyone else is doing."

"Because I'm weird," I say again.

"Because you're creative."

"I think that's why Jeremy and I were never going to be together. Not for long. He saw me fitting in to his life in a certain way, and I never really could."

Lila Beth's cheeks are turning pink. "I did that to you, too. I saw you as a brooding artist who needed to get away for school or to study abroad or whatever."

"You meant it in a nice way, though."

"Maybe Jeremy did, too."

I let that sink in. "Do you think I made a mistake breaking up with him?"

"No. If there's a guy for you, he needs to get you from the start. He's got to be perfect from the get-go." She gives me that half-smile again. "Doofus older sisters get more leeway."

25

Halloween dawns gray and cold. Cold enough that mothers all over town will demand that their children wear sweaters and parkas over their Halloween costumes. Cold enough that the high schoolers headed to the bonfire tonight will throw on extra wood and snuggle under layers of blankets rather than give up the tradition. Cold enough, I'm hoping, that some of Miss Paula's steaming hot rage will simmer down.

In other years—normal years—the Historical Society would be gathering in Mama and Daddy's front parlor, drinking punch and sitting on the uncomfortable but historically accurate furniture. Miss Paula would be giving long toasts about the Legends of Eagle Valley. Mr. Carson would read boring passages from letters and journals he discovered in the library. Mama would be the perfect hostess. Daddy would make as many sarcastic comments as he could while Mama raised her eyebrows at him.

This year, my parents are in Roanoke, getting bags of sugarless candy and watching a costume parade put on by the local Girl Scout troop. Daddy may or may not remember where he is or that he's there to stay. I wonder what Mama is thinking. Whether she misses the old life or if there was enough hurt at the end to make her happy to move on.

If Miss Paula's planning and scheming had worked, this year's Halloween would have been a real celebration. Today would have been the day for Eagle Valley residents to clink their glasses and toast themselves for raising enough money to buy back the land from the developer.

There is not enough money. There isn't even three-quarters as much money as they needed to get the matching grant. Miss Paula kept that poster board thermometer up in the museum window until the bitter end, but they never hit the goal. I guess a celebration's off the table. Don't know what the Historical Society will do this Halloween instead. Nurse their wounds, I suppose.

As for McCrae's Antiques, we'll be having our own kind of party. Lila Beth and Janie both promised to help me pack up, which is true friendship if I ever saw it. Eliza can't because the boys are going trick-or-treating tonight. She promises to drive up once they're in bed, if I still need help. "If not, I'll be up tomorrow morning," she says over the phone. "I'll bring some of the boys' candy. They'll have such a sugar high they won't notice if any of it's missing."

"Better yet, take the boys with you and leave me the candy," John calls over the phone, and I have to smile.

Lila Beth and I got most of the major work done yesterday and this morning. Had to do something to keep our minds off the estate sale happening just over the hill in the house that used to be our parents'. Still is, I guess, until November first. It feels strange to see cars parked in their fields and people going inside and picking off things we used to live with every day. So we don't think of it, or try not to. I spent my last Friday morning off here at the store, wrapping things in newspaper and putting aside furniture for Bryson to take with him.

The estate sale is over now. I know from the way the cars have disappeared from the fields and from the way the house has gone dark and lifeless. Bryson and his sons will be heading back to Roanoke with the truckload of things that didn't sell. They'll be back to pick up the furniture from my store. It's been a good month for business for Bryson.

As empty as I should feel about closing the storefront, I'm actually in a pretty decent mood. I got an email this morning from Sylvie Harris. She remembered me from my trip to the jewelry store weeks ago, and was asking if I had any more pieces like the ring I had sold to her. I didn't, but on a whim, I sent her some pictures of the pieces I'd made from the broken antique jewelry. She e-mailed back within the hour to say that she loved them and wanted to set up a lunch to talk about teaming up with me.

I used to think doing business over the Internet was harder. I couldn't guess the stories the customers might want to hear and couldn't tailor my sales pitch just for them. Turns out, in some ways, it's a little easier. When I'm working on my own things, buffing and polishing and finding just the right finding, it's all about making a piece that has a story worth telling. I don't have to worry about whether anyone will want it. I just have to trust that somewhere, out in the World Wide Web, there's someone whose story will match up.

That's kind of how things are on the Alzheimer's forum. I haven't checked it so often in the last week, now that Lila Beth's here and I've been working on closing the store. But I know it's there, and I can log on anytime. Whatever we're going through with Daddy, and whatever we will go through in the weeks to come, there's somebody who's bound to understand on the forum. I feel a little less lonely, just knowing that.

Lila Beth and Janie have been loyal to the end, wrapping and packing while the sun sets and the wind picks up outside. Golda and Cliff bring by sandwiches and sweet tea for lunch and a piping hot lasagna for dinner. "You girls have made a lot of progress since we were here last," Cliff says, surveying the empty shelves and one bare side of the store.

"Can I hire y'all to clean out our basement?" Golda asks. "I've been trying to get it organized for years. I reckon you three could have it spic and span in an afternoon."

"Or get caught under an avalanche," says Cliff. Golda swats him on the arm, and they leave us to it.

I eat my lasagna standing up, holding my plastic fork and plate high above Thor's quivering nose.

"Is he hungry? Can I give him something?" Lila Beth asks.

"He has a whole bowl of kibble in the stockroom," I say. Thor's gaze doesn't waver from my plate. He doesn't want kibble.

It's getting dark outside now, just like it did the day of my first premonition. The first time I stood in this store and saw Main Street split in two and my parents' house go up in smoke. I shiver. It's almost exactly like that day, right down to the glowing street-lamps and the glass-like, frozen feeling settling over the town. Like everything's about to change.

Well, of course it is. I'm starting over, for better or worse. I gulp a hot bite of lasagna too quickly and cough.

Out of the corner of my eye, I see a light go by the window.

"Are they doing another ghost tour tonight?" I ask. Lila Beth and I both look at Janie, who looks uncomfortable.

"Kind of," she says.

Another light goes by. I catch a better look this time. It's a person holding a candle, all right.

"What do you mean, kind of?" I ask.

Janie sighs. "I didn't think I should tell you. Since the Gala is off because they didn't raise enough money, Miss Paula decided to host a last Eagle Valley Ghost Tour. They'll do the tour again, only instead of anyone acting it out, Mr. Carson will read the story aloud."

"If they want to hear it all again in the freezing cold, more power to them," Lila Beth says.

Janie is holding something back. I can tell by the way she's squirming. "Anything else?" I ask.

"They're framing it as a last goodbye to Historic Eagle Valley. A last look at the town and its history before it's gone."

There's an amazing silence before Lila Beth asks, "Are you serious?" Her lips are twitching. "They do know that it's just the view that's changing, right? As in, they could literally turn their backs to the new houses, look up Main Street, and see a perfectly restored historic hamlet?"

"Did you just call us a hamlet?" I ask.

"I'm sorry," Lila Beth says. "*Township.*" She drawls out the word for all it's worth.

Janie bursts into giggles.

Another shadowy figure with a candle passes by the window.

"Let's keep packing," I say. I'm wearing gloves for the occasion, trying to get everything wrapped up and moved without getting bogged down with its personal history. Janie and Lila Beth are, too, because they assume it's some kind of protocol for keeping the artifacts clean. Thank goodness it's not. Lila Beth has wiped sweat off her forehead with her gloved hand twelve times. Not that I'm counting.

Janie, for her part, is focusing a lot less on her job of cataloging and a lot more on asking Lila Beth about D.C. She's thinking of applying to both Georgetown and George Washington University. She also has William and Mary, Virginia Tech, and University of Virginia on her hit list. I feel a little surge of jealousy toward Janie, listening to her chatter on about all the possibilities. When I was her age, all I wanted was to be safe and hide away from new experiences. I wish I'd been like her.

I can be like that now, I remind myself. *What would Daddy say? The show ain't over til the fat lady sings.*

Lila Beth went to George Washington University, so she's busy trying to talk up all its merits. She sends me sideways glances every so often, like she's wondering if I'm okay. If this is too close to reminding me about the trip she wanted to take with me.

"You should try going up to D.C. I bet you'd like it," I say to put her mind at ease. Janie looks electrified with excitement at the suggestion.

Two more candle-lit figures pass by. I think I recognize Gordon and Miranda Johns.

The first time I saw Jeremy was through this front store window. That first time when I saw him and realized–saw, really–that this was it, my first love. Come to think of it, the last time I saw Jeremy was through this store window, too.

Maybe there will be a next love, I think. But if not, if it is just me, I feel like that could be okay, too. I look over at the corner where Thor is sleeping. He perks up an ear whenever someone pops the bubble wrap. It could be okay. It is okay.

An hour goes by before the boxes start to outnumber the shelves left to be packed. Janie gets a hand cramp and switches cataloging duties with me. Lila Beth runs out of bubble wrap and starts packing things in crumpled newspaper instead.

I feel it coming. Not settling in, like usual, but roaring so loud and strong it nearly knocks me off my feet. Thor carefully dodges through the supplies and sits down next to me, his chin quivering on my knee. I take some deep breaths. I feel like I'm drowning.

"Miss Arden?" asks Janie. "Do you need to take a break?"

"Step away for a minute," Lila Beth says. "We can get the rest, if you need it."

"I'm fine," I say thickly, but Lila Beth is looking past me now, her head cocked to the side.

"Is that...?" she asks, holding the bowl she was wrapping in mid-air. Lila Beth has probably forgotten about the sirens. The firehouse is just outside town. Whenever Eagle Valley has an emergency, they blare the siren so the rescue squad or the volunteer firefighters can get on the scene and help until the ambulance or the fire trucks get there.

Janie glances down at her cell phone. Kids these days. They're texting each other all the news before the rest of us can catch up. "Nothing yet."

I hear voices gathering on Main Street. *The ghost tour,* I think, but the sinking feeling in the pit of my stomach says it's not.

Janie looks out the window and then darts out the door, holding it open and letting the cold, smoky fall air inside. "Miss Arden!" she yells. "Quick! There's a fire!"

26

I see the smoke first—billowing and black, just at the horizon. I jog down Main Street, squinting as I quicken my pace a little when the wind blows again. At the end of the street, I see it.

Orange flames are licking out the windows of my parents' old house. Even from here, I can see firemen pointing hoses at the kitchen, the sitting room, my childhood bedroom. The smoke billows darker.

Just past where I'm standing, where the pavement turns to gravel road, a crowd is gathering to watch. A month ago, I would have been part of that crowd. I would have walked over and traded whispered news and let myself be hugged. Now I'm standing off to the side. Leaving myself out before anyone else can leave me out, I guess.

"Miss Arden." Janie appears at my elbow. She's breathless, her cheeks bright pink in the cold wind. She must have run after me. "I'm so sorry."

Lila Beth appears half a pace later, holding Thor by the collar. He looks wild- eyed, frantic, and his nails scratch against the brick sidewalk. Janie takes Thor.

Wordlessly, Lila Beth wraps both arms around me and pulls me tight. I lean in.

In the flurry of phone calls that evening, Mama had been awakened. Told, I suppose, that the house that was still hers until tomorrow had gone up in smoke. She'd called us sleepily and asked if the fire marshal could talk to us about the details instead of her. It had been a rough day with Daddy, and they both needed rest.

I suppose that's fair enough. The fire marshal, grave-faced, meets with us sisters instead.

"Electrical fire," he says. "With the wiring in this house, it's a wonder it didn't go up in flames sooner."

"But why now?" I pester. "When no one was even home? I'm sure everything was turned off after the estate sale."

"Mouse chewed through a wire, probably," he says. "Or one light might have been left on, or the applianc-es were still running." He claps his hand on his knee and shakes his head. "Sometimes things just happen. Times like this, you just have to thank God no one was inside."

"What happens now?" Eliza asks. She drove up in the middle of the night, as soon as we called her. The boys were tucked in bed already, but she hadn't taken off her Halloween costume entirely. She went as a witch. She has smears of green cream makeup behind her ears and under her chin.

The sheriff shrugs. "Nothing. The new owners have been contacted, but they were going to bulldoze the house anyway. As long as there's no sign of foul play, there's nothing more to do."

"And you're sure there's no sign of any-thing...wrong?" Lila Beth asks.

The sheriff cocks an eyebrow at her. "I know it was Halloween, ma'am, but this is a clear-cut electrical fire. No harm, no foul. Thank God your parents had the good sense to move out of the house and count your blessings."

Maybe the firemen and the sheriff were okay with "no harm, no foul," but Eagle Valley started buzzing with theories before the last flame died out.

"I collected the candles," Paula Abernathy is telling everybody that will listen. "After the candlelight vigil, I stood right there with the box and made sure all those candles were returned."

"Nobody is blaming you, ma'am," says the sheriff, finally. "They said it was an electrical fire." Which is the point when Miss Paula has the good sense to shut up.

"Do you think it was a bonfire?" others are asking. "It was Halloween..." The kids' bonfire happened on the other side of town, though, as it always does.

"Karma, if you ask me," some people are saying. "That house was built by Vaughn McCrae's granddaddy, and he wouldn't have stood for having it sold and torn down to make room for new housing."

Give it time, I think. Maybe more than a year, but give it ten years, or twenty. The story of the fire at the McCrae's will join the Eagle Valley Legends. It'll start with suspicions, suggestions, like it is right now. Then the story will become its own animal. Its own piece of Eagle Valley history, the Story of the Mysterious Fire. There's no truth to it, but it's interesting, and interesting is true enough for most people.

Mama looks wrung out. Soon as it was light out, we all three drove up to fill her in on the details. "Honestly, that house has caused me more trouble in the last month than in all the time I lived there," Mama says.

"Amen to that," mutters Eliza.

Daddy wakes up then. He starts up before he's fully awake, jerking and sinking back into the couch. Mama is at his side within seconds. I look at Eliza, remembering the way Mama was when they were at the house. She was so tired then. Worn out and worn through.

I can't make out what he's saying. Mama rubs a finger over his jaw until he unclenches it then rubs his shoulder until he unwinds. Eliza and I walk over slowly while Lila Beth hangs back.

"I brought him a little something," I say, pulling the wooden dogwood flower out of my pocket.

Mama takes Daddy's hand and folds the flower inside his palm. He runs his fingers over the smooth wood, across the indents of the petals.

"He loves it," Mama says softly. "I don't think he understands the significance, exactly, but I do."

"And who knows? Maybe he does," Eliza says.

Another day, at another time, I'll fill Mama in on the e-mail I got from Sylvie, my plans for the online business, and my new hobby of woodcarving like Daddy. She'll be proud of me. She'll be happy to see I'm striking out on my own and trying new things. She's always wanted that for me.

Daddy would have been proud, too. I hate that I'm finding my place in the world right when Daddy's withdrawing from his. That's life, I suppose.

From behind me, I can feel Lila Beth gathering her courage. "Daddy," she says softly, crossing over to sit on his other side. "Daddy. I'm going to go back to D.C. today. But I'll be back soon. I promise."

Daddy glances up at her briefly before he goes back to running his fingers over the flower.

"Okay, Daddy?" Lila Beth says. "Okay? I'll be back real soon."

"We'll be happy to see you when you come back, Lila Beth," Mama says, standing up and guiding her away. "Maybe for Thanksgiving?"

Lila Beth nods quickly, the same way Eliza does when she's trying to hold back tears. They're more alike than they think.

"It's almost time for Daddy's medicine," Mama says. "I'm so glad to see you girls."

We say our goodbyes and move back towards our respective cars. Lila Beth and Eliza hug tightly.

"Tell those boys I say hi," Lila Beth says.

"Thanksgiving's at my house," Eliza says. "Come stay with us. You too, Arden. And Thor. The kids will be wound up anyway. Might as well get the dog in on it, too."

"Speaking of," I say. "I need to go get Thor before he decides to live in Golda's diner permanently."

We drive out in a small procession. Lila Beth turns first, honking and waving before she goes north up the highway, back to D.C. Eliza is next, turning south towards John and the boys.

Me, I keep driving until the mountains loom closer and the cars are spaced farther and farther apart. It rattles me a little, coming back into town. I look one more time at the fields that used to be Mama and Daddy's and the burned skeleton where our house used to be. Then I turn and drive up Main Street, past the bookstore, past the hardware store, past my old store. The streetlights are coming on at the same time that the sun is setting, giving Eagle Valley a warm, golden glow.

I feel change come rolling over me, covering my skin with a fine dust of anticipation. I stop and breathe it in.

It's over, I think. *Everything's going to be different now.*

I can't wait.

ABOUT THE AUTHOR

Ellen Smith is a freelance writer and first-time novelist. When she isn't writing, she can be found reading, sewing, or avoiding housework. She lives with her family near Washington, D.C.

www.ingramcontent.com/pod-product-compliance
Lightning Source LLC
Chambersburg PA
CBHW051122120726

47905CB00005B/1388